MISTRESS OF THE STORM

MISTRESS OF THE STORM

TERRI BRISBIN

BRAVA

KENSINGTON PUBLISHING CORP.

www.kensingtonbooks.com

DEDICATION

My first trip to Skye in 2002 was a special one. Staying on after a group tour left, I traveled west with two new friends, Sue-ellen Welfonder and Lisa Trumbauer. Both were writers and aficionados of all things Scottish. They were great guides and the places we visited have become the basis of many of my books.

While visiting Eilean Donan, we met guide Alex MacKay who told about all the wonderful medieval (and older) ruins on Skye, even drawing a map for us to follow . . . which we did!

Duntulm was one of those places. We climbed the ruins, looking over the Minch to Lewis and Harris and took dozens of photos. I visited again in 2009 but, due to the deterioration of the ruins, I couldn't get close to it, peering through and over the fence to take more photos.

Lisa Trumbauer passed away not long ago, but I will always think of her when I think of Skye and Duntulm—as I did while writing this book and during that last visit. So this book is for her. Her love of Scotland inspired and guided me on my first trip and each one since. Thanks, Lisa, and God bless.

And to Alex MacKay, who still works at Eilean Donan, who sent us on our way that day to find the wonders of Skye. Thanks!

Prologue

Only by using the intensity of her will did Isabel force out a few sounds to convince the man thrusting into her body that she enjoyed his touch and having his body in hers. Moaning again and tossing her head from side to side seemed to work, for he paused, holding his massive body still for a moment before she felt the hot spray of his seed within her. He collapsed on her, his weight forcing the breath from her lungs, but she waited before moving.

If she moved away too quickly, he might see her distaste and her need to leave. If she moved too slowly, he would fall asleep on her as he had before. When a few minutes had passed, she eased out from under him, the sweat on their skin making it possible to escape. Isabel slid to the edge of the pallet and dropped her legs over it to touch the floor. She tried to ignore the way they trembled and the bruises that formed in the shape of a man's large handprint on her thigh as she reached for the remnants of her shift. Allowing herself to believe she could get away before he stirred, she made the biggest mistake—she hurried.

"Ah, sweetling," he whispered as he placed his hand on her

neck, tugging her back against him. "Your stepfather told no false tales when describing your skills."

Isabel sat completely still, waiting for the man's next word or action.

"Come back." He pulled her to face him. "He is a man of his word."

Seeing the proof of his arousal before her eyes, Isabel accepted the inevitable and let out a long breath, masking it as one of deep appreciation for the size of his maleness. "Lord Malcolm, I did not wish to disturb your rest."

"Rest?" he asked, laughing in his deep voice as he pulled her face to his and kissed her. "I will rest when I am dead."

Isabel began the silent ritual that allowed her to leave her body behind and hide behind a wall in her mind. He gave her no chance to resist or to stop, so she just let go, allowing her body to react as it would until he finished with her.

As the sun rose over Duntulm Keep, he finally slept soundly and Isabel dragged her body from his. Tugging her gown on and leaving behind the torn pieces of her chemise, she walked barefoot from the chamber, down the steps, and out through the back door, nodding to the guards who recognized her and allowed her through the gate.

Following the path to the south, she continued until she reached the narrow strip of beach below the walls of the keep. Though the sun's light crawled up the sides of the keep, illuminating the flecks of quartz within the dark stones, the beach would remain shadowed for some time.

Time enough for her.

She dropped her shoes and stockings on the sand and pulled the gown and undertunic over her head. She tossed them down before she walked into the icy water. Only when she'd scrubbed the feel and smell of him from her skin would Isabel retreat from the icy water and return home.

Home.

Nay, not home, but the place where she lived now.

Home was the distant memories that kept her separate and her soul safe while her body was used to satisfy the desires of the men who fed the ambitions of her stepfather.

Home was where she had lived with her mother and younger sister, safe from the machinations of those who used anyone for their own success.

She sank under the surface, the cold water stinging her skin, until she could hold her breath no longer. She rose and then dipped once more, waiting for the icy chill to penetrate her limbs and remove all memory of the causes of her pain. The third time was the worst, for there was always a moment when her soul urged her to stay beneath the water and seek the comfort that its depths offered. Isabel could almost leave everything behind to seek that comfort, if not for the knowledge that the fate of her sister lay in her hands.

When that happened as it always did, she burst up from below, gasping and pulling air into lungs constricted by the freezing grasp of the water. Then, covered in gooseflesh but no longer Malcolm's scent, she struggled back to the beach on legs so deadened by the cold they did not move easily. She was shivering so much that every breath was a fight. Shaking and shuddering with every step, Isabel wrung out her hair, tied it with a strip of leather and pulled her clothes over her trembling limbs.

Her stepfather would be waiting, ready to punish her sister for every moment Isabel delayed. He would demand the details of the tryst, his eyes smoldering with an unholy need as he poked and prodded until everything that had happened was laid bare before him. Any attempt to avoid his questions or hold back a detail would find him making threats about Thora's future. *She is safe and well cared for, for now. . . .*

When he was satisfied he knew all, he would nod and then go off to plan his next conquest, deciding to whom he would pimp out his whore of a stepdaughter as a token of appreciation or esteem, and she would be left to continue to live out the nightmare.

Isabel gathered her control, and put her hand on the latch. Letting out her breath, she searched for and found the sense of calm she needed when facing down the man who'd turned her life into hell on earth. Bowing her head as she entered, she never realized that someone watched her from high above on the ramparts of the keep's tower.

Chapter One

Duntulm Keep
An t-Eilean Sgitheanach (Isle of Skye) or
Skiô (as it was called by the Norse), 1098 AD

Duncan, son of none, watched the storm grow from the window of his chambers at the very top of Duntulm Keep. It rushed across the Minch from the outer islands of Lewis and Harris toward those who lived on the rocky cliffside. They would all seek cover from the dangerous winds and lightning.

But he would not.

As the storm grew in size and ferocity, Duncan left his room and climbed to the roof, bracing himself against the stone wall that encircled the tower, and waited. The rumbling thunder warned him of the strength of the worsening storm and the first rain, blown by those winds, began to pelt him with drops as sharp as daggers.

He ripped open his tunic, baring his chest to the worst of it, waiting, praying he would feel the slicing rain cut his skin or sting his eyes.

Nothing.

He waited, not moving from the path of the rain and hail that tore at him. On and on it went, red welts appearing on his skin everywhere the hail or rain struck.

And still, he felt nothing.

The desperation he'd felt only weeks ago at the changes in his body and spirit was dull and he searched for the anger and pain that should be coursing through him. He found only a growing emptiness. Prepared to suffer the onslaught of the storm until he felt something, Duncan knew naught but someone with strong arms wrapped them around him and dragged him inside.

Though he could not feel the cold, it must have penetrated deep into his muscles, for he could neither resist nor help the efforts to get him out of the storm's way. Soon he was flung onto a bed and his soaked garments were pulled from him.

His senses of pain, hunger, and any other feelings or needs were dulled, but his hearing was as good as ever. He heard every word and curse rained down on him by his manservant. Ornolf spared no insult to Duncan's intelligence, his plans to kill himself, or his ability to follow instructions.

Duncan could not fight the strong trembling that shook his body—most likely from the cold. Ornolf fretted and fussed, pulling off the soaked layers of clothing and tossing them away, even as he layered blankets on top of his master.

"What did you hope to gain by that?" Ornolf asked his first actual question that had not been rhetorical.

Duncan tried to move, but his limbs refused to answer his mind's commands. "I did not hope for anything, Ornolf. 'Twas simply a test."

When Duncan did not explain more fully, Ornolf crossed his arms over his chest and glared down at him. "And, young master, what was the test?"

The ritual Duncan faced when the moon reached its fullest

each month, allowed some unknown power to flow into him, to become him, and to heal those who were sick. He spent hours in agony as the cauterizing fire of the power burned out every feeling and sensation in his body, leaving him numb for days and days.

And he was . . . still.

He did not want to voice his purpose before he understood more about the changes happening within him. To put his fear into words made it real and he must find out the full extent of the changes before the next step could be taken.

But, even as he comprehended that the changes were dire ones, his body did not react with the customary rolling bile or nervousness. No, his heart continued to pump along at an even pace and his breathing changed not at all. Though he should feel frightened at the realization and wished he did, he was empty of all emotions.

Finally Ornolf gave up any attempt to get answers and went back to fussing and muttering under his breath. Duncan lay there empty of fear, empty of pain, completely empty, yet knowing he wanted to feel something. *Anything.* That had been the reason he'd stood out in the storm and let it inflict its worst on him.

It was hours before he could climb from the bed and hours more before his body stopped shaking. Ornolf shoved a bowl of steaming porridge into his hands, placed a cup of ale on the table, and left without another word. Tempted not to eat, for no hunger assailed him, Duncan realized another change as he scooped up a spoonful of the porridge.

Although he could taste every ingredient in the thick concoction, none of it appealed to him. The flavors of the oats, cream, butter, seasonings and even a dash of spirits rolled over his tongue with each spoonful, but it made no difference—he neither liked the taste nor disliked it. He drank from the cup—a well-aged ale, kept for his consumption as a gift from a wealthy benefactor, but it was nothing special, simply a liquid to wash down the thick porridge.

Had all his sensations been burned from him during the ritual? It seemed that when the fires in his body went out, everything else ceased, too. Would his senses return? Would he feel emotions again? Duncan realized he would have to wait. He would have to recuperate before he could discover the answer and the extent of the changes.

Days and nights marched on for nearly a week. Though the welts had long since disappeared, Duncan's skin could not feel, his appetite had vanished completely, and the numbness in his soul and heart deepened.

When the moon reached half full, the familiar need returned. His scent poured out, bringing women to his door to fulfill some part of what he called "his curse." Though no hotblooded man would ever think having a never-ending stream of willing women at his beck and call was a bad thing, Duncan learned it was not necessarily a thing to be coveted. Endless need without satiation could lead to madness, and he feared that would be his fate.

Spring flowed into summer as the Norse king Magnus and his noblemen and warriors continued their travels throughout the western isles, fortifying their allies and smiting their enemies. When they moved south to deal with the Welsh and to bargain with the Scots king, Skye quieted. But those who held land, titles, or power all began planning anew, for the Norse would pass that way on their journey home and favor was to be gained.

Duncan's arrangement with Lord Davin remained a secret few knew and fewer questioned. With the changes wrought in him the last months, Duncan knew the truth—he had no idea of his curse's origin and less about its eventual end. He used his accumulated wealth to seek out knowledge, but there seemed none to be had.

Every possible space in the hall of Duntulm Keep was filled. Many of those who owned land in the surrounding areas attended the early autumn feast hosted by Davin to meet the men from Orkney and take their measure. Though invited to sit at table with him, Duncan declined Davin's invitation, choosing to sit away from the guests so he could observe them. It seemed the fires of hell had left his sense of curiosity intact when they burned away all the rest, so he listened and learned much about the visitors from the north.

Greeted as cousins, they were related to Davin through the marriage of their grandparents or some other ancestor, and the welcome he gave was warm. Foodstuffs and ale were plentiful and everyone ate and drank their fill. Ornolf placed a bowl and cup before Duncan, bothering him every so often so he would eat and drink. The smoke grew thick as the fires burned lower, offering heat but not much light. The torches and rush-lights added what they could, but Duncan could see clearly through the dimness and the haze.

It was a strange effect he'd noticed the last few months, and served him well in his attempts to watch and learn. He was studying the similarities in appearance between Davin and the one called Ragnar when the woman arrived. The room suddenly grew brighter and the chatter lessened as though everyone wanted to see her at once.

Nothing she wore was ostentatious, but the cut of her gown drew every man's eyes to her body. He could not identify the material of it, but it draped her curves as though painted over her flesh instead of being a garment. Duncan noticed the tightened nipples of her very full breasts as the gown molded to them and the way it fell into the junction of her thighs.

When she turned to sit down, he and every other man noted the way it hugged her arse, flowing into the indentation of the cleft and outlining her strong legs. Watching her move in it, he did not have to imagine what her body was like—he could see it.

He let his gaze wander over her, waiting for her to be seated so he could see her face.

Something he had not felt in months coursed through him in the moment their eyes met. A heat, a need, a wanting made him ache. Her eyes widened as though she knew her effect, but she looked away when someone spoke her name.

Isabel.

Who was she?

What was she?

How could she cause him to feel the blood heating and rushing through his body when he'd thought himself empty of such things? Duncan shifted in his chair and continued to watch as the attention of those gathered began to drift back to the honored guests. But he realized every man eventually turned back to watch Isabel.

She'd gathered and arranged her hair in a way that made her look well bedded. Its black waves accentuated every move she made and framed the creaminess of her skin perfectly. It was her mouth that sent waves of heat through him; her lips were bow-shaped and red as though well kissed. The blush in her cheeks added to the display—one he could tell was orchestrated carefully for its effect. Tearing his gaze from her, Duncan looked at the people she had followed into the feast.

Strange.

The man and younger woman she'd walked behind had taken seats much closer to their host, while she remained farther away. Was she the girl's maid? Neither of the women resembled the man in any way for he was as light as they were dark in hair and eye coloring. Duncan thought the women might be related based on the frequent glances they shared, cousins probably, though mayhap even sisters.

But, if sisters, why did they so clearly separate themselves at table?

The meal continued and Duncan resumed his perusal, watching her as she ate the food placed before her, and as she spoke to others, seeming to watch every move made by the man with whom she'd entered. It was only when she lifted her chin, gazed up at the ceiling of the chamber and closed her eyes that Duncan realized he'd seen her before. Searching his memory, he finally remembered where and when.

In the early hours just as the sun rose, when unable to sleep, he would walk the battlements of the keep, gazing down at the sea and the village outside the walls. Several times in the last months he'd noticed her leaving the keep just before dawn, and walking to the south beach.

With nothing more than curiosity to keep his attention, Duncan would watch as she took off her clothes and flung herself into the water. Her practice was the same each time he'd watched—dipping twice under the surface of the water and scrubbing her skin as she did. Then she would plunge down and remain in the freezing waters until he thought she'd perished. He remembered several times when he began counting how long she stayed under the water, wondering if she would rise from it at all.

Over the months he'd witnessed her behavior, the changes within him making any tension he felt as he counted out the seconds lessen until he'd watched in complete disinterest, no matter how much he knew he should be concerned.

Watching the way she tilted her head, he was reminded of the way she looked up at the sun as she walked, sometimes struggling, out of the waves. In the earlier times he'd seen her, he'd thought she might be a selkie or water spirit. But, lately,

he observed her actions from an emotional and physical distance—until she lowered her head and gazed at him through
her lashes.

That heat seared him again, letting him feel things he'd not
felt in months. Was she a selkie risen from the sea or some
otherworldly creature capable of giving him back all he'd lost?
His moments of disinterested watchfulness were over, for his
body and his soul knew she was more than she appeared, and
his mind knew he must discover her secrets and their link to
his own. Standing, his feet moved before he could think on
what words to say or what he wanted. All he knew was that he
wanted . . . her.

Unable to understand or explain what was between them,
Duncan stood in front of her, his gaze never wavering from
hers. He did not stop when the entire crowd noticed and quieted. He continued even when she tore her gaze from his for
the slightest moment, then met it again. He did not let the
fact that every eye in the room fell on their encounter concern
him at all.

"Who are you?" he asked, unable to form his thoughts and
the newly-returned needs into anything more complex.

She looked away, turning her head and her eyes, and he followed the direction of her gaze. The man with whom she'd arrived frowned at her, then looked over at Duncan, assessing
him before nodding to her.

"I am called Isabel, my lord," she said in a voice that sent
chills through his numb body. She bowed her head as she
spoke.

"Isabel," he whispered, savoring the sound and feel of it on
his lips—something not possible just minutes ago.

"Duncan?"

Duncan acknowledged Lord Davin with a tilt of his head,
but dared not look away from her. Fear had returned as well as

sensation and he was afraid all of it would end if he turned from her. "Lord Davin?" he replied in the same manner.

"Is aught amiss?" Davin asked. "Has she offended you in some way?"

"Nay, my lord." From the reactions of those in the room when she'd entered, *offended* was not the word Duncan would have used to describe her effect. In a moment of clarity, the whole of the situation became clear—her entry, her dress and sensual manner, her position away from others, her early morning departures from the keep, the gazes filled with lust that watched her every move, her habit of looking to the man for permission.

She was a harlot and the man her whoremaster.

"The lady intrigues me," Duncan explained. The bold guffaws from those watching and listening confirmed it. She was no lady.

Davin leaned in and explained under his breath. "She is only tolerated here because of her father's worth to me. If she interests you, I will order him to send her to you. No coin need be exchanged for her."

The discovery that she made her way from man to man and bed to bed ought to have dampened his interest, but it did not. Harlot or lady, she brought his body to life under her gaze. He felt the blood in his veins and the fabric as it pulled against his erection—sensations gone for months. Being a harlot made it easier somehow to want her just for physical release.

Not daring to leave it to chance or willing to delay, Duncan looked over at the man who'd brought her in and waited for his answer. When Davin crossed his arms over his chest and turned as well, a nod was hastily delivered. Duncan held out his hand to Isabel and waited for her to accept it.

His stomach clenched even as his cock surged with anticipation and his skin ached. He held his breath, unsure if the pride he saw in her eyes would allow that public declaration of what was to happen. The moment spun out between them, drawing the silent observation of everyone around them until he could see nothing but her. He could almost hear the sound of her shallow breaths as he waited. Then, as though moving with exquisitely slow motions, she lifted her hand and placed it in his.

A wave of heat and a shock pulsed through him in that very moment. He gasped at the intensity of it, for it burned without harming as it coursed through his body. Her matching gasp and the surprise in her gaze told him she'd felt it as well. Duncan closed his fingers around her hand, guiding her out of her seat and along the table until she could step closer.

Her scent flooded him with a mix of flowers, arousal and something unexpected, a hint of innocence. Duncan inhaled again as he drew her to him and placed his arm around her waist. She shook her head, but he sensed it was more out of confusion or surprise over the growing attraction between them than denial. When they reached the corridor outside the hall, he hastened their pace. He guided her up the stone stairway to his chambers in the tower and could not help that they were almost running when they reached his door, both out of breath. He flung the door open, surprising Ornolf, who remained within.

"Out."

Ornolf glanced from Duncan to Isabel, squinted, and frowned before offering a cursory bow and leaving them.

Duncan faced her and waited for some sign of hesitancy or refusal before closing the door. A whore had no choice, true, but he did not want to think she was there against her will. He needed to believe she felt the force between them and wanted it, needed to believe it almost as much as he wanted her naked beneath him.

After months of feeling less and less until nothing remained within his heart or soul, the flood of feeling nearly over-whelmed him. Usually it was the power surging within him as he neared the fullness of the moon that drew women to him. But that would not begin for another sennight or so. Duncan did not understand the need he felt for her, the hunger to have her, but he could not deny it or stop it any more than he could stop breathing.

The door slammed closed and it was only the two of them.

Chapter Two

Isabel could not breathe.

She tried to tell herself it was from running up three flights of stairs to reach the chamber, but she knew it for the lie it was.

Shame had assailed her belowstairs for she had been forced to accept the man's invitation while her sister watched. She never wanted Thora tainted by what she'd done and never wanted her to witness it. Isabel did not fool herself into believing her sister was ignorant of what she was and what she did, but for the first time it had been done in Thora's presence with no way to blunt the embarrassment she must be feeling.

In the chamber, a storm built around and between Isabel and Duncan. Heat poured through her as his gaze burned into her. She feared for her soul and her sanity as that storm beat against the defenses she'd built around herself.

She tried to control her breathing, drawing in several deep breaths and letting them out slowly. The slamming door made her jump in surprise. The man stood there staring at her and she wondered if he felt what she was feeling. Would he want a whore the way he wanted other women who shared his bed?

He entwined their fingers and tugged her closer. She

stepped away to gain some power over the situation before it spun completely out of her control. He would not allow it, drawing her back to him and wrapping his other arm around her waist once more. When she expected to feel his mouth on hers, he leaned toward her, closed his eyes and inhaled deeply as though there was some scent.

Isabel found herself unable to resist the temptation to do the same and discovered the smell of him drew her in. Falling into his embrace, she lifted her face to his. It was she who leaned up to touch their mouths. With the first touch of their lips, the storm that brewed between them exploded into something uncontrolled and unknown to her.

Flames of a never-experienced desire leaped to life deep within her and Isabel wanted him in a way she'd never felt . . . and never wanted. She needed to pull the veil of self-control back into place, but every touch of his mouth to hers and every caress pushed it away. If she did not regain control, she would be destroyed by the very thing she wanted most in that moment—him.

Lying down with other men had been like acting for her. She knew just when to sigh or moan, when to stroke flesh, when to resist and when to comply. But every ounce of confidence she had in her ability to keep herself separate from the acts of the flesh and safe from the demeaning nature of it all was being destroyed by Duncan. She knew his name, and he threatened it all with a look of longing and a hand held out in offering.

She could not find the strength to leave his embrace and put an end to whatever was happening between them. Her traitorous body leaned against him, urging him for more.

He did not hesitate, possessing her mouth as he released her hand to wrap both arms around her. He stole her breath with his lips and tongue, tasting her, then nipping along her neck, as her gasps kept pace with his kisses. Her breasts swelled, their tips chafing against the fabric of her dress. *He* had chosen it because of the way it rubbed her nipples and made them hard and visible to any man looking at her, but now the friction sent spirals of pleasure through her body. When Duncan moved his hand up to cup one, she could not help but arch against it, seeking more.

He kissed her then, laughing against her mouth and she craved to hear it again. The deep rich sound echoed in her mind as her body reacted to it. The movements she usually had to force herself to perform became no chore. Isabel let her hands glide over the strong muscles of his back and down until she reached his buttocks, squeezing the muscular globes of his flesh. It was his turn to arch against her, and the proof of his readiness thrust against her belly.

He lifted his mouth from hers, his breathing ragged and quick. He searched her eyes, then held her gaze as he reached down and gathered the folds of her gown in his large hand. The tension of it—knowing what would follow and both wanting and fearing it—made breathing difficult for her. She placed her hand on his arm, whether to stop him or to hasten him to his target she could not tell, but when his fingers slid between her legs, she found herself pushing him to go deeper still.

Duncan smiled, realizing she did not want to enjoy what they did. He could feel it in his soul, though how, he knew not. Isabel leaned her head back as he thrust two fingers deep into her woman's cleft and massaged the swelling folds.

The heat of her core so near to his fingers threatened to burn his flesh. He could feel the moisture that poured from her as he rubbed and teased the bud within the folds. He felt her body pressing against his as he fought the need to lay her on the floor and plow into her as he wanted to. In that moment, he realized what he wanted most of all. Like a man dying of hunger, he needed to feel her touch on his skin. More than him touching her, Duncan needed her hands on his body. He pulled away from her and stepped back, holding her arms so she did not fall.

When she stood without danger of tumbling over, he loosened his tunic, shirt and trews and pulled them off. Standing naked before her, he whispered his command to her as the very air around him caressed his flesh in a way he'd not felt in months.

"Touch me."

Duncan closed his eyes and waited, praying to any god listening that he was not mistaken or fooling himself about her ability to restore all that had been lost to him. After a few moments, he opened his eyes to see if she had changed her mind. Like a siren of legend, she stood before him smiling. She reached up and tugged the laces of her gown and tunic loose, then gathered both up and pulled them over her head, leaving her in a shift so sheer it covered little of her temptress's body.

He could see the darkness of her rosy nipples and the triangle of hair at the junction of her legs. She slid her hands over her body as she reached for the hem of the shift. Then, she paused and reached up to take her own nipples between her fingers and thumbs. She twisted them, arching her head back, letting the length of her hair swing behind her.

His cock surged, thickening and growing harder each time she flicked her thumb over the tips of her breasts and he swore he could feel her touch on his erect flesh. Finally, she pulled the shift over her head and revealed the rest of her womanly curves to him. The breasts he'd held in his hands were high and firm, tipped with large, rosy nipples that drove him to madness. Her waist narrowed only to have her hips flare out becomingly. The strong legs he'd seen from afar could ride a man all night . . . and he wanted them wrapped around his waist as he filled her flesh with his. Duncan took a step toward her but she waved him off. Not daring to risk her displeasure, he waited and watched as she took one gliding step toward him. Then another brought her to within an arm's length of him. He closed his eyes once more, returning to his silent prayers.

The sharpness of her nails grazing down his flesh shocked him into opening them. Beginning on his chest, she flicked her fingers across his nipples, making him shudder with pleasure. With her gaze capturing his, she moved lower and lower, avoiding his cock but touching his balls until she stopped on the skin of his thighs.

He felt every inch of his skin as she touched it!

When she cupped him, he gasped out of sheer shock and watched as her green eyes glimmered and her lips curved into a wicked smile. He feared and prayed her next move and held his breath waiting . . . waiting. . . . Instead of leaning down, Isabel fell to her knees, grasping his legs to support her as she moved. Without shifting her gaze, she licked her lips and touched the tip of her tongue to his turgid flesh.

Duncan could not hold back his loud moan. It echoed through his chambers and was joined by another and another as she took him into her mouth and suckled him. Her hands never stopped their intimate torture, cupping his sac and moving over his thighs and arse. He felt the flicking of her tongue along the length of his cock and her teeth as she nipped it.

He'd felt nothing like that before. Not even before his senses began to dull months ago. Not even during the wild nights of passion and pleasure in the years past when his power drew women to him to satisfy his growing need and desire. Whether the intensity was greater simply because of the absence of feeling for those last months or whether it was something else entirely became a moot point, for his flesh screamed out for more and she provided it.

She released his cock and trailed a path of wet, hot kisses

over his flesh, down his thighs, and around to his arse. Shudders of pure pleasure coursed through him as she reached around and stroked his shaft from behind, her skin rubbing against his as she gradually stood. Her head did not rise to his shoulders, so her breasts pressed against his arse and then his waist and back as her hands encircled his cock. Duncan reached around, grabbing her arse and pulled her against him tighter. The curls at the junction of her thighs teased his skin.

Overwhelmed by the sensations she created and by the sheer thrill of feeling everything once more, he was surprised at how quickly his release came. She covered the tip of his cock, pumping the length of it until every drop escaped. His seed may have spilled, but Duncan was in no way finished. He turned, taking her by the waist and tossed her onto his bed, climbing in and covering her with his body. The musky smell of his seed added to that of her arousal and it spurred him on to further pleasure for both of them.

He moved over her like the fog as it covered the hills and glens of Skye. Gently at first, with caresses so light she thought she must have dreamed them, then increasing in pressure until she cried out from the pleasure. His mouth tasted and licked and even bit her skin, from her neck to her feet. He turned her like the waves of the sea, over and back, this way and that, until no part of her was untouched by him. He buried his face between her legs. He suckled her there, pausing to incite and then to soothe, until she screamed out a release unlike any before. Her body ached from it yet hungered for more and he gave it to her.

All pretenses dropped and Isabel absorbed the pleasure, allowing her heart and soul to partake as she never had. Her mind warned of the danger, but she ignored it. Long past the point of stopping, she let him have her, have everything that she was.

She tried to tell herself she had no choice—a whore did not choose her way—but when he gazed at her with such wonderment and hunger and desire, she could deny him nothing.

She wanted to deny him nothing.

Release followed release, pleasure upon pleasure, until he rolled her onto her stomach, lifted her against his body and spread her legs with his knees. He slid his hand down, opened the folds of flesh between her legs and guided his cock to the place that ached to be filled. With a thrust that took her breath away, he plunged in so deeply he touched her womb.

Isabel tried to move with him as he drew back, but he held her tightly, his hand teasing the bud between the folds. Filled with him, his hand pleasuring her all the while, she felt the tightening spiral of pleasure deep within her. His cock stretched her and she wanted to slide along it, to ease his way inside her, but he held still. The strength of his arms wrapped around her not allowing her body to arch.

He paused then, resting his head on her shoulder from behind, inhaling and rubbing his face in her hair. Isabel felt as though she stood overlooking the sea from a cliff, waiting to fall free into the abyss. She held her breath as her body tensed, her inner muscles tightening around his flesh.

With one stroke of his finger against the engorged, aching bud, he pushed her over.

She screamed as she fell, spiraling downward as her body and spirit found release again. He followed her—plunging deep within and then out, deeper and deeper with every thrust—until she felt him grow harder still. He bit the place between her shoulder and neck, impossibly increasing wave upon wave of pleasure rolling over her. His seed spilled again, drenching her womb.

He would not relent or release her, continuing to stroke her until she screamed out again and again, until she begged him to cease in a voice hoarse from too much pleasure. His deep laugh from behind her echoed through her body and she convulsed again with waves of satisfaction. Still buried deep within her, he neither released her nor withdrew.

When their racing hearts and ragged breathing eased, they collapsed together, him on top of her, until he rolled them onto their sides. Though she drifted asleep, he never let go of her, touching her constantly and remaining within her until he was hard again.

The second time was slow and gentle. He prolonged the touching and tasting and caressing until she ached and then brought her to release without a sound, his own release a quiet thing.

The third time he was relentless again, not content to seek satisfaction of his own until she screamed and begged him again.

The fourth time happened in a blur of pleasure her body could remember feeling but her mind could not.

By the time the sun rose, Isabel knew only that what had passed between them would never be forgotten. She swore it would never be repeated.

She would never survive if she allowed such a thing to happen again.

Chapter Three

As was her custom, Isabel barely dozed and roused at the first light of dawn, dazed and confused when she opened her eyes. It took but one movement to bring the memories of the previous night rushing back to her. Every muscle of her body felt sore as she moved away from the sleeping man and eased from his bed.

She crept around the chamber quietly, seeking out her clothing, dressing quickly and silently. Only as she tugged the door open did she allow herself a glance at the man she was leaving.

He lay sprawled across the bed, his nearly blond hair in disarray covering most of his face. She remembered his eyes as he'd gazed at her throughout the night, almost glowing in their intensity. His muscular body spoke of a man well trained in fighting, though talk was that he was not a warrior but some kind of healer. Her body remembered the strength in his arms and legs even while her mind tried to push that all aside.

Isabel closed the door quietly and was surprised to find his servant waiting in the corridor. She lowered her head and walked past him as she usually did, but he placed his hand on her arm and stopped her.

"Are ye well?" he asked in a quiet, gruff voice that made her want to cry for the father she never knew. No one ever asked how she was. She straightened up and nodded.

"Well enough." Her practiced reply seemed a lie, for in some ways she was exceedingly well and in others terrified at what had happened. It mattered not, so she turned to go. The man stepped in front of her, blocking her path . . . her escape.

"Thank ye, lass," he whispered.

Isabel shook her head and shrugged. "For what? I did nothing unexpected." A whore did what a whore did.

"Thank ye for being what he needed."

She frowned. What had he meant by that? "What did he need?" she asked, unable to stop her curiosity over the man within. She knew little about him, other than the talk of his being a healer. She wondered why he had chosen her.

"You."

He stepped out of her path and smiled at her as she passed. She held her tongue, not allowing the questions she wanted to ask to slip free. She needed to regain control and put the . . . incident in its proper place if she was to move on with her life.

She hurried from the keep and down to the beach. The sound of the waves soothed her as she approached. Submerging herself always seemed to empty her mind of all worries and concerns and memories. As she began to lift her gown over her head, Isabel stopped. The winds blew her hair wildly and tugged at her clothing as though trying to speak to her. She gazed out over the sea and realized she felt no need, no compulsion, to enter its waters.

Confused, she sat on the sand and pushed her hair from her face, gathering its length in her hands and tying it back. She always needed to go into sea when she left some man's bed. It cleansed her body and eased her spirit and heart, but that morn, the urge was not there. She turned and peered up at the keep's walls. What had happened between them? Could it have changed her so much and so deeply?

The winds gentled into soft breezes and her exhaustion began to catch up with her. She closed her eyes, drew her legs up, wrapping her arms around them and leaning her face to rest on her knees. She lost track of everything and when she roused it was difficult to tell how much time had passed. Glancing behind her, she tried to estimate how high in the sky the sun sat and suspected she'd been lost in thought and sleep for over an hour. From the sounds of activity in the yard of the keep and the village, she knew her stepfather would be pacing the floor awaiting her return.

How had she let things get so out of her control? She would suffer in more than one way for the lapse in judgment, for only the steely control she exerted over her mind and her soul prevented her from being destroyed. From being changed irreparably by the vile things she did for her stepfather in return for the safety and future of her younger sister. And from losing that last bit of herself lying dormant under layers of protection until she had seen her sister set in the life Thora should have.

Surprised by the tears flowing down her cheeks, she rubbed them away and stood, righting her clothing and stretching her arms above her head to ease the various kinks and cramps in her muscles from last night and from sitting too long. Isabel stumbled a few steps across the sand, then walked quickly the rest of the way to the cottage her stepfather owned.

Sigurd did pace as she expected he would do, turning to face her as she stepped inside. With his massive arms crossed over his chest and with his height and girth, he could intimidate with a simple glance. When he raised his arm or his hand, any person with sense cowered before him.

Isabel had and would, she suspected, do it again very soon.

She closed the door, not willing to allow the sounds of their encounter to be heard by those she must face when he left.

What surprised her was the tone of voice he used when he began.

"What did he want from you?" he asked, stepping closer and watching her as she answered, as though trying to discern truth from lies. She'd tried to lie once and his wrath when he discovered the truth made it not worth trying again. Ever.

"He wanted pleasure, just like every man before him." She delivered the words in an even tone—neither challenging him nor acquiescing.

"And . . . ?"

"I did what he asked, however he asked." A bit of an untruth for she had sometimes not waited for him to ask.

Sigurd paced a few times, then nodded at her. "Did he ask you to return?"

Isabel swallowed to ease the tightness in her throat. She'd left before Duncan had said anything. Unsure of what Sigurd wanted, she went with the truth. "He slept."

His dark eyes narrowed and unease crept down her spine. "Did he offer you gold? Coins?"

"Nay." She shook her head, holding out her hands and opening them to show she clutched only her clothing. She kept nothing given to her and had few belongings or trinkets other than the clothing Sigurd provided.

"He is not known to be wealthy or have lands," Sigurd admitted. Those were the usual reasons he gave her to men to be used—wealth and lands. Or . . . power.

"Who is he?" she asked, passing him to put down her cloak. Loosening the tie on her hair, she lifted her brush and began to ease through the tangles caused by the wind.

"No one would say," he reported. "He is known to be close to Lord Davin and in his favor. His attendance last night and his place at Davin's table speaks of that."

"Is he from Skye? Or the mainland?" she asked, pouring water into a bowl to wash.

"No one would say, or no one knows. He stays in Duntulm Keep when he is here."

Isabel dipped a cloth in the water, twisted out the excess and wiped her face and neck. She would never prepare a hot bath while Sigurd was there; that would have to wait. As she continued to wash, the silence between them grew and a shiver warned her more was at stake than she'd thought. She finished her ablutions and faced him—better than having her back to him and not knowing what he would do.

" 'Tis perfect, really." He smiled, neither lightening nor softening his expression. "You will discover his secrets and bring them to me. I will use what is important to gain control so he will do my bidding with Lord Davin."

Bile rolled in her stomach at his pronouncement. She hated her role as spy and secret-gatherer more than sleeping with the men he chose, knowing he would use such information to pull another man into his web. Isabel fought the rise of bile into her throat by pouring some ale into a cup and drinking it down quickly.

She must refuse him. It was not right to use and betray another man for Sigurd's benefit. She understood to the marrow of her bones how it felt and how he destroyed those from whom he could gain nothing. After sharing Duncan's pleasure and something else she could not explain, Isabel did not want to be the instrument of his downfall. But any intent or desire to show resistance was ended as the door to the cottage opened and Thora stood there outlined by the growing sun's rays.

The tightness in Isabel's heart eased as she watched her sister enter. Ignoring a whispered warning from Sigurd, Thora walked straight to her and pulled her into a rib-crushing embrace. Isabel closed her eyes rather than let him see her tears as she clung to Thora. Months had passed since she'd seen her sister and they'd had no time for words when they had arrived at the feast. Nor would she have approached Thora in public.

"Isabel, you look pale." Thora brushed the hair from Isabel's face and kissed her cheek.

Isabel could not think of a word to say. She swallowed and tried to clear the tears from her throat but she could not. Though she wished to release her sister and get her out of that meager place, she found her fingers clasping the folds of Thora's gown tighter. Thora hugged her again before stepping back.

"I am well, sister." Amazed that she could even speak, Isabel smiled through her tears. "And how do you fare?"

"Well," Thora whispered back.

"Thora," Sigurd began with a growl. "I told you not to ever come here." He took hold of her and pulled her free, tossing Isabel to one side of the room. When Thora moved toward her, he blocked her and pointed to the door. "Out. Now."

The gentleness in his voice when he spoke to her sister always shocked Isabel. How in one moment he could be so brutal to her and in the next seem warm and caring to Thora. But, that was their arrangement—saving Thora in exchange for her. She shook her head and watched in sadness as Thora left, turning to give her one more glance as she followed his orders.

"Wait for me at the cart," he told Thora as he closed the door behind her.

Isabel underestimated his ability to change in an instant. But she remembered as he grabbed her by the hair and pulled her back to him, slamming an arm around her chest. She fought to breathe under the pressure of his hold and the pain in her head.

"Do not disobey me, girl, or she will pay for it." He gave a hard tug on her hair, then flung her to the floor.

Gasping, she could not rise. Her hair flowed around her, covering her face.

"Prepare yourself and be ready when you are summoned."

"But . . ."

He moved quickly to answer her hesitation in following his orders, crouching down and menacing her with his curled fist. "Do not think to naysay me or neither of you will survive."

Isabel nodded her understanding without moving. Sigurd stood and stomped away, leaving the cottage and following her sister. She could hear them speaking in low tones as she collapsed, allowing her anger and grief to flow unimpeded.

Thora understood she'd angered her father in going to her sister's cottage, but it had been months since she'd seen or spoken with Isabel. Too long for sisters to be separated. He'd looked stern as he'd left the cottage, holding out his hand to help her climb into the cart. But as she settled on the bench across the cart next to Erlend, who would drive her out to their farm, she watched as her father's expression softened.

"You should not come here, Thora. Your reputation and your value as a wife will suffer if you are seen with her," he warned.

"She is my sister and I want to see her, Father," she answered. "You must understand."

He smiled and patted her hand. "When you were younger, it was another matter. But now, she will ruin any chances you have for a good marriage. I allowed you to be at the feast last evening and look what happened. She spared you no thought as she followed that man off to . . . to do whatever she does when she whores herself to men." He lowered his head and shook it, his eyes and face filled with sadness.

"Ah, Father," she said, touching her hand to his cheek. "As you said, she made her choice when she ran from home and sought this life. 'Tis not your fault."

He lifted his head and nodded. "At least you are a virtuous

and dutiful daughter. Your mother would be pleased by the young woman you have become, my Thora." He glanced over at Erlend. "Now, you have a journey before you and I want you back at the farmstead safe and settled before nightfall."

"When will you return?"

"Well, a few days at most I think. And, from the talks last night after you sought your bed, I should have news of an offer of marriage for you to consider." He winked at her as he tantalized her with that bit of news.

She smiled at him as he stepped away and waved his hand for Erlend to set off. They'd spoken many times of her feelings about marriage and she knew he'd have a care for her preferences as he bargained for her hand. He walked off and it was only as she turned to wave that she caught sight of Isabel's small cottage. A tear trickled from the corner of her eye and she reached up to wipe it away.

Isabel had always been the strong-headed and stubborn one. She had fought her stepfather on everything until the day she'd run away. By the time he'd found her, she had fallen from respectability and into a sad life. Thora would never understand why she'd done it, why she'd not accepted her father's, Isabel's stepfather's, offer to return home and seek forgiveness for her sin of pride and disobedience. The separation had torn her own heart in two.

He had promised to help Isabel in any way he could as long as Thora obeyed him and behaved as a daughter should. If that was the only way she could help Isabel, she would do so. And for the last year she had. She only hoped that her small lapse that day would not cause her father to turn his back on her sister.

Thora could not bear the thought that Isabel would be harmed because she could not keep her part of the bargain. She considered all the possibilities of how she could aid Isabel herself while Erlend guided the cart and horse through the hills away from the coast. When they reached the farmstead, she'd come up with nothing—except to continue to obey her father and allow him to chart the path of her life.

If that would help her dearest sister, that was what she would do.

It was exactly what she would do.

Chapter Four

Duntulm Keep

Duncan woke from the first deep sleep in months to find his bed empty and Isabel gone. He raced to the battlements to search below for her, seeing her on the beach, pleased that she did not enter the sea to wash his scent from her skin as she had so many times before. He stood above watching her, experiencing a panic and sorrow he could not explain.

That was remarkable in itself, but the fact that his skin was alive once more was even more so. The rough surface of the stone wall scratched his palms as he slid them along it. The chill in the morning air raised gooseflesh and he felt the tightness of his skin as it puckered and his hair rose. His stomach growled its hunger for the first time in months and he laughed aloud at the amazing sensations.

He was alive, more alive than he'd been in so long and he knew for certain she was the cause of it. He must keep her at his side to find out the extent of her influence on the curse he bore. Caught up in things that should be mundane, he missed her standing and leaving the small stretch of beach below.

When he realized she was gone, he ran to the other side of the roof and gazed down on the small village, seeking out any movement on the narrow pathways between cottages and outbuildings that would give away her position.

Finally! She moved slowly along the path to the south, heading for the cottage that sat separate from the rest, far enough away to almost be outside the village. Even from a distance so far he saw her shoulders were slumped forward. Once more, waves of pain and sorrow echoed across the space between them and his heart ached in response.

His intentions of meeting with the men from Orkney disappeared as the need to discover the source of her pain overwhelmed him. Had he hurt her during the night? He remembered relentless passion and pleasure. Overwhelmed by it, he might have hurt her and not realized it. A whore would never mention such things.

His feet were running before he knew where, the sharp stones that covered the roof tearing into the skin on the soles of his feet. Only when Ornolf blocked his path did he skid to a stop.

"Out of my way, old man," Duncan said, trying to push his way around his servant.

"Ye cannot leave yer chambers naked as the day ye were born, Duncan. And clean the blood from yer feet or it will leave a trail."

Only then did Duncan realize his feet were bleeding. And they hurt! A mystifying and wondrous—and unexplained— change. He laughed again, the thrill of the pain rushing through him.

"Fix them," he ordered as he sat on a stool in his chambers.

Ornolf worked quickly, wrapping Duncan's feet with strips of linen, then shoving short boots on over them. Every wince was cause for celebration. Without a word being said, Ornolf handed him clothes and helped him dress. It took only a few minutes, but those were minutes Duncan did not wish to waste. He ran through the keep and the yard and the gate and finally, stood in the shadows observing as Sigurd spoke with the young woman he'd brought to the feast the evening before. The exchange between them was nothing like the glances Duncan had witnessed between Sigurd and Isabel. These were filled with soft feelings and concern while those were of ownership and possession.

How could a man treat one so lovingly and the other so callously?

Thinking on the matter would not change a thing, for the world was made up of men such as Sigurd—hard men whose only concern was making their way in the world, reaching above themselves with others paying their way. Men who sold their own brothers into slavery to gain from it. Men who would change allegiances and fight for whomever promised the greater reward.

Duncan watched the cart carrying the daughter leave and Sigurd stride off in the direction of the keep, no doubt to meet with Davin to curry more favor or find ways to do so. After waiting until he was certain Sigurd was not coming back, Duncan walked the last few paces to Isabel's door. He knew which of the small dwellings was hers after watching her from high above as she made her way there . . . more times than he could explain or care to think on.

He placed his hands on the doorframe and leaned his head against the door, trying to calm his racing heart and his breathing. Waves of anguish poured over him from within, forcing him to his knees. Gasping for breath, the affliction pierced his heart and caused storms of pain in his head. The feelings reminded him of the beginning of the healing ritual—the part when he was still conscious of his own body, before the power flowed through him and erased all that he was. But the power did not build or flow, only the pain.

Pushing himself to his feet, he knew he needed to get to Isabel. Something was wrong, terribly wrong. Lifting the latch of her door, he eased it open and peered into the darkened cottage. He fought against the ever-increasing waves of pain, trying to see into the shadows, hearing the sounds of weeping echo in the tiny dwelling.

Isabel was crying, weeping so deeply he thought her physically wounded. She lapsed into coughing, then vomiting from the intensity of her cry. When he would have stepped inside, something stopped him from going to her. Clearly she thought herself alone and his interference might not be warranted or welcome. He realized he knew nothing, *less* than nothing, about the woman other than her skills in bedplay. He suspected much, but knew nothing about her family or her connections in Duntulm.

In spite of feeling her pain and her sorrow, he stepped back and closed the door. The action did nothing to ease the suffering he felt, but he could not help her if he did not understand. He knew in the heart and soul he could now feel that he wanted to help her. He wanted to understand what she was to him.

He wanted her.

As he walked away, the pain lessened but did not dissipate completely, leaving an ache in the pit of his stomach he suspected would continue until her pain was gone.

He stopped as the revelation struck him.

He'd never felt the power flowing in his veins between full moons before. He'd never wanted to let it flow, to unleash his ability to heal bodies and souls, because of the terrible cost he paid for its exercise. Yet, he'd stood in her doorway wanting to heal her, wanting to erase the anguish that lived deep within her. Wanting to take her pain into himself and banish it.

Duncan shook his head, trying to clear the confusing burst of thoughts and desires and needs from his mind, unable to

sort through it all after the months of emptiness. To call forth
the power he had was courting disaster. To even think of such
a thing frightened him.

He must discover more about her. He gazed up at the sun,
estimating it to be mid-morning. He smiled at that, since he'd
not slept past dawn in ages, but his soul filled and his body satisfied and exhausted, he'd not wanted to wake. Then he'd
rolled over to pull her body beneath his and seek that moment
of perfect satisfaction and peace . . . and found her gone.

He took and released a deep breath. Ornolf was excellent at
gleaning information, so Duncan would set him on that task.
His usual caution reared then and he knew he must find out
more about her before allowing her close enough to discover
the truth of his curse and his ability.

Walking back to the keep, he knew the moment something
changed. All the pain that had flowed into him disappeared as
though the flame of a lamp had lost its oil and gone out. It was
not diminished, but extinguished as though never there.
Breathing did not hurt. Existing did not hurt. The pain was
gone, mimicking the moment in the ritual when he came back
to himself and the person involved felt nothing. He felt nothing, too, but knew that moment was simply a pause before all
the pain that had been drawn out flooded into him.

This time, it did not.

Quickening his pace and filled with an anticipation he'd not
known for months, he made his way to his chambers and sent
Ornolf off on various tasks. When the men visiting from
Orkney arrived to share his noon meal, he thought he might
discover something about his origins. He had never known his
family, only that he'd come from Orkney originally. But, by
nightfall, he'd learned little or nothing except that the Earl of
Orkney had a truthsayer, a man who was called on to determine the truth whenever it was in question.

Not one of them could give more information than that, and

with the earl about to sail south in the king's company, Duncan had no time to pursue the matter. Ornolf suggested sending someone north and he gave his permission, even knowing it could take months to find out more.

Duncan watched for Isabel to appear at the feasts held each night over the next sennight, but she did not. Nor did the man called Sigurd. As the newly returned sensations began to fade in his body and soul and the cold detachment spread again, terror of going back to that empty state became his only emotion. He sought out Davin for advice on how to handle the task of arranging to take Isabel as his leman.

He might not yet know why she was different or how she managed to bring about such changes in him, but he could not let her slip from his grasp. He rarely called in favors, but Davin owed him many and it was nothing compared to what he could request. If not for Duncan's ability to heal anyone from injury or illness, Davin's wife and firstborn would be dead. Procuring a leman was nothing by comparison.

He found Davin training with his men outside the wall and joined them for a few hours, hours in which he learned his ability to feel was diminishing by the day. Every hour since he'd bedded Isabel sensations and emotions were being stolen from him.

"Come, Duncan," Davin said, handing his sword to one of the young boys in training, "Walk with me."

Davin also held out a scrap of linen for Duncan to use. Glancing down, Duncan noticed the cuts on his arms and legs that he had not felt before. When they reached the small beach, he tugged off his boots and walked into the seawater to wash away the blood. The saltiness in it did not bother him, though Davin winced as he saw to his own injuries.

Another change. Duncan walked from the water and waited for Davin on the sand. They sat down and Duncan accepted the flask offered by Davin. Swallowing a mouthful of the powerful brew, Duncan thought on how to begin.

His friend, always perceptive, said, "So, you want my help in getting this woman?"

Duncan laughed and nodded. "That obvious, am I?"

"Aye." Davin met his gaze and shrugged. "Though you have sought out women before, this one is different. You seem to care about finding her and having her."

Duncan ran his hands through his hair and nodded. "I cannot explain it, but I know I need her."

Davin shoved him and laughed.

"Nay, not in that way, though aye, in that way too."

"You are not alone in wanting her in your bed," Davin added. "Every man who has had her bargains with Sigurd to get her again. Does she offer something any other woman could not give you?"

Pushing himself to stand, Duncan tried to explain it to the man who was the closest thing he had to a friend.

"She has undone some of the changes." He spoke boldly, not trying to explain more than that.

"Undone them? But, look at the wounds you sustained just this morn because you cannot feel. How is that changed?"

"I could feel. Last week after spending the night with her, my skin hurt, my appetite returned, my emotions . . ." He paused. "And more, I wanted her, Davin. I wanted her."

Davin looked over the sea toward the outer islands and remained silent for a few minutes. He never responded in haste, a quality that kept him out of many battles and other troubles when others plunged in headlong.

"Did my cousin's men tell you anything? Is there some link between you and their earl's truthsayer?"

Duncan kicked the sand at his feet toward the water. "Nay.

I think not, though Ornolf is sending someone north to learn more."

"The full moon approaches. Will she be . . . enough?"

The only appetite that remained when all else was burned out at the full moon's rising was his need for countless, nameless women in his bed. And though he sought and used any and every woman who arrived at his door, he remembered none of them, only the emptiness that resulted from it.

"I know not, Davin. I know only that she is different. And tied to this somehow."

"You know I will do whatever you need. I am in your debt." Davin stood and began walking. "Her stepfather asked to see you."

Duncan grabbed his friend and pulled him around so they were face-to-face. "He did? When?"

"He is not a fool. He has waited until he knows you are frantic to have her and will make it worth his while for you to get her."

"Where is he?"

"I told him to speak to you before the evening meal. He will be there."

"Will she?" Duncan asked before thinking about revealing so much to his friend.

Davin laughed and slapped him on the back. "He is a good merchant. Surely he will put the goods on display before telling you the cost of them . . . of her."

So many thoughts filled Duncan's head, he could think of little else. He was like a man knowing he is about to starve whose need for food soars above the reality of how much his stomach can hold. Duncan craved the sensations she caused— he wanted to feel again. After knowing the complete emptiness he faced, he wanted his heart and soul to be satisfied and full.

"The cost matters not to me. I will have her."

"Duncan! That is what he is hoping for," Davin warned. "Let Ornolf do the bargaining. One thing you must consider. If you wish to keep her for longer than one night, or make it more permanent, you must find another place. My wife would object to you keeping her in our home."

"And her wishes matter?" Duncan asked the question already knowing the answer—Edda mattered more than life itself to Davin.

"Any smart man with a wife who wishes for peace in his home abides by her wishes. You would know that if you had a wife."

The heartfelt words hung between them. Davin loved his wife. There was no mistaking the soft feelings he had for her or the lengths to which he would go to make her happy. Duncan could never have one—not since he changed from a normal man into something driven by unknown forces and was still changing with each phase of the moon. He would never lay claim to a woman when he knew not whether he would survive the next ritual or the one after that.

What wife would endure the endless women in his bed he needed each month to ease the wild craving in his blood?

None. So he had none.

"And you are nothing if not a smart man," Duncan said, trying to ease the strain between them. "Come, at least I can arrange for a leman to see to some of my needs."

They were almost at the gate when Davin stopped him.

"Have a care around this man, Duncan. Though no one has complained, there is something strange about him."

"The way he whores out his stepdaughter?"

"The way others support him for no discernible reasons," Davin countered. "Her skills in bedplay may be good, but men would not back him for only that."

Duncan could think of no reply, so he remained silent, his mind slipping back to memories of that night with Isabel. Still, a bit of pleasure should not influence a man's loyalty as Davin's words indicated was happening. To most men, one woman was the same as the next.

"How many men did you send with the king, Davin?"

"Half of them . . . and Askell."

The king had taken many hostages from among the families of those ruling the western islands and Skye to ensure their loyalty and their help in strengthening his claim and control over those lands so distant from the rest of the Norse holdings. With his only son accompanying Magnus south, Davin would do nothing to further upset his wife and would do even less to anger the king.

"So you are relying on those men who stand with Sigurd for defense?"

"Aye." Davin nodded. "More than I would like."

"Watch your back," Duncan advised. "And send to your cousins in Orkney and over in Lewis for men you can count on."

"I have already, though I like how you think."

"I will try to learn what his plans are from Isabel."

"She may only be a pawn in his plans and not know what he is about." Davin had a soft spot in his heart for the gentler sex.

"I suspect she knows much and I plan on finding out whatever I can. You are not the only one who owes a debt of honor."

Their lives had been entwined since they were but boys and they'd saved each other more times than he could remember. Davin had not shunned him when the strange power had begun and had protected him from those who would misuse it. Davin was his only true friend, more like a brother;

Duncan owed him loyalty and more. He would do what he could to protect Davin and his family from Sigurd's machinations.

Even if it meant not having the one person he thought might save his own life.

Chapter Five

Sigurd was determined, Isabel realized. No amount of questioning or cajoling had made a difference. When he was intent on something, he accomplished it. And when Sigurd wanted to bend her to his will, he did. His command to be dressed and ready at sunset was not to be ignored or refused.

They walked in silence, Isabel following several paces behind him, never acknowledging anyone they passed. Harder to ignore were the whispered comments as they entered through the gate and made their way to the hall. A guard spoke to Sigurd, who told her to follow the guard to a different place to wait.

'Twas not unusual—whores were not welcome in the homes of the nobleborn. Only Sigurd's high standing and Lord Davin's need for his men made her presence less an outrage than it might have been. Without raising her head, she followed until they reached a small chamber near the stairs that led to the tower. He stopped and stepped aside for her to enter. She prepared herself for the inevitable groping or touching that happened when she passed too close to a man, but he did nothing. Glancing up, she understood why.

Duncan stood across the small chamber, watching her every

move, never giving away any sign of his mood. It was the first time they'd looked at each other since that night filled with passionate abandon, but there was no hint of desire in his gaze.

"My lord," she said softly, dropping low before him. He might not carry a title, but he moved in higher circles than she or even than Sigurd, so courtesy was a good first step.

Though he might not remember, her body surely did, for with each step he took closer, more heat raced through her— along her skin where every inch had been his to touch and taste and thrill, through her body and into her core, which throbbed in anticipation of his possession. Isabel began to slow her breathing, to regain the control that seemed to disappear when in his presence and to calm the raging heat that threatened everything. His hand before her eyes offered help to stand. She stood by her own efforts and nodded to him.

She concentrated to gather her control, protecting her from the damage he could do. Damage that was far more dangerous than any Sigurd could mete out. Isabel knew Duncan wanted her, knew he would have her, several times before the sun rose again, but in order to escape unscathed, she must seek that place of emptiness within her where she could hide her soul.

"Isabel," he whispered. The sound felt like a stroke across her skin as he repeated it. How could a sound be physical? Yet every word he spoke felt like a touch of his hand or his mouth.

"My lord," she repeated, using courtesy to prevent familiarity from battering down her defenses so early in their encounter.

Apparently unwilling to allow her such refuge, he took her hand and lifted it to his mouth, kissing the back of it, then turning it to expose her palm. Her nipples tightened and pressed against the scratchy fabric of her gown as he first kissed, then licked, the sensitive skin of her wrist. As he kissed down the length of her arm, she realized how defenseless against him she was. Frightened by her inability to control her reactions to him, she did the unthinkable and pulled out of his grasp.

She waited to see if he would strike her for such insolence, but he did not. Instead, he smiled and stepped back. That the smile did not reach his eyes worried her, but it was too late to give in.

"If you wish me to return to your bed, you must speak with—"

"Your father?" he asked, interrupting her.

Was that what he thought? "He was my mother's husband," she explained for the first time ever. *Not my father.* She cursed under her breath, turning away for a moment. She'd never responded to anyone's questions about Sigurd and never spoke about any rumors or stories of how their arrangement had come about. She must not speak on it now. "Sigurd. You must speak to Sigurd." Isabel turned back to Duncan in time to see him frown.

"Ornolf is speaking to Sigurd and making the arrangements with him." Duncan stepped closer, never taking his gaze from hers. "And I am speaking to you."

Would she ever be at ease with him? No man wanted to speak to her. They wanted her mouth to be doing something other than spilling words.

"Speak to me?" Her palms grew damp. "About what?" Her breath caught. Looking around her, she noticed there was no bed in the chamber, just a small table and two stools. The guard had shut the door behind her and the room began to close in on her.

"I wish your . . . company over the next few weeks," Duncan said in an even tone.

"Company? Do not call it what it is not, my lord." Better to have the truth between them. "I will pleasure you, if you wish, my lord, but it will not take weeks."

He laughed then, the gesture making his face come alive and the sound of it forcing a smile to her own lips. How did he do that to her? No other man had made her resolve so fluid and changing.

"I do not think I could survive your pleasure for all the time I plan to be with you, Isabel."

Confused, unused to feeling out of control, Isabel knew she did not like it. He seemed to be teasing her and commanding her presence all at the same time. Was his servant truly bargaining with Sigurd at the moment? Sigurd would not be happy to be relegated to dealing with an underling and he would take out his anger on her when next he could.

"I am traveling to my farm and will remain there for some weeks. I wish you to accompany me there."

So many thoughts filled her mind in that moment—why, where, how, and why again. What did he mean to do with her for *some weeks*? Would Sigurd consent to such a thing? With enough gold crossing his palm and promises of influence, Sigurd would sell his soul . . . or hers.

"And if I decline your invitation?" She truly had no choice, but wanted to watch his reaction to measure his control.

"It is your choice. Though I confess, I will be disappointed if that is your decision."

She sensed he would allow her to refuse. But what then? Face Sigurd and the consequences? Mayhap if she spent some time with Duncan she would not feel so overwhelmed by him and by his power to distract her from everything. Mayhap it would be less of a shock to her and she could regain control and see him as she saw every other man—someone to pleasure in order to avoid the consequences of not doing as Sigurd commanded.

"You think your servant can convince Sigurd of this?"

He laughed again. "You have a habit of answering my questions with questions of your own. Do you never speak your own mind?"

She let that go unanswered for the truth of it was no, she did not. In those encounters it was best to simply deflect questions so the man thought she only considered his requests and interests and never her own. It went better that way.

Dare she accept? How would Sigurd get messages to her? Was it safe to leave the keep and village with the man? On a farm, out somewhere on the isle, she was more defenseless and less able to call on others for assistance as she had when . . . She shook her head to avoid thinking on that night.

"Nay? You will not?" he asked, misunderstanding her gesture. His face lost its smile and his eyes darkened.

"Nay!" She touched his hand. "I will go with you," she agreed. "If Sigurd allows it."

Duncan smiled once more and placed his hand on hers, the heat of that simple caress spreading into her body. "He will. I have something he wants."

Isabel kept her face from reacting to his words. Did he know Sigurd's plan? Worse, did he know her part in it?

Before she could choose careful words, he spoke. "Gold, certainly. And enough of it to satisfy his appetite for it." He watched her as he said it.

"He likes gold." She nodded.

Without a doubt, she knew he had not meant gold. The way his gaze flickered she knew he meant something else entirely. He had something Sigurd wanted, something other than gold, and he knew she was playing him to gain it.

Though she might have been insulted by such knowledge, in many ways it made it easier somehow. Nothing to entangle them. Nothing to fool them into believing it was more than a practical arrangement to benefit all of those concerned. Nothing more than a few weeks of pleasuring the same man rather than many different ones. Once the novelty wore off, it would mean simply bedding him and being done with it.

Her heart and soul knew better, sounding off a warning from within that there was much more at stake than just an exchange of flesh for coin.

"Do we leave now?" she asked, not knowing where his farm was.

"Nay, we leave at first light." He stroked her hand and she understood he wished to bed her that night before leaving in the morning.

"Should I send word to gather my things?"

His fingers caressed her hand and her arm, tugging her ever so slightly in his direction. She could not take her gaze from the movements of his hand and, for a moment, she thought of him stroking her naked body instead of touching her through layers of cloth.

"Nay," he said in a roughened voice. "You can pack for yourself and be ready at first light."

"You do not wish to bed me now? This night?" she asked, completely confused and surprised. She knew he was aroused, the scent of it nearly intoxicated her. She thought . . .

"I wish to bed you, Isabel, but have matters to see to before I can leave on the morrow."

She nodded, accepting but not understanding. "Very well, my lord," she said, easing her hand from his grasp. "I will be ready at first light."

"You do not believe me?" His voice was quiet with a hint of something she could not name. "Let me show you how much I want to . . . bed you."

With no more warning, he took her by the shoulders and drew her to him, taking her mouth in a searing kiss. He claimed her mouth and possessed it, rubbing their lips against each other's and tasting her deeply. His arms wrapped around her, holding her so tightly against him she could do nothing but fall into him. His mouth released hers and she sucked in a ragged and deep breath before he kissed her again . . . and again until she had no breath and no will to leave. Then he took her hand and placed it over the ridge of hardened flesh below his waist.

"I want you, Isabel," he whispered as he kissed a path along her chin and jaw to her ear, where his breath heated her. "I do not intend to bed you this night, but soon I will take you in every way a man can take a woman. I plan on touching you, licking and tasting you, at all hours of the days and nights to come."

Her body arched against his, moisture pouring from that place between her legs. Her flesh ached and throbbed at his words. Her fingers curled around his erection.

"And I will fuck you so deeply and so many times that you will forget where you end and I begin."

Isabel was lost.

She wanted him.

She wanted all he promised, all he threatened.

But, she could not allow it.

Pulling away, she stumbled to the door, trying to escape the madness he created in her before she lost everything she'd worked so hard to gain. Her control slipped dangerously and she needed space and time away from him to ready herself for the challenge he presented.

"On the morrow, my lord," she said, lifting the latch without looking back at him. "At first light."

Isabel pulled the door closed behind her, ignoring the sound of his footsteps as they followed her, knowing she must get away or she would be the one begging for his touch that night. She followed the path around the hall and left the keep, making her way back to her cottage at a near-running pace.

Sigurd would not be happy she'd left without his permission, but she did not care.

If it were not already dark, she would have gone to the sea and swum in its soothing waters. For longer than she could remember, she always sought out water when she was worried or upset. Since the arousal of her body did not lessen as she entered her cottage, she decided to go down to the shore, knowing sleep would be impossible. Taking off the costly gown she wore and putting on a plain one, she walked quickly to the path leading to the beach. Where other women feared the night, she relished it for she had nothing to worry over losing. The men of the village avoided her because they had to answer to Sigurd for anything done to her.

Though the half moon lit the sky above her and the glow of thousands of stars added to it, Isabel could feel a storm coming from across the sea. It whispered to her and she closed her eyes and let the breezes ease the tumult inside her mind and her soul. Breathing deeply, she cleared all of it away and focused her thoughts on the coming storm and the sounds of the sea at her feet. It took only moments for her to shed her clothes and dive into the water, going deep and swimming away from shore.

Sigurd had beaten her the first time he'd witnessed her skill at swimming. It had happened so long ago, she remembered thinking how much he cared and worried over her. Had her mother yet lived?

Returning to the surface, she kicked as hard as she could, pushing her body out of the water, landing with a splash. With another deep breath drawn in, she spun and dove again, skimming just under the water as she swam to the calmest place before the waves began to lap the shore.

Turning onto her back, she floated, watching the moon and stars above, hearing only the sounds of the water as it surrounded her head with calm. Unlike the small lake where she'd grown up, the sea was cold and she could not tolerate it for long. Unable to stand its chill, she rolled and dove under once more, all the time offering up the prayer she always did—to whatever god would listen. As before, she did not know for what she prayed, only that she did. One word echoed through her thoughts as she began to swim to shore.

Please.

The litany of words added to that one had grown and grown and not even a holy sister spending all of her days in secluded, silent prayer could have voiced them all. So Isabel held onto only that one, hoping that any god powerful enough to answer her would know and understand the rest.

She walked the last few yards to the beach and gathered her hair in her hands to wring the water from it. As she made her way to the pile of clothes she'd left behind, she saw him, standing there watching every step she took.

Duncan had followed her as she fled from him—unsure whether his crude words had frightened or aroused her. They were true, every one of them, and they were only the beginning of what he wanted to do to her. A few weeks would never be long enough. Months would not, but he did not have more than another two if what he suspected came to be.

Duncan had only wanted to find out if she would go with him of her own will and not because Sigurd ordered her to do it, so he'd had her brought to him while Ornolf met with Sigurd. And he'd watched her reaction. Though she'd tried to remain calm, he heard her heart racing, saw her skin flush with arousal when the scent flowed from him.

He felt the fullness of his own arousal—his skin aching once more for her touch and experiencing the pain of his earlier injuries on the field. It felt remarkable after the numbness had begun creeping back in.

Though she'd put him off with questions meant to distract

him, he could tell she wanted him as much as he wanted her. She'd used no whore's tricks.

She rose from the sea like a goddess of old, her skin tightened from the cold. Duncan could see how her nipples puckered as she walked toward the place where she'd dropped her gown. He was rock hard, fighting the urge to run to her and do at least some of the things he'd told her about earlier. But that would undo what he had followed her to accomplish.

He fought his wayward desire. Mayhap he should run into the frigid water to cool the desire rushing through his blood.

"My lord?" she whispered. Her voice shook from the cold seeping into her muscles. She waited for him, pausing in the act of picking up her clothes.

Duncan walked to her side, picking up her gown as he passed it. Gathering it up he tugged it over her head, noticing it was not the same one she'd been wearing at the keep.

"Are you mad? Swimming in the sea at night and when it is so cold?" He rubbed his hands over her arms, trying to ease the cold from her skin. Unfortunately, it brought her into his arms and he wanted nothing more than to ease her to the ground and fill her with his aching flesh.

"It soothes me."

So, she had been disturbed by his invitation. Good, for he, too, was bothered by the thought of having her at his beck and call for the next few weeks. Most likely, though, for reasons different from hers.

Duncan wrapped his arms around her, absorbing the cold from her body and wondered at her admission. She entered the sea every time she left the keep and left a man's bed—except for his that first time. He'd watched her do it, countless times, wondering at her reasons and her ease in the sea, regardless of the change in seasons or the growing iciness of the water.

"Drink wine," he barked. "It has remarkable medicinal properties."

"You said you had things to do, my lord," she said, easing out of his arms. She walked away and gathered the rest of her things together.

"You left abruptly."

She paused then, before turning to face him. He did not feel the overwhelming sadness he'd sensed that first morning after, but 'twas almost as though he could feel her emotions. Usually that sensitivity was reserved for the ritual, but with her, it seemed to occur naturally. As he watched her face, he felt ripples of confusion and fear and wonder passing through her.

"I did, my lord." She schooled her expression and the whore's face appeared, one he hated to see on her features. Her eyes went blank, her lips pursed temptingly, her skin flushed, all to increase her sexual attractiveness to men. "Have you changed your mind?" She rolled her shoulders, which made her breasts appear larger. Her nipples were still taut against her thin gown.

"Do not do that!" he said, shaking his head. "Do not play the whore with me, Isabel."

Though she was surprised by his words, she did not lose the vapid expression or whore's stance, offering herself to him without a word. "But that is what I am, my lord. A whore whose time and attentions you are buying. Do not mistake our arrangement for something it is not."

For some reason, Duncan knew the warning offered by her was speaking to her own fears. She was trying to convince herself of it, not him. He only knew it for the lie it was and something much more important was building between them.

"I will keep that in mind, Isabel. Now, let me see you to your cottage."

"I can make my way there, my lord. I have before."

The implication being that she would again, without him.

He did not want to think on that, nor did he want to think about her being with another man now that he had found her. There would be time before he had to deal with it all.

"Until the morning then," he said. He had no intention of letting her make her way back alone, but she did not need to know that. Once she was in her cottage, he would return to complete the negotiations with Sigurd. Ornolf was keeping the man occupied for him until he returned.

She nodded, then walked past him, not waiting for him and not looking back to see if he followed. He dogged her steps, remaining far enough back she would not hear or see him, but close enough to reach her if she needed him. He did not fool himself that she was not used to watching out for herself.

In less than an hour, Duncan was seeing to those tasks he'd mentioned to Isabel—things needing to be done before he left in the morning. Sleeping was not one of them.

Chapter Six

When Duncan arrived at the cottage, Isabel stood at its door waiting for him. From the look in her eyes, she had slept as little as he had. Sigurd was nowhere to be seen, which was exactly what Duncan had ordered when paying the exorbitant amount of gold coins asked in exchange for having Isabel to himself for the next month.

"Is that all you bring?" he asked, nodding at the small sack in her hand.

"Aye, my lord," she said, eyeing the horse he rode with a skeptical expression.

"Give it to me then." He held out his hand. He secured the sack to the front of the saddle and turned back to her. "Now, come up."

For a moment she looked as though tempted to refuse. She walked around the horse, a large, powerful gelding, and watched it closely. Duncan released a foot from the stirrup and positioned it so she could use it to climb up behind him. He leaned over and reached for her hand.

"Put your foot there and give me your hand," he directed.

"I do not like horses, my lord."

It was the first time he'd heard her express a preference and it startled him. She hadn't uttered a word no matter what he had asked her to do with him during that bliss-filled night, but a horse had wrung the confession from her. Before he could offer any reassurances or words of encouragement, she gathered the length of her gown in one hand and took his with the other, hefting herself onto the horse.

Though he controlled the horse's movements, the animal shifted to accommodate their combined weights and he heard her gasp with each side-step, clutching at his back. He calmed the animal, then helped Isabel to settle behind him. Duncan touched his feet to the horse's sides and they were on their way.

He felt her hands fluttering as she tried to find something to hold onto, something sturdier than the layers of clothing she held. Lifting his arms, he told her to wrap her arms around him. There was no hesitation as she did as he suggested, but he felt the tension in her body. She sat straight up, not adjusting to the horse's gait as they left the village and keep behind.

"How far is your farm?" she whispered.

"Do you fear reaching it, Isabel?" he teased.

"Aye."

He laughed and reached up to cover one of her hands with his. "How do you travel from Duntulm?" Surely she must have ridden before.

"I do not leave Duntulm."

Her words stymied him. "Not even when Sigurd returns to his farm?"

Her silence answered him. He thought back to her original question. "My farm is to the north of the hills surrounding Uig."

"You live near the bay?"

"Aye."

"We could have taken a boat," she whispered.

Her tone was disgruntled, again the first time she'd allowed anything but compliance to enter her words.

"You are at home in the water, but I am not," he explained. "Hold on until you are at ease."

The mists swirled around them as he guided the horse along the path into the hills that headed south and east toward Uig and his farm. It would take most of the day to reach it, but all he could think on was the coming night. Though she held on tightly, she did not relax or lean against him.

The sun tried to burn off the thick fog, but the day remained dreary and cool as they covered the miles. She did not say a word or ask him to rest, but sagged behind him when he stopped a few hours later. He lifted his leg over the horse and jumped to the ground, turning back to help her.

Heavens protect her, she sat alone on the back of the huge animal and had no idea how to get off. Her legs were numb from hours of clenching the sides of the mighty beast while trying not to fall off. Duncan stood watching her with amusement at her discomfort. She struggled to lift her leg over the horse as he had, but her muscles chose the wrong time not to obey her commands and she ended up toppling off and falling. Duncan broke her fall, cushioning her as she landed on the ground.

Isabel lost her breath but soon realized she was straddling his body. Her gown and cloak were twisted around her, exposing her legs almost to her hips. She pushed up on her arms, shook her head to get the hair out of her face and gazed down on him. His eyes were closed and she was not certain whether she'd knocked him unconscious or not. Reaching down, she touched his cheek with her hand and rubbed her thumb along his jaw.

His lips curved ever so slightly, into the hint of a smile, and his eyelids twitched as he tried to keep them closed. He was pretending! Bedeviled, she leaned over and kissed him. It was a simple, gentle kiss that said nothing of passion. But his reaction was swift and she found herself on the ground with him covering her, his eyes lit with lust and his body hardened and ready to take her.

As quickly as it had appeared, he banked the heat in his gaze and rolled off her. Holding out his hand, he helped her to her feet and dusted the dirt and mud from her cloak. He was unlike any man she'd met before—one who would ignore his body's readiness to couple and delay his own pleasure for . . . for what she knew not.

Isabel looked around the area where they'd drawn to a stop and noticed he seemed familiar with the place. He led the horse to the nearby stream to drink, then let it graze. He pointed to a thick stand of trees where she could see to her own needs, and when she returned, he offered her a skin filled with ale, and pieces of bread and cheese.

She thought him stranger with every action he took.

What man would see to such tasks when a woman was there to perform them? He did, and did it with good cheer when another man would have been swiving her on the ground where they'd fallen. She remained a bit apart and watched as he tended to his horse and saw to his own needs, leaving her alone.

Isabel walked a wide circle around him, eating the food he'd given her as she tried to work the pain and tightness from the muscles in her legs and her back. She was stiff from riding for longer than she ever had before. Worse was the knowledge she would have to get back up on the horse and continue their journey.

He did not hurry her, though he could have. He watched as she walked by him, offering the skin to her as she passed.

Duncan knew they needed to leave soon, but he noticed the way she limped as she took each step. He waited until she seemed to move with less pain, before calling to her.

Their journey would last several more hours, along the stream and into the hills, but staying south and east of the Quiraing escarpment. His farm was not large and he did not rely on its income or crops, but it was his. If everything else he owned disappeared on the morrow, the farm would remain his.

Isabel passed him once more on her circuitous path and he handed her the skin of ale. As she drank deeply from it he noticed the way she tilted her head back and the lines of her graceful neck. Her hair fell in waves over her shoulders and, after handing it back to him and walking away, he also noticed the sway of her hips as she moved. Touching her, kissing her, or simply being with her freed his body and heart and soul from the damage wrought by the curse he bore.

When the horse had been watered and grazed, Duncan put the remnants of their meal back in the sack and tied it and the skin on the saddle. As she approached once more, he nodded and tried to ignore the funny expression she made at the news that it was time to get back on the horse.

"You are still not at ease on his back," he said, as he held out his hand to her.

A shake of her head was her only response.

"Here. Go up first and I will sit at your back."

She did not take his hand at first, but it was only a momentary hesitation. He realized she didn't hesitate to obey his words long enough to be considered a refusal. He wondered at that as he helped her climb into the saddle.

The horse shifted as she sat and she splayed out across his neck, grasping his mane as she did. Though terror filled her eyes, she did not utter a word of complaint or refusal. 'Twas clear to him she had been trained, like a hound, never to refuse an order and that her will did not matter.

Like a good whore.

Her body sat rigid when he climbed up behind her. She didn't relax or lean back against him as he guided the horse at an even pace along the stream that wound through the valley. Though his arms encircled her to hold the reins, she did nothing that either welcomed or hindered his embrace-of-a-sort. They rode in silence, covering the miles as the skies grew cloudier and the air cooled. Finally, as she drifted off to sleep for the third or fourth time only to awaken with a jolt, he whispered to her.

"Lean back against me, Isabel. Sleep if you need to," he urged.

She did as he directed and soon he felt her body melt against his. He shifted her in his arms, so she rested more fully on him as the horse followed the path to his farm. It felt right holding her and caring for her. Keeping in mind that she was a whore being paid to accompany him home became difficult.

Isabel slept through the rest of their journey. He woke her as they approached the lane that led to his house. At first she did not move, then she startled, sitting up straight and looking around as though she'd forgotten where she was.

"Here is my farm," he said.

She stopped moving and asked, "How long have I slept?" Her voice was roughened by sleep and his body responded to it. "Your pardon, my lord."

Confused by the apology, he shook his head. "What have you done to beg my pardon?"

"I should not have fallen asleep."

In other words, a whore did not sleep while with a man. Whores were not paid to sleep—they were paid to pleasure.

"We must set some new rules between us, Isabel. A month is a long time to go without sleeping."

"A month?" she asked. "Sigurd agreed to a month?"

Duncan heard the shock in her voice and saw it in her expression when she turned to face him.

Any further discussion between them was forestalled when his arrival was noticed. Several men working in the yard called out greetings and he knew it would only be moments before—

"Duncan, you should have sent word!" Harald exclaimed as he ran over to meet them. He stopped just a few paces away and stared at Isabel. Having visited Duntulm several times recently he recognized her.

"Isabel is my guest, Harald," Duncan said, cutting off any questions before they could be asked. "Let the others know."

"Aye, Duncan," the young man said, nodding. He would still ask questions, but understood to wait for a time more private to do so. The real problem would be Gunnhilde.

Duncan slid off the horse and turned to help Isabel just as that young woman burst out of the house in her customary exuberant fashion and ran to him. She barely waited for him to step back and turn before she threw her arms around him in a rib-crushing embrace. The younger sister he never had, Gunnhilde was always filled with vitality and joy. Because she'd nearly lost her life in an accident, she valued her days. Seeing her made his heart glad.

"Duncan! We did not know you were coming or we would have been ready," she began. She released him and turned to call out orders to the girl who helped her in the house and to the younger man in the yard. "See to his—their—things, Gawen. Eara, make certain Duncan's chamber is clean and his linens fresh."

"Ornolf follows a day or two behind, Gunna," Duncan said, calling her the name he always used. "Worry not over the room."

"And who is this?" Gunna asked, as he'd known she would.

He'd turned back to help Isabel from the horse and did not answer until she was on her feet and not wobbling.

"This is my guest Isabel," he said once more, making it clear that no one would treat her otherwise. "She will be staying for a few weeks."

Gunna did not hide her surprise. Her gasp was heard by the others in the yard. Though they would not dare to express it, she had no fear of showing her reaction. Duncan did not think she understood what Isabel was, but Harald did, as did the other men who stood by listening and watching.

Harald walked over and put his arm around his sister's shoulders, drawing her close to him. She said, "I meant no disrespect, Duncan. 'Tis just not your habit to bring *guests* with you."

Gunna understood more than he'd hoped she would.

"Isabel, come, let me make you welcome in Duncan's home." Gunna held her hand out.

Duncan turned to watch Isabel. Once more, after gaining his nod of permission, she obeyed, following Gunna into the house. Once they were gone, Duncan untied the sacks from the saddle and started to follow them.

Harald stepped in front of him. "You bring her here, Duncan? Is that wise? The full moon approaches."

"I had no choice. She is involved in some way I do not yet understand."

"Has she told you something?"

"Nay." Duncan stared at the closed door. "But I will have weeks to find out what she does know."

Or what she is.

"She is an outsider. 'Tis too dangerous to have her here now," Harald warned, stepping closer so no one else could hear his words. "I cannot allow her to witness the ritual."

Davin had selected Harald for his trustworthiness and dependability. And his complete and utter devotion to Duncan for saving his sister's life.

"We will observe her and decide if she is a threat," Duncan offered.

"She *is* a threat," Harald replied, stepping out of Duncan's path. "I just do not understand why you want her here. Other than the obvious charms she offers."

"I have decided to bring one woman with me to see to my needs during this time. Who better than a woman who makes her living on her back?"

Harald remained silent, not arguing or offering his opinion and Duncan worried over the trouble that could signal. They reached the door, but Harald remained there, not entering. "What about Gunna?"

"Gunna will be who she is, Harald. She will try to adopt another lost soul and care for her."

"Is that what the woman is then? A lost and wounded soul who needs you to heal her, and Gunna to nurse her back to life?"

Duncan reeled back from that revelation. Was that it? Did the healer within him recognize the need in her to be healed? He'd noticed it happening more and more as the months passed—his healing abilities leaking into the days between the ritual, which always occurred when the moon reached its fullness. Did his power simply want to heal whatever was broken within her?

Relieved somehow at that explanation, he lifted the latch of the door and stepped inside. It was the main building on the farm and where his private chamber was located. The others slept elsewhere but the cooking and eating were done there. The house was not like others on most farms, for Duncan had designed it according to his needs and not the usual ones of a farmstead. He ducked his head as he entered and found Isabel sitting at the table while Gunna put food before her. A place had been prepared for him as well.

No matter the time of day, Gunna had something cooking in the pot over the fire. Porridge in the morning and a stew throughout the day. Anyone stopping there would be given a hearty meal before they continued on their journey. Her task in life was to collect and care for those in need and she relished it. Truth be told, he'd encouraged her for she made him feel as though he had a home.

Isabel did not raise her eyes from the table, nor did she begin to eat. Though he knew she must be famished from the day's travel and meager rations, she waited without a word. He touched her hand and she startled, then recovered, allowing his hand to cover hers without moving it away.

"Eat," he whispered as Gunna prattled on without pausing for anyone to answer the questions she posed. She didn't notice the silence, but he did. Isabel spoke not a word except to murmur her thanks when Gunna placed another cup or bowl within her reach or refilled the one before her.

He ate, listening to Gunna's lively chatter, picking out bits of news about the surrounding neighbors, about the villagers in Uig, and Gunna's concerns. But he never took his eyes off of Isabel. He sensed she had closed herself off from him. Duncan asked a few questions of Gunna and watched as Isabel finished eating.

"Has Gunna showed you my chamber here?"

"Aye, my—" Isabel paused for a moment, not knowing whether or not to address him as lord among his people, who seemed more like his family than servants. All of them, from the field hands to the woman who kept house for him, treated him like kin, or the way Isabel thought kin would treat each other.

The woman Gunnhilde stopped and stared at her then, and

Isabel knew she'd misstepped in some way. She knew the young woman was special to Duncan, and he would not have told her of his arrangements or of Isabel's true place there. Whores were a fact of life but were not tolerated in a man's home or around his kin.

Duncan squeezed her hand. As she dared a glance up at him he spoke softly, guiding her way. "Duncan."

"Aye, Duncan. Mistress Gunna showed me your chamber." Isabel also realized Gunna wanted to please Duncan more than anything in the world, so she continued. "And it is most pleasing."

The woman smiled and nodded at Duncan.

"I thank you for worrying over my comfort, Gunna," Isabel said softly. The warm surroundings gave a sense of intimacy to their conversation that almost put her at ease, but she knew better.

Every possible warning sounded to keep her from feeling too at ease there, among those people, with him. She needed some time and some space to gather her thoughts and her resolve. Looking around and then at him, she wondered if he would give her leave to go outside without him. Taking a chance, she rose from the stool and stepped away from the table.

"May I walk for a bit?" she asked.

Silence filled the house, only the crackling flames in the hearth making any noise. Isabel worried her lower lip, waiting for his permission, not daring to meet his gaze or to look at Gunna.

"You are my guest, Isabel. You may come and go as you please," he said quietly.

She nodded and smiled at Gunna. "My thanks for the meal."

Then she fled, one slow step at a time.

Chapter Seven

Isabel left the house and followed the path away—the one they arrived on though she had no memory of the last half of the journey. Her body ached from the hours spent on the horse and each step she took began to ease the pains in her back and legs. She passed the men who'd been working in the fields and the one named Harald who'd spoken to Duncan in a frank manner.

He knew who she was.

He knew what she was.

Isabel felt his gaze remain on her long after she walked by him, but she kept on walking. His attitude she understood, more than she comprehended Duncan's. He confused her more with each encounter. A man buying a whore's time for weeks? A man taking a whore to his home and among his people? None of that should have happened. She offered him nothing more than any other woman could—a night of pleasure, a bout of bedplay that would last for a few hours.

She turned her face up to the sky and watched the clouds gather and swirl. The storm had followed them from the coast inland and would strike soon. She tried to determine how

many hours of daylight were left, but the darkness of the
growing disturbance above prevented that. The winds grew
stronger, blowing down the valley and over the farm. As her
hair whipped around her she closed her eyes and let the power
of the storm surround her.

The rains would be coming soon. They would be strong
and would last for several days. She did not question how she
knew—it had been part of her since . . . she could not remember when. Long-ago bits of memories came to her of her days
as a child when she would warn her mother and their neighbors of the approaching rains. She shook her head to clear her
thoughts. Thinking back too far only made it harder to face
the present.

Opening her eyes she found Duncan standing just yards
away from her.

The winds caught his shoulder-length fair hair and blew it
wildly. His amber eyes blazed like hot metal and she could
feel wave after wave of desire pouring off him. Whatever feelings of lust he'd banked last evening, they were back in full
measure. Clearly he was ready to claim that for which he had
paid dearly. Looking around the area where they stood, she realized it was a secluded glen and not visible until one took the
turn in the road to the east.

His people would have seen him go after her and would
know not to follow them. Harald and the men knew her purpose there, for certain, and Gunna at the least suspected it. Isabel had caught her surreptitious glances, but did not want to
speak of such things to such a young and innocent woman.

He took a step toward her and then another, and she found
it difficult to breathe and impossible to move. How would she
survive such an onslaught of sensations and pleasure if that
happened every time they joined? Over the next weeks, every
shred of control that she'd built up would be stripped away.

She would be left with no way to protect herself, her heart and soul, from the damages of the life she led.

She'd sworn never to lie to herself and she just had. The control she'd fought so hard to develop as a defense was stripped away whenever she was in his presence. For whatever reason, she could no more play the whore with him than she could refuse him. What would become of her once they finished? What would happen to her with the next man and the next and the ones after those?

He stood but a few paces from her. He lifted his hand up and loosened his cloak, tossing it to the ground at his feet. Isabel's body heated at the knowledge he would take her on it. The blood raced through her veins and her skin began to ache for his touch. Her breasts swelled and the sensitive folds in that place between her legs grew moist and throbbed at the thought that he would put his mouth there to lick and suck until she screamed out her release.

He tugged his tunic over his head and reached for the ties on his breeches. Her feet moved toward him before she could think. Her usual way of planning and carrying out a seduction was useless, for she followed her body's commands and did what it wanted, pushing his hands away.

Giving in to the inevitable and accepting that she could not defend herself against the draw of the man, Isabel reached out and took hold of the laces of his breeches and untied them. His indrawn breath excited her and she fell to her knees to do exactly what her body was urging her to do—pull his trousers down and kiss a path down his thighs as the fabric gave way. Consequences be damned, for she would have to deal with them later, at a time when she had no choice but to face them.

Duncan had waited behind to speak with Gunna, to try to ease any fears she had about the woman he'd brought with him. He was not certain how to explain Isabel's presence, for he doubted Gunna had been exposed to women like her before. She'd grown up in the small village of Uig, in a large protective family. She'd spent little time anywhere but within walking distance of the cottage where she'd been born.

But, as she had so many times in the past, Gunna told him that Isabel was a lost soul. She would not explain more than that. She'd reminded him Isabel could become disoriented in the thick woods at the turn of the stream and he'd accepted her dismissal.

However, he'd followed Isabel for his own reasons, too. He could tell she was still out of sorts from the journey, from waking up among strangers, and from being placed in the middle of a situation unlike any she'd experienced before. He'd made the final turn on the path and seen her ahead. She stood with her face lifted up to the sky and her eyes closed. A habit it would seem, for she stood just so on the beach when he watched her there.

As she knelt before him, he noticed the dark smudges of exhaustion under her eyes and the paleness of her skin. The position accentuated the graceful lines of her neck, her shoulders, and the womanly curves of her breasts. His hands ached to touch them. His gaze went back to the evidence of her lack of sleep and he swore to himself if she gave any sign of reluctance, he would stop.

But when she opened those earthy green eyes and met his gaze, he read her hunger and her need. Not to be the whore to him but to be the woman. His body was long since ready for her, ready to join with her and to claim her. Nothing, not even the strong winds swirling above and around them, not the threatening storm, would stop him.

Duncan felt the touch of her tongue on his hot flesh. He shuddered, then leaned his head back and let the sound of the pleasure she caused echo through the glen.

Thunder rumbled in reply and lightning flashed across the

sky as she used her mouth up and down his prick. His hips arched, thrusting his flesh deeper into her mouth. He slid his fingers into her hair, freeing it to the wildness of the winds. She pushed him to the edge of release, then eased back, peering up at him from where she knelt on the ground before him.

He did not want her like that, in a position of serving him; he wanted to be deep within her, making her scream as he pushed them both to satisfaction. Duncan knelt down with her, removing her cloak and adding it to his. Then he guided her onto the ground and knelt between her legs. She opened to him, her legs cradling his hips. Sliding her gown out of the way, he eased into her, watching every move of her mouth and her eyes to gain some understanding of the woman he wanted with a growing desperation.

Her lips opened slightly and a breathy sigh escaped, making his blood heat. He surged forward, filling her until he could go no further, and his flesh swelled against the constriction of the throbbing muscles within her. He felt the sensations pulsing through him with each passing second.

Her gaze met his and neither moved nor breathed as their bodies remained joined. Lighting flared again in the distance and the rolling rumbles of thunder grew closer and louder.

Duncan smiled at her. "Not a good time?"

"There is time," she whispered as she returned his smile with one that made him want to possess her mouth. "The rains will not reach us for nearly an hour."

She'd spoken the words with such a tone of authority, it sounded to him as though she was ordering the storm to remain at bay. He leaned down and kissed her mouth. When she entangled her hands in his hair and held him to her, he tasted her deeply, enjoying the warm, wet heat of her mouth with his tongue the way his cock had.

He angled his hips and thrust again into her welcoming flesh. Ignoring the winds and thunder, he slid in slowly and withdrew at the same pace, trying to bring her to the edge of release. He paused and rolled, guiding her up over him. As she straddled him, he reached down and teased the sensitive bud that lay hidden inside the folds of flesh.

She arched at every caress, every touch of his fingers, and her deeper muscles clenched his cock. Isabel's legs tightened around his hips as she lifted her body up, then plunged down to slide on his length. Clouds swirled above them, the patterns of dark and light mixing, making it appear as though she moved slowly over him. Her black hair outlined her body and her green eyes caught every burst of lightning, reflecting it back at him, giving her an otherworldly appearance.

He ignored the thunder. He ignored the winds. He ignored everything that was not Isabel, forcing them past caution and into the oblivion pleasure offered. She tossed back her head, crying out as her body shook and spasmed around his, causing his own release in that moment. The storm answered back. Lightning rippled through the thundering mass overhead and Duncan wondered once more about her affinity to water and her knowledge of storms.

She collapsed on him and he wrapped his arms around her, caressing her back as she, as they, regained control and their breathing returned to a slower pace. He remained within her, despising the feel of his cock gradually withdrawing from her heat. They lay in silence for a few minutes, but the storm grew louder and wilder around them.

"We have to go," Isabel said as she straightened up. Still straddling him, she gathered the length of her gown and tunic and pushed herself to stand. "I was wrong—the rains are coming now."

Duncan shielded his eyes and looked in the same direction she did, but could see nothing to indicate the rain would commence.

Isabel did not hesitate—grabbing his tunic and tossing it to him. "We must hurry."

He climbed to his feet and tugged the shirt back into place. As he tied his laces, she shook out their cloaks and held his out to him. Instead of putting hers on, she began to walk away from him, back toward the farm. Duncan felt the first drops as he caught up with her.

As he watched she leaned her head back and let raindrops land on her face. Then she laughed and ran off ahead of him on the path. Her speed was no match for his, so he took her by the hand and led her, half running, half walking, along the narrow dirt path. Before they reached the outbuildings that might shelter them from the worst of it, the skies opened and torrents of rain poured down.

For a moment, he felt as though he was a child again, racing against the rains, trying to get home before a storm. Memories swirled in his mind much like the clouds—gray and white, dark and light, clear and muddied—as he tried to remember exactly what had happened. He had been thinking back on those tender years for some time, for it was difficult to face the end of one's life without contemplating the earliest and happiest days of it.

With each step he took, holding her hand like the anchor it seemed to be, joyful memories flooded through him. His friendship with Davin, finding and saving Gunna, discovering his ability to heal others. The good things in his life. It was as if the rain washed away the fear and the doubt and the pain of all he'd lost and all he would lose if things proceeded as he thought they must.

For a moment none of that mattered, for her strength flowed into him and refreshed his spirit and his soul. If he was the one known for his healing powers, what was she?

They raced along, finally reaching the fence that marked

the first of his fields. Soaked through to the skin, they ran to the door of the house and twisted out of their cloaks, letting the water drip on the ground. Duncan opened the door to check if anyone was within. When he found no one, he peeled off his clothes, then hers, and carried her inside.

He would have laid her on his bed, but she fussed about ruining the linens, so he set her on her feet and found a drying cloth. Wrapping her hair in it first, he drew out all the excess water, then rubbed the rest of her dry. He would have done it for himself, but she pulled the linen from his hands and dried him. Though it was not meant to, the feel of the fabric over his skin pushed him to arousal once more.

He would have taken her in that moment, but he remembered her exhaustion from the journey. To pursue her again would be cruel. Duncan told himself he had a month of her time and her attentions and he did not have to rush with her, but his body wanted more—and worse, his soul did, too.

She watched him in silence as he took the cloth and tossed it in the corner of the chamber. He walked around her, moved the blankets and furs from the bed and offered her his hand. As always, she did not hesitate to accept it. Duncan settled her in the bed, tucking the covers around her. She undid it all by lifting them for him.

"Nay. I want you to rest," he explained. His cock disagreed, surging as he gazed down on her body in his bed.

A frown marred her face, her brows raised and her lips downturned. If he did not know the amount she'd cost him, he would have thought her a lover instead of a paid companion in his bed. He was about to tell her of the dark smudges beneath her eyes that gave away her exhaustion when he realized they were gone. Her skin was unmarred.

How could that be? The sound of the storm outside drew his attention as thunder rumbled around them. He spoke his question before he could stop the words. "What are you?"

She began to speak. "I am"—

He knew what her words would be before she uttered them, so he spoke them with her. "A whore," he finished. "But you are more than that, Isabel. And I would know the rest of it."

He knew there was more to her than simply what she did for Sigurd. Duncan could feel something deep within her that hinted at a sharp mind and a caring heart. Something she hid and protected from everyone. And something without which she could never be whole.

"Stay there," he ordered in a calm voice. "The storm rages and everyone has sought shelter for the coming night. I would have answers from you now."

Then, to give himself time to sort through all the questions he had for her, he left, planning to return with wine and food.

Chapter Eight

She'd failed.

And that failure would cost her dearly.

Isabel gazed around the chamber, twisting her fingers in the bed linens. Tears burned in her eyes as she contemplated the price of the misstep.

Had Duncan been warned to be watchful for Sigurd's machinations? Did he know she was there more to lure him into Sigurd's net than into her bed?

If he discovered and exposed Sigurd's dealings, Lord Davin would take action against her stepfather, even call for the earl's or king's justice against him. If that happened, she would be turned out or worse, and all Sigurd's properties would be forfeited. Thora would pay for the failure.

Drawing in a slow breath, Isabel gathered her thoughts and focused. She was smart. She could control the situation. She thought back on their exchanges and tried to remember when she could have slipped up with Duncan. They'd spoken so little, she could not pick out a mistake.

She needed to dress. Handling him while sitting or lying naked before him would not work. In spite of his command to remain where she was, she scrambled out from under the covers and sought a garment to wear. Sigurd had told her to take few clothes, expecting she would spend most of her time pleasuring the man or waiting in his bed for his return. Without knowing how long her stay would be, she'd followed his instructions.

She found her sack but could find no other gown. The only one she had was rain-soaked, outside until she could hang it to dry. Opening Duncan's trunk, she found one of his undershirts and began to pull it on.

The door behind her opened. Duncan held two cups in his hands and stood watching her tug his shirt over his head. Without saying a word, he kicked the door closed with his foot and placed the cups on the table near the hearth.

"If you dig a bit deeper, you will find something warmer than that." He gestured with his chin at what she wore.

Now that he'd given her permission, she opened the wooden trunk and searched through the layers of clothing, guided by his voice.

"Not that. To the left. You are looking for something green."

She found a green garment, dark in hue as the forests around them. It was made of a soft fabric she did not recognize. Unable to resist the feel of it, she rubbed her hands over its surface and found it pleasing. She slid it out and stood, shaking it and holding it before her.

"A robe," he said, walking closer. "It will keep you warm while here in my chambers."

Isabel slipped off the undershirt and let the robe slide over her. It caressed her skin, making her shiver, as it fell over her body. She could not stop from touching it, wrapping it around her fingers and sliding them over its soft texture.

"It was a gift from the East," he explained, his eyes not missing a thing as the fabric clung to her and displayed every curve of her body. "I had no use for it until now."

Isabel startled at the revelation. Was she the first woman

he'd brought to his home? It simply could not be! And she a whore. Sigurd had discovered Duncan had no wife and no family to speak of, but she wondered why not. He was in his prime years, in good physical condition and wealthy. He should be setting about starting his own family. Truth be told, he should already have children.

"My thanks for allowing me to wear it," she said.

"It is yours," he offered.

Isabel smiled. No one gave her gifts, for Sigurd made it clear anything of value should be given to him, *in safekeeping* for her. Though she treasured a small trinket—a pin a man had made himself for her—she'd managed to hide from Sigurd, any other valuable object or jewelry disappeared from her possession as soon as it arrived at her cottage. The robe would always remind her . . . of the kindness she was certain Duncan meant by it.

But she understood she should not read more meaning into it than just that—a kindness shown. Too many times since her nightmare had begun, she'd thought someone, some man, would come along and save her from the life she lived. Someone would value her for herself and not only for the pleasure she could give.

The first time she believed a man who'd promised to take her from Sigurd, then left without keeping his word, she was devastated. The second time, she thought she knew the man and thought he meant what he said, but when faced with Sigurd's anger, the man abandoned her. The punishment from Sigurd crushed any remaining traces of hope she might have been foolish enough to hold in her heart. It was clear that to try again was worse than foolish—it would be dangerous to her and to Thora.

Lost in her thoughts, Isabel realized she had not thanked Duncan properly. She swallowed down the wisps of hope that would not die and accepted the gift.

"My lord, you are a generous man to give me something so valuable." She bowed her head, waiting for an indication he expected pleasure in return for the magnificent garment. Truly, she would not mind giving him release to thank him for it. She stepped closer and reached out her hand, stroking his manhood, which seemed to always be ready for joining.

"If this is in exchange for the gift," he began as he removed her hand from his hardened flesh and stepped away from her, "then I would like something else for it."

Isabel reached down to remove the garment so they could join. He did seem to prefer that to finding release in her mouth or with the play of her hands. So be it.

"You misunderstand me, Isabel." He stopped her from removing the garment and handed her one of the cups, pointing to a chair near to the hearth. The entire chamber was a luxury, with an additional hearth to keep it warm. "I wish answers from you."

She fought against the inclination to gasp or appear nervous before him. Taking a sip of wine to keep from blurting out anything she would regret, she was surprised to find it to be of high quality. She sipped again, enjoying the flavor of a wine she rarely was given a chance to savor. "I will answer your questions, my lord."

He stared at her for a moment and she could feel the bile grow in her gut. He must know her true purpose.

"How did you know about the storm?"

She blinked and looked at him. Was he jesting to distract her? "From years of watching the skies and from living on the island." It was how she always explained her ability. Most never asked past that basic question.

"It is more than that." His gaze was intense.

For a moment, she thought he could hear her thoughts and know the truth or lies within her. Dare she tell him the truth?

Even if he did not believe her explanation, would he sense she was being honest with him?

"I have never spoken of this to anyone," she began. Another sip of wine eased the tightness in her throat. Isabel had to dredge up memories that were long hidden away. Ones that could cascade into others she did not want to think on.

"Go on." He watched her over the rim of his cup.

"When I was a child, we lived near a lake."

"You and Sigurd?"

Isabel looked away. She hated to be coupled with him, even mentioned in the same breath, but that was her lot in life . . . for now, at least. "Nay. My mother and I, I think."

Truly, she did not remember the exact timing or how old she'd been, for she was just a wee one and all her memories bled together in a blur. But it was before Sigurd entered their lives, she knew that.

"Go on," he urged as he stood and leaned against the wooden beam over the hearth, listening but not watching. The tension between them did not ease and she knew he was paying close attention to every word she spoke.

"My mother always warned me to stay away from the lake, but I wandered from home one morning and somehow found my way there. I remember hearing sounds and seeing flickers of light and color near the water and I went to see what they were. I fell in."

Isabel could feel the cold water swirling around her as her garments soaked up water and their weight dragged her down. If not for the lights and the voices in the water she would have been terrified. Could she tell him of the voices?

"Could you swim? Did someone see you fall in?" he asked.

She shook her head. "Nay. I was too small. My mother kept me close to her, except for that day."

In her dreams, she saw those glimmers of light and heard the voices that swirled like music around her. She called on them to calm her and to help her block out what was going on around her.

"What happened?" he asked, interrupting her reverie.

"I only remember someone being in the water next to me, pushing me back up toward the sunlight. It was a woman and she lifted me onto the shore and told me not to fear the water. She said she lived in the water, so I would always find it to be my friend."

He said nothing. Isabel knew how silly her words sounded, but her story would seem even more so before she finished. "I was but a bairn and that's all I remember. Ever since then, water soothes me. I can sense storms approaching. Other things like that . . ." She trailed off waiting for him to laugh. She looked up when silence met her words. His expression was not one of disbelief at all, but rather curiosity.

"It heals you?" He walked over to her and examined her face.

She raised her hand to the place he stared at, feeling for some bruise or injury she'd not felt before. Isabel shook her head. "Nay. Not heal so much as strengthen and refresh." She tried to make sense of how she felt after being in the sea or even, as that day, after being caught in a shower.

"It makes no sense." She shrugged and met his gaze. "I cannot explain more than that."

"The bruises around your eyes from too little sleep and the hard ride here are gone. I wanted to know." His gaze moved to her lips and her breath caught.

His words were not demanding, nor did he scoff at her explanation. His ways were simply as different from other men as she knew herself to be from other women. Good thing that, for her stomach chose that moment to rumble almost as loudly as the circling thunder above them.

"Do you never eat your fill?" he asked, as she put her hand over it to muffle the sound.

"I . . . I . . ." What could she say? She had little time when with a man for anything but pleasuring him. If that included food, to be consumed or to be used to tease his other appetite, she ate it or used it. But it was not her place to ask to eat once a man had paid Sigurd for her use.

Isabel stumbled over words to answer his question, but Duncan already knew the answer: she did not. She never sought to fulfill her own needs, never spoke her own mind and never sought or expected anything a whore would not. For someone who had not yet two score in years, she had learned the limits of her life and did not question them. But from the expression in her eyes, he knew she wanted to burst out of it in so many ways.

"Come," he said as he walked to the door of the chamber and opened it. "We should see what Gunna has left behind for us."

She hesitated but he sensed it was more because he'd surprised her with his actions than because she objected. From watching her, he was certain her desires were never considered first. Though he'd promised their time together would be no different from her time spent with other men, Duncan wanted it to be different. He watched as she walked past him, the robe gliding over her, covering everything yet hiding nothing from him. His hands twitched, wanting to touch the lush fabric and her but he grabbed the shirt she'd discarded instead and pulled it over his head.

"Gunna does not live here?" she asked as they walked into the larger of the three chambers in the house. "This house is big enough for many people."

"I wish them to live elsewhere. Fear not, their house is comfortable and large enough for their needs."

She turned to face him, her cheeks flushed and a frown wrinkling her brow. "Your pardon," she whispered.

Her constant apologies, offered for every real or imagined

offense, angered him. It was not, however, anger at her but rather anger *for* her. Duncan had watched horses being broken, being stripped of their desire for freedom and forced to obey their masters without thought. She reminded him of such animals. Worse, though, was the growing need within him to find out the sources of her fears and to protect her from them.

Sigurd was only one he knew, but there had to be others. Other people who pulled the strings of her life, who made her dance to their tune whether she wished to or not. Isabel never complained, never rebelled against the things Sigurd obligated her to do.

He watched as she took bowls from a shelf in the cooking area of the cottage and scooped some of the stew into them, giving herself a portion that was half as much as the one for him. He cleared his throat, gaining her attention, and nodded at the smaller amount. "That is not enough to sustain a bairn, let alone a woman. Double it."

She did it quickly, obeying his command much as his horse did. Trained to it, she was. Duncan nodded and pointed at the stool nearest the table. "Sit and eat all of that."

Once more, she followed his orders, scooping one spoonful of the stew after another into her mouth, barely pausing to chew it, until the bowl was emptied. He handed her a cup and she drank from it. As ordered. He'd found the key to her behavior and would use it until he found the secrets behind it, too.

Surprised that she would share the story about the lake in her childhood with him, Duncan wondered as they ate in silence, if she understood the significance of such a tale. The islands were rife with remnants and symbols of some ancient race who had lived there before the Gaels or the Norse ever did. Standing stones heralded their places of worship; strange hills marked entrances to places not usually seen and rumored to have no exit. Because he did not know the source of his power and had suspicions about its origins, a story such as hers was not too hard for him to believe. Had some spirit or sith who lived in the lake saved her life? Could he have some link to the sith as well?

Isabel finished her meal and Duncan decided to begin their time together as he wished it to be, not as she was trained to act.

"Will the storm blow over soon?" he asked, taking the last mouthful of wine from his cup.

She looked up at the ceiling of the cottage and closed her eyes, appearing for a moment as though she was asleep. Then she shook her head. "It will storm through the night and end at dawn."

Her wistful tone caused him to smile. Almost as though she longed for the rains and winds to continue for as long as possible, which in the case of weather on that isle could be days long.

"And what do you wish to do while the rains pour down?" He gave her a choice. "I do not care to be outside in the worst of it," he admitted.

"Do you have duties to see to, my lord?" she asked, while gathering the bowls and cups together. "Must you leave here this night?"

He could not tell if she flirted or if she was now the curious one. "I am not your lord, Isabel," he corrected. "I am just a man who wanted you."

"And could pay the high price demanded for me," she completed. "Surely you must be wealthy and powerful to pay that cost."

Duncan watched her eyes light as she spoke. He sensed a game had begun. A counter move was needed.

"Aye, I am wealthy and powerful, but choose not to give the appearance of such. Unscrupulous men would seek to separate me from both if they knew," he explained. Something flashed in her eyes as he made that statement and he recognized either guilt or surprise at his admission. "Again, what do you wish to do this evening while the rains make remaining inside so appealing?"

As she considered her words carefully before speaking he felt her retreating within herself, almost as if building a wall around her innermost thoughts and desires and needs so no one could touch them. The whore's expression returned to her features and he wondered if she even knew when she used it.

"You," she whispered in a husky tone. "I wish to do you."

It was safer to retreat into the persona she knew and could control than to let him get closer, so Isabel did just that. Pleasuring him, even when she allowed herself to enjoy it, did not threaten her soul as did answering his questions. Already she'd revealed something she had never spoken of to another except her mother on that day and she could little afford to let out anything else she kept inside.

Having sex with him would be no hardship for he gave as much pleasure as he took. She shook her head so her hair tumbled across her back and over her arse and she stood taller, pressing her breasts against the luxurious fabric of the robe she wore. Then she did the one thing that seemed to make him lose control—she slid the tip of her tongue over her lips, drawing his attention and reminding him of all the ways she could and would use her tongue on his flesh.

His response was fast and almost furious as he crossed the few paces between them, pulled her into his arms and dragged her onto the surface of the table where they'd just shared a meal. When she tried to ease her hands free so she could touch him, he took them in one of his and held them above her head. Before she could say a word to him, he kneed her legs apart, pulled the robe and his shirt out of his way and thrust into her.

Isabel gasped in surprise, for he'd never done that in all their joinings. With no prelude and no attention to her at all, he shoved his cock until it could go no further and then relentlessly sought his own release. Her body adjusted to his, her inner walls relaxing as they accommodated his length and thickness, pouring out moisture to ease his way. Just as her body fell into rhythm with his movements, his cock hardened and released his seed into her. His breaths were shallow and quick, but he did not pause to relax after his release. Instead he withdrew from her and stepped away.

Lying exposed, her legs spread and his seed still escaping from within her, she felt like the whore she was. In a way, that was cold comfort, for she knew how to be a whore with any man. She drew her legs together and pushed up on her elbows to watch him for a sign of his next intended move. With another man, she would have cooed and coddled and complimented, but Duncan befuddled her. She eased the robe down and slid off the table's rough surface, having a care not to catch the delicate fabric on it. When she raised her head, he was staring at her and she felt naked once more.

"Now that Isabel the whore has had what she wanted," he began in a low voice.

His words hurt her for some reason she did not wish to examine too closely.

"What does Isabel the woman wish to do this evening?"

Chapter Nine

Truth be told, Isabel wanted to sink to the floor, huddle in a ball, and cry until she was spent. That rarely happened and it was *not going to happen*. She took in a deep breath and prepared herself for whatever he had planned for her.

Her legs shook and she leaned against the table to regain her balance. He'd simply been teaching her a lesson by swiving her as most men did. He would have his way and seemed intent on breaking in to find what she hid behind her whore's mask. She could not allow him to do that.

"Have I angered you in some way?" she asked. Always best to deflect and learn more before proceeding in the dark.

"If and when you act the whore, I will fuck you like you are one," he replied in a calm voice that did nothing to ease her discomfort. "Like that." He threw a glance at the table, reminding her of the mindless, selfish manner in which he'd taken her—seeking only his own release and having not a care for her. Like a man treated a whore.

With others, she knew not any other way and cared not, but he'd shown her something completely different in their previous couplings and that difference stung her.

What did he want from her? She was a whore and she

needed to remain only that with him. The small weakness displayed when she'd explained about her affinity for water should never have happened. Did she dare tell him what she wanted? No one ever asked; Sigurd punished her for making any demands or requests. Watching Duncan as he stood with his hands fisted on his hips, she wondered if he would accept her words. Or was it simply a ploy to learn more of her weaknesses?

He raised his brow, waiting for her to ask for something. Thunder crashed outside as though prodding her on, so she took a deep breath and blurted out the thing that was uppermost on her mind.

"I would like to sleep," she admitted, looking away and fixing her gaze on the floor.

Silence filled the space between them until his footsteps grew louder and closer as he paced across the stone paved floor. She could see his legs and the edge of his linen shirt as it hung over his thighs but feared looking at his face. She'd fallen asleep once while bedding a man and he'd complained to Sigurd, demanding his coins back. She'd learned the folly of sleeping and never repeated that mistake . . . until on the ride to Duncan's farm.

The gentle touch of his fingers beneath her chin, lifting it so she had no choice but to meet his gaze, surprised her. Once more. "Then go now and sleep." He nodded toward the other chamber and stepped away, no longer blocking her path.

Did she dare? Would she be able to sleep? Her blood raced through her veins; the heat of his fast and furious coupling lingered. So many questions plagued her she doubted she would indeed get any rest. And, when he did join her in that bed, he would expect her to satisfy his needs. Why bother then? Why even make the request and expose another part of herself, another weakness to him?

When she delayed leaving, he reached up and touched the

skin below her eyes. "The bruising of exhaustion is back, Isabel. Seek your rest now."

The kindness in his voice made her control waver, and other emotions threatened to burst through. She needed to get away from him, for her own sake. She took the first step and then the second before he spoke.

"In the coming days I will have need of everything you offer. I will need the passion and oblivion found in relentless pleasure, but not now. Sleep well."

His words aroused her in an instant. The place between her legs, so recently used, throbbed in response and her nipples tightened. Her body ached for what he threatened and what he promised with his words, but her mind grew curious at what he'd said. What would happen to cause such things? Why would he need physical release soon but not now? What could he mean by relentless pleasure? He had taken her so many times the first night they were together—could he mean to repeat that?

She never took her gaze from him while walking past him. He was a young man, vigorous and healthy, in the prime of his life, so she did not doubt he could repeat such a night over and over again. Isabel pushed open the door to the bedchamber and stepped inside. Other than the trunk of clothing, there were few belongings there to give her any clues or information about him.

Regardless of any respite offered, Isabel found herself thinking on her true task there—not only to seduce him with pleasure but also to find out his secrets so Sigurd could use them. Mayhap a night of good sleep would clear her mind. Then she could figure out how to discover why he had so high a standing with Lord Davin and what his value was.

She slid the luxurious robe off and climbed into his bed. Pulling the bedcovers up higher, Isabel closed her eyes and hoped sleep would come.

*   *   *

Duncan did not enter the bedchamber until he'd regained control of himself. He was appalled by the way he had used her. Knowing he'd been trying to make a point did not lessen the disgust he felt. Even when she had not resisted, even when her body had adjusted quickly to his invasion, even as he spilled his seed within her, he'd known he should not treat her so. But he had and she had taken him without complaint, her body growing wet and hot around his cock with each stroke.

He feared she was so used to being a whore to men's desires and wants that the woman inside was lost forever. Though he was sure there was someone different within her, someone she most likely did not even know, it was folly to think he could change her in one day. He did not know why he wanted to do such a thing. His month with her would be over and she would return to Sigurd and his machinations. Duncan would face death alone.

Just because she seemed to stave off the effects of the curse that afflicted him did not mean she could banish the end result of it. His death grew nearer with each day and with each use of the power that began to bloom and beckon from deep inside his soul. He had spoken the truth to her about his growing need over the next weeks. With the full moon less than a fortnight away, he would soon become unmindful of things like consideration for her needs. The terrible power would seize control, exuding the scent that would pull her or any other woman within a short distance into his web of need and desire. Stronger with each passing month, it was reaching some apex and he knew with a frightening certainty that it must soon end and cause his death. From observing the progression of his abilities over the last months, and the resulting inability to feel any emotion, Duncan believed the culmination would come two full moons hence.

Opening the bedchamber door with care, he saw her asleep on the bed . . . his bed. Though he had come inside her twice already that night, he could have done it again. He closed the door, dropped the latch and walked closer to the bed. The robe that had flowed over her skin like shimmering liquid lay on the floor waiting for her to don it once more. His hands itched to rub it while she wore it and feel the way her body roused to the sensations of the delicate silk.

Strange that. He'd had the robe in his trunk for years and never had the impulse to give it to someone. But everything about the woman and his reactions to her had been strange and different.

She moved then, stretching under the bedcovers and moaning softly as though in pain. Whispered words he could not understand floated on the air. They were garbled, but the pain behind them made him hurt. He closed his eyes and opened himself up to the waves of anguish coming from her. Duncan saw it in his thoughts—bands of gray and black that rippled across the distance between where she lay and he stood.

As in the ritual, he pulled the pain from her, silently, wordlessly, until he hit a barrier he could not break. He pressed against it and could feel it swirling beneath his power, but he could not lift it or get inside. He pulled back and opened his eyes. The strength of her will to maintain that wall was not something he could overcome without the full release of his healing powers, and that only happened during the ritual. This small sampling was, again, something he'd never experienced before. Could he blame or credit it on her though? Or was it simply his powers spilling over?

He noticed the dark smudges under her eyes were gone and she murmured less and slept deeply as he pulled off the shirt he'd put on. He blew out the lamp so the room was lit by only the low-burning peat in the hearth. Lightning continued outside, occasionally sending flashes through the seams in the shuttered openings high in the wall of the chamber. Thunder crashed, continuing to ebb and flow around them. Duncan lifted the bedcovers and slid in beside her, barely disturbing the bed.

She turned on her side away from him as he adjusted the thick, warm layers of blankets and he lay on his back considering all the changes in him since he'd found her. Whether seeking the heat his body gave off or offering hers to him, he knew not, but Isabel rolled back against him, rubbing her arse against his thigh. He'd thought her asleep, but when her hand reached back and touched his erect cock, he knew otherwise. Still, he did not want her to service him, so he brushed her hand away, whispering for her to sleep instead.

Duncan knew she did not understand his actions. Truth be told, he did not completely understand them either, but knowing she was there, that she was his and would remain for several weeks, lessened the rampant need that usually assailed him as full moon approached. He placed his arm over her and leaned closer, sharing his warmth and enjoying the moment of intimacy. The smell of the rains scented her hair and he inhaled it.

Though his body ached for sleep, he got little through that night. Too many questions and too many things to ponder kept him awake until the light of dawn crept through the crevices around the shutters.

Chapter Ten

The morning that dawned was rare in the tumultuous autumns those living on Skye experienced. There was a sunny, pleasant breeze, few clouds in the sky, and no mist rolling over the hills. Isabel woke alone in the bed, not remembering how or when she fell asleep. She stretched, her muscles reminding her of the hours spent on a horse's back during the journey there. Pushing herself up on her elbows, she noticed a few changes in the chamber.

The shutters high on the wall were opened a bit, letting light and air in. The other side of the bed was still warm, telling her that Duncan had risen not too long ago. And a pile of clothing lay at the foot of the bed. For her. She shoved back the covers, slipped off the bed, and examined the clothing. Nothing like the provocative garments Sigurd provided for her, they were well made yet attractive gowns and tunics constructed in the Norse fashion. Warm stockings and shifts lay at the bottom of the pile.

Duncan had noticed her lack of appropriate clothing and provided them.

She glanced over to find the gift he'd given her folded on a stool near the bed. Isabel could not help skimming her hand over it, enjoying the smooth feel of the fabric. How would she ever keep it a secret from Sigurd when she returned? Her body shuddered at the thought, so she pushed that fear and worry aside and returned to the clothing on the bed.

Dressing, she understood why Duncan had given them to her. They were the sort of things any woman, any good woman or wife, would wear while going about her daily tasks. As she pulled the warm shift and then the gown and tunic over her head and adjusted them around her, Isabel wondered how it would feel to wear clothing like that every day. To never have to worry over exposing too much or the results of men seeing the curves of her body because of the cut of her garments. What would it be like to be respectable and live and walk freely among other respectable people? To have friends and share . . .

She shook her head and rid herself of such thoughts and dreams. Such a life was not for her. Pining for it would do no good and could lead her to harm. She pulled the stockings on and tied them up, then laced her shoes. She was ready, and presentable enough, to leave the chamber and discover what Duncan had planned for the day.

Lifting the latch and pulling the door open a crack, she was greeted by the enticing aromas of a well-cooked meal. Gunna moved around the main room, serving several men from a pot of steaming . . . porridge. Crocks of butter and loaves of bread lay on the table waiting to be eaten. Three of the men she did not recognize and one she did—Harald, who seemed to be the overseer for Duncan. A moment of silence when all heads turned in her direction ended quickly when Gunna noticed and approached her.

"Duncan said not to disturb your rest," she began, taking

Isabel's hand and leading her to an empty stool at the table. "Sit now. Break your fast with us."

Isabel accepted the bowl and inhaled the wonderful scent of cooked oats and some spice she could not name. One of the men moved a bowl of butter and a small jug of cream closer to her, so she could add it to the steaming porridge. Another handed her the loaf of bread. Only Harald sat without taking his gaze from her. Well, she understood her position there, even if Gunna did not, so she nodded her thanks and ate head down in silence.

One by one the men finished and left, until it was only she and Gunna in the house. Isabel stood and began clearing the table, gathering all the bowls and cups and taking them to the wash bucket to be cleaned. Gunna accepted her help and smiled, once more causing an emptiness in the pit of Isabel's stomach. So long had it been since she was part of a household where such menial tasks were appreciated and accepted it made her want to cry. Shaking off the growing need within her, Isabel cleared her throat and focused on the reason she was there.

"Where is Duncan?" she asked. "I must thank him for these garments."

"Oh, he and Ornolf had some things to see to," the young woman answered. "I thought they would fit you."

So, his manservant had arrived sooner rather than later. "I should have realized you had a part in this," Isabel said. "My thanks to you as well." She smoothed her hands over the tunic and smiled at Gunna to show her appreciation.

"Duncan thought you might want to accompany me to the village today."

Whether Isabel cared to or not was not the issue. If Duncan had suggested it, especially after the new consideration he'd shown her, she knew it was what she must do. Her task, one that extremely large amounts of coin were being paid for, was to do as he bid her to do. The suggestion was more than that—it was an order which she must carry out.

"When do you wish to leave?" she asked. She kept her gaze on the table as she wiped it clean, so Gunna's hand on hers surprised her.

"Worry not, Isabel. You are here as Duncan's guest and no one will utter a word against you."

Clearly, Gunna had no idea how much talk her presence could ignite, even under the protection of Duncan.

"It matters not to me what they say," Isabel admitted. "I have heard it all. But you have not." She slid her hand free of Gunna's comforting gesture.

"If you do not wish to go . . ." the young woman began.

"Nay." Isabel shook her head. "Pray do not think I am refusing your request, Gunna."

"Duncan said the choice is to be yours. If you wish to remain here, all is well." The tone of her voice gave the impression she knew too much and understood even more.

Isabel paused. Though she wanted to speak to Gunna and learn more about Duncan, exposing the young woman to embarrassment would not help her and might anger him. "I—"

"Stay then, Isabel. I will be back before noon and you can help me prepare the meal." Gunna did not dawdle or hesitate, but grabbed a large basket and left.

Isabel took only a few moments to decide she should go, after all. The walk would feel good and she could speak to Gunna alone. If things happened in the village, she would leave Gunna and wait for her along the path back to the farm. Spying another basket, Isabel picked it up and ran after Gunna. As though expecting her to follow, the woman waited just along the path. When Isabel reached her, Gunna turned and led the way, in the opposite direction from the stream and the farm.

They walked in silence for a bit before Gunna began talking about their path, the village of Uig, and the errands she ran. Isabel did not for a moment think Gunna would ignore other topics, feeling as though Gunna was easing her way onto topics she wished to discuss.

Good, for Isabel had much she wanted to ask as well.

"How long have you known Duncan?" Gunna asked.

While considering how to answer, Isabel decided to tell the truth. There was less chance of tripping over lies when answering other questions.

"Nearly two weeks, I think," she said.

"And he is so taken with you that he brought you home with him."

"I do not think that is the situation, Gunna."

The young woman must be of a romantic inclination, one who expected to marry for love rather than under the guidance of her family.

"I know his habits, Isabel. I know his ways. He has never brought a woman here before. Ever." Gunna stopped and turned to face Isabel, looking at her with the eyes of a woman much older and wiser that her years. "He probably does not even know why he brought you here."

"He knows," Isabel began, but then paused, unsure of what Duncan wanted Gunna to know and what he would be angered by her knowing. "And I think you know." She tested to see what Gunna might understand. At her nod, Isabel smiled. Better to both be on the same ground and not speak of such things.

"So, how long has he owned this farm?" Isabel asked.

They reached a split in the path and Gunna led them down

the one to the right, to the south. Uig sat on the coast, named after the sheltered bay that allowed boats large and small to dock safely there. Isabel knew her mother's family had lived south and east of the village, in the hills, but did not know the exact place. When her mother had died, Sigurd took Isabel and Thora to a new place to live and everything changed. She'd not returned to the area again until that day. With grief and humiliation and the past threatening to overwhelm her, she forgot about the question posed until Gunna spoke again.

"He has owned the farms and lands to the north for about five years now," she said. "A gift to him and one that he has shared with many."

"Are you kin then?" Isabel watched the path, which had begun to climb higher and become more rugged.

"Harald is my brother." That much was clear from the expression in Harald's eyes when he deemed Isabel a threat to the young woman. Their resemblance spoke of a blood connection.

But not to Duncan.

"Have you lived here long?" Isabel paused to take in a deeper breath. The incline of the path made it difficult to climb and talk at the same time. Though Gunna did not slow or seem affected, Isabel found it a hard climb.

She realized it had been years since she'd had to walk such terrain. Her only walking involved going to the keep or another cottage and finding her way back to her own. The few journeys out of Duntulm were by cart when Sigurd had her delivered to this man or that one.

They reached the crest of the hill and the view of the bay spread out before them. The day was clear and she could see for miles in all directions. The outer islands lay to the north and west while the other peninsulas of Skye lay south and

east. The ancient mountains stood between her and the mainland of the Scots. Shielding her eyes from the sun, she stared
at the expanse of earth and sea and sky.

So many places she had never seen or visited, nor would she
ever in her life, for she suspected her life would be a short one
and its end coming soon.

"I have lived here for nearly five years," Gunna answered,
standing at her side, looking out over the scenery before them.
"My brother pledged to him when Duncan healed me."

In the process of taking a careful step down the steep incline, Isabel stumbled a few paces before regaining her balance. "He healed you?"

Duncan was rumored to be a miraculous healer though
none ever said more. She'd seen no evidence of herbs growing
near his house nor a room of concoctions and elixirs such as
most healers had. Nothing that would make the claim seem
warranted.

"Aye," was Gunna's only reply.

The path became harder and a wrong step could result in a
fall, so Isabel paid attention as she walked, all other questions
put aside for the moment. Even after reaching level ground,
they walked on in silence until they came to the outskirts of
the village. Isabel felt as though she should warn Gunna about
the possibilities of an encounter since many men traveled to
Duntulm and traded with Lord Davin. All it would take
would be one to recognize her before the story would spread
and the offers made.

Like her sister Thora, Gunna should never be exposed to
such things and Isabel would prevent it if she could.

"Gunna, wait for a moment, I pray," she began. The
younger woman stopped and turned to face her and Isabel
could not find a polite way to explain what could happen.

"You are Duncan's guest, Isabel," Gunna said plainly. "Too

many here owe too much to him to ever make his guest feel unwelcome." As though that would put her at ease, Gunna turned and began walking again, following the path into the main street of the village. Isabel grabbed her arm and pulled her to a stop once more before they reached any people.

"It is never that simple, Gunna. You know what I am, but mayhap you do not know how others will react to me. I think this was a bad idea. I should wait for you here."

"You are under his protection here, Isabel, just as I am. Fear not." Gunna peeled Isabel's fingers from where they clutched her arm and smiled. "You are safe here."

Isabel wanted to cry. She could not believe herself to be safe—not while Sigurd wielded such power over her. Not while Thora was at his mercy. Facing hatred and humiliation and vile threats and insults was easier than trying to accept the kindness Gunna and her words offered. All Isabel could do was nod acceptance, or rather compliance, and follow Gunna down the street.

Not lifting her head when the first person, a woman with a child, approached Gunna, Isabel stood off a pace or two to allow them to converse. When Gunna invited her into their discussion, she hesitated. Gunna drew her over with a question about the condition of the path they'd walked and then the woman continued to include her. Isabel averted her gaze and could not talk to the woman. Her heart pounded and her stomach rolled with fear, making it almost impossible to draw a breath.

Never speak to a respectable woman. Never soil her reputation, her honor. Never approach a child. Look away. Step away. Avoid.

She could hear Sigurd's ranting threats if she did any of those things he forbid. She felt the sting of the lash when he thought she'd disobeyed. It took months and so much pain to learn those lessons, but she had. Now, Gunna tried to make her forget and overstep her place.

Isabel could not. She simply could not break the first rules that Sigurd had beaten into her just because the woman offered her a taste of kindness. A change while there would result in a slip when she returned to Duntulm. Someone would be insulted by her words or her glance or her presence and the punishment would be harsh.

Isabel withdrew from the conversation and waited for Gunna or the woman to move on. Unfortunately, the child, a girl of about five years, reached out and touched the skirt of Isabel's tunic, tracing non-existent patterns in the fabric to amuse herself. Wisps of pale hair encircled the girl's face, giving her an angelic appearance. Something else Isabel would never have in her life—a child.

She'd given little thought to the reasons behind her apparent barrenness, for in her life it was a good thing. She'd never gotten pregnant in spite of the dozens, nay hundreds, of times men had spilled their seed within her. As the child drew nearer, ignorant of everything about her, Isabel felt a longing within unlike any she'd felt before.

A child. A home. A place of her own and a person who depended on her alone.

Grief for all the things that could not be broke free, forcing her feet to run away from such thoughts and the people who caused them. Gunna's voice calling out to her went unheeded as she ran, tears blinding her path, her chest tight, unable to expand and breathe. She followed the same route back into the hills and did not stop until she could go no further.

She stared out at the expanse of water before her, trying to understand what had happened. Since the first moment she'd met Duncan, her control had been slipping. A small crack here, another there and soon she could not keep her soul hidden behind the wall that she'd built to protect herself from the life she led and the things she did. If it continued, if she allowed it to happen, she would be destroyed by the time she returned to Duntulm.

Sigurd would be waiting, expecting her to reveal the secrets she'd gathered, then move on to the next unsuspecting man she would draw into Sigurd's web of deception and control. She'd known for some time that he would never let her go, never let her stop, for she was too valuable a part of his machinations.

If she knew for certain Thora would be safe and settled regardless of her own obedience—or disobedience—to his dictates, she would end her life and be glad of it. Isabel would give in to the impulse to dive under the water and never come to the surface again, finding peace and safety in the depths.

When the tears ceased and she regained her sense of control and balance, she understood what she needed to do to survive the latest challenge. No matter the reasons for his kindnesses, no matter the expectations he had for the next weeks, Isabel must remain what she was—a high-priced whore who drove men crazy with lust and used their passion against them. That path was much clearer to her than the quagmire Duncan offered her.

She made her way back to his farm and into his house and found the clothing she'd brought with her. Removing the garments he'd given her, she put the whore's gown and tunic back on, feeling a sense of control returning to her. She arranged her hair so it appeared to threaten to tumble free at any moment and she rouged her lips. The roughness of the inner layer of fabric teased her nipples to tighten and she felt her body prepare itself for what she knew would come. She would make it happen the same way she always did and she would control the situation, control the man, and seduce his secrets from him.

When Gunna returned and Isabel opened the door of the chamber to help her prepare the meal as she'd planned, it was Isabel the whore who entered the main room.

Gunna's gasp stung only for a moment, until Isabel reminded herself that it must be the ways of things. Duncan's eyes widened as did each man's as they entered to share the meal, but their reaction did not sway her from her purpose. Though she did not ignore the others, she made it clear that Duncan could have all she offered whenever he wanted it.

They all took their leave after eating; only Gunna remained behind to clean up and ready the evening meal. Duncan left without saying a word to Isabel through the whole meal, which suited her. Once the men departed, she offered her help but Gunna refused, never meeting her gaze. Waves of hurt and confusion poured off the young woman, but it was for the best. Ignoring reality was a mistake and not one Isabel was willing to knowingly make.

The evening meal proceeded the same way and when everyone left to go to their own dwellings, including Ornolf, Isabel went to the bedchamber to prepare herself. She'd seen the signs of Duncan's arousal—his erect cock visible through his trousers when she looked. The scent he gave off when his passions were high filled the room, even if she seemed the only one to notice.

She peeled off her clothing, lay on his bed and began to touch herself to ready her body for him. It took little time; knowing what would happen between them aroused her. Even so, when he opened the door and saw her there, the fingers of one hand holding open the folds between her legs and the fingers of the other sliding in and out, drawing forth her body's moisture and rubbing it along them, he stopped and stared.

His body reacted, but she witnessed disappointment in his expression before lust took control. Like any man, he watched as she opened wider and spread the folds, moaning softly with every touch. She knew where to touch, how to touch, whether it was her own body or another's, to bring forth the heat and pleasure. And so she did, enticing him to approach. Step by step he came closer and closer until his legs touched the side of the bed. Her fingers never stopped teasing herself, making the flesh throb and ache for more, readying it for the pleasure his cock would give her once he plunged deep inside.

She lifted her hips, angling them so he could see more as she moved her fingers and began to tease the tips of her breasts. Rubbing the nipples between her fingers and thumbs, she pulled on them, moaning each time and arching her hips to invite him in. Yet he did not move toward her. The essence of arousal filled the chamber and she breathed it in deeply, allowing its intoxifying scent to add to the anticipation.

As she watched, he loosened his laces and let his trousers drop. One tug and he removed his shirt, tossing it aside. He slid his hands down, lifting his hardened flesh forward, offering it to her, but as she began to move toward him, he climbed between her legs. Instead of his cock, he pressed one knee between her thighs, rubbing against the flesh she'd readied. Though it felt good, true release hovered just a bit away as she lifted her hips and rubbed against him.

She waited for him to offer his cock and when he did not, still staring at her with an inscrutable expression, she leaned up to take hold of it. As her hands curled around its length and she massaged the sac and balls beneath it, he reached out, taking her head in his hands and guided her mouth to it.

Though her body screamed for release, she was trapped. Sliding him into her mouth, she suckled on his cock, then drew back to tongue her way along its length. His hands held her face there, so all she could do was take it in, sliding it deeper and deeper as he thrust forward. Isabel grabbed his thigh to keep from falling and tried to rub his knee and the hard muscle of his thigh against her heated flesh, but he would not relent.

It was another lesson. She was a whore and only his pleasure mattered. As he fucked her mouth, thrusting into her throat with each movement, she understood and let him. He grew thicker and harder and she knew his seed would spill in only moments. He held her there, and she swallowed as it burst forth from him, sucking until he was drained. He withdrew and leaned back on his heels.

"Finish it," he ordered in a gruff, sex-filled voice.

"Would you not like to . . ." she began, lifting her hips to offer her body to him. In truth, she wanted to seek the release he'd refused her thus far.

"Finish it yourself. Now."

Chapter Eleven

Duncan watched her with a sense of profound disappointment which confused him. She was a whore, trained to it, and one who could not or would not see that she was so much more. He reminded himself he'd bought and paid for a woman who would be able to keep up with his increasing sexual needs over the next weeks.

That she was more than that somehow had obscured his perspective and his idea of how the weeks would unfold. But if he'd thought he could change her, he was learning that he was wrong.

Upon her return from the village, Gunna had told him of Isabel's behavior, told him about her abrupt departure and the incident with the woman and child. He remembered the way Isabel walked around Duntulm—head down, never engaging or speaking to anyone who crossed her path. Avoiding others, staying in her place. Never presuming to sit amongst the respectable, but only among those who served them.

Watching her service him once more, emptying his seed into her mouth, had given him no satisfaction. Though watching her touch herself would have excited him to another bout of pleasure at another time, it had left him unsatisfied and un-

interested. Though he'd ordered her to see to her own pleasure, he climbed off the bed and walked to the table, which
held a jug of wine.

From the looks of it as he glanced back, satisfaction eluded
her as well.

Her movements became frantic, her fingers plucking at the
nub of flesh that refused her efforts to arouse it. He realized
she would continue because he'd ordered her to do it. Shaking
his head, he poured some wine and drank it down.

"Cease, Isabel." He said it softly but his words seemed
louder in the quiet chamber.

He did not look at her just then for he wanted to give her a
chance to regain her control and her composure. At the sound
of her approach, he held out the second cup without a word.
Her hands shook as she took it from him.

"Is this the way you wish it to be between us?" he asked.

"It cannot be any other way," she answered. "I am what I
am, just as you are."

The thought that he might have been mistaken about her,
that he might have seen or felt something more because he
needed or wanted to see more, crept into his mind. Were his
needs causing him to think wrongly that she knew more than
he did about his situation?

"You said you needed what I offered, that you brought me
here to pleasure you. You said you would need me in the coming weeks. Why?"

It was the first time she'd asked him a question outright.

Did he answer with the truth? Would she use it against him
as he suspected?

"I change as the full moon approaches. My body will have
needs I cannot deny nor control. I have powers I cannot control."

He turned to face her then, searching her eyes for some sign
she believed him.

She wore the blank expression he hated so much. The only sign she was thinking anything was the slight twitch in her left eye. "Powers?"

"Gunna told you I am a healer." He walked closer to her and poured more wine in her cup. "My power to do that seems tied to the phases of the moon."

She drank a mouthful before she met his gaze. "How do you heal people? I see no herbs or concoctions that most healers use. I do not understand." He sensed she was speaking the truth.

"I do not know how it works. The power grows as the moon reaches its fullest and then wanes until the next full moon. It has been so for a number of years."

He waited for her to laugh or to look at him as though he was the madman he sometimes felt he was, but she only watched through guarded eyes. "The power to heal someone," she began. "How do you heal people?"

Suddenly, he knew he should not tell her more. A feeling swept over him, sending chills down his bones and making his flesh freeze. He'd told her enough. He walked past her and sat on the bed, drawing her attention there.

"I know little of how it works, only that it does." He left his reply vague.

"Can we begin anew?" He nodded at the bed and held out his hand. The need in him grew each day and he had not lied about the ever-increasing appetite. Watching her and taking her as he had simply made him want her more. "I will ask nothing more of you than I paid for, save one thing," he offered.

"And that one thing?" she asked, her expression guarded once more.

"Wear the garments I gave you when you leave this chamber," he said. "The men . . ."

She hesitated only a brief second before nodding acceptance. That momentary pause signaled to him a slight change in her since they'd met. Before she'd obeyed every order implicitly.

Duncan walked to the bedside and took the green robe in his hand. Holding it out to her, he watched as she drew it on. It flowed over her skin and her body like water sluicing over her flesh and his body came to life as the robe covered almost every inch of her.

He wanted her. He wanted to pleasure her and satisfy her. At the moment, though, he realized he wanted to enjoy her company. To take her to bed felt too much like using a whore to him, so he pulled on a shirt and trousers and held out his hand to her, leading her out of the chamber and out of the house.

The moon's light shone brightly, illuminating the area around them. Peering up at it, Duncan saw it was past its third-quarter mark and would soon gain its fullness. The power surged in his veins, urging him to call it forth. Was she so wounded, so injured in spirit and soul, she brought it close to the surface and made him, in spite of the terror of his power, want to risk all to use it for her?

He guided her along the path that led to one of the storage barns, the one he would use for the ritual in just days, but walked beyond it. Leading her up a small hill, he stopped where there was a view of his lands and the surrounding area. The stream flowing along his boundaries crept south and east, creating a waterfall not far from there, then it meandered through a scenic glen on its way to the bay. She might like to visit the waterfall.

"How much of this is yours?" she asked when they stopped.

It was such a clear night, he could see for miles from there. Unusual for the season, when misting fog was the norm. He pointed at another hill in the distance.

"That marks the end of my lands to the north," he ex-

plained. "And that outcropping of trees to the south and east."
He owned extensive lands on Skye because of his gift. "When
we crossed the stream on our journey here, we entered my
lands."

"You are a prosperous farmer then?" she asked.

"I can support a number of families on my lands, aye," he
replied.

"And do you? Support kin on your lands?" She looked away
as though not attentive to his answer, but he could feel her interest.

"Not mine, but families.

"Tomorrow I think we should walk to the glen." He
pointed off in the distance toward it. "You will like it there."

"Why?" she asked.

Duncan laughed as he took her by the hand and tugged her
to walk with him back to the house. The air around them
cooled quickly now that the sun had set. They'd not brought
cloaks.

"If my memory is correct, there is a lake there."

She walked in silence with him, back to the house. All the
others had sought shelter for the night and only the sound of
night birds floated on the air between them. Their footsteps
sent small, loose stones scattering along the path before them.

"Do you have no other duties to see to?" she asked as they
reached the main house.

"Ornolf is here and will see to things," he explained.

He released her hand and allowed her to enter first. Closing
the door behind them, he watched as she walked directly to
his bedchamber. The green silk flowed over her and he
watched as it touched her hips and her breasts . . . as he
wanted to.

The time for trying to change her was over. The need for
her surged in his blood even as the power did, pushing him to
take her. Would it be different when the scent overwhelmed

everything and called women to his bed? Would it affect her? As though she knew he was thinking of her and of what he wanted to do to her, with her, she turned and faced him.

Her eyes seemed to shimmer, changing in the low light of the hearth and glimmering from pale to bright and back again. The scent did that to women—lured them into a sensual oblivion so his needs came first and memory of what happened between them dimmed. Her body shuddered, the material swaying softly over her skin, over her breasts and erect nipples and across her stomach and hips. She would do whatever he wanted and needed, as any woman did when that part of his power was released. Whore or not, no woman could resist the call in his blood.

Then, the most extraordinary thing occurred. Isabel's gaze cleared and she watched him step closer. He closed his eyes and wanted her, sending more of the scent across the chamber, swirling around her, calling to her.

Her eyes shimmered for a moment, before they cleared once more.

Duncan laughed. She could conquer the pull of his power as no other woman had before. He'd known there was something unusual about her from the first moment he'd seen her. Then, as she began to slide her hands over the fabric, and over her body, accepting the sensations he caused and heightening them, he realized she used his power as if it was an elixir capable of making their joining even more pleasurable. Her eyes closed and she leaned her head back, but her hands never stopped moving over the garment.

He flexed his hands, fisting them, then releasing them, trying to resist the call of her body to his and failing. Duncan crossed the chamber in a few paces and placed his hands on the fabric, pushing hers aside, feeling the smoothness of the silk and the curves of her body beneath it.

Isabel arched into his hands as he caressed her through the

robe. Decadent arousal simmered in her body as she enjoyed every touch, waiting for something heated and dangerous to explode. She tried to remain still, but her body arched and shuddered as he slid his hands over her breasts and stomach. His fingers teased the hair between her legs through the silk and when she would have spread them for his further caress, he moved his hands to her thighs and then around to her bottom.

Her body took over then, inhaling the scent that poured from him, allowing it to take control of her senses. Time seemed to slow as he drove her mad with pleasure, even though they were yet clothed. Isabel understood it would not be like the last two times when he'd sought his own pleasure without regard for hers. As the change he'd referred to earlier took over, he could not deny either of them pleasure. What confused her was the power flowing from him, a power she could feel, one that called to something deep within her. She let go of all restraint and gave herself over to that call.

The feel of the silk as it moved over her made her ache. Her skin wanted more, her body wanted more and readied itself for all that would come. With her eyes closed, she felt every caress, never knowing where his hands would move next but falling under his power and control.

When he gathered the robe in his hand and touched her flesh without its sensual barrier, her body melted. His finger slipped into her cleft, sliding in deeper, touching the sensitive bud that lay within its folds. She clutched his arms, for her legs began to shake. His deep laugh sent shivers through her blood and she opened her eyes to watch his face. He was looking at her, his face intense in spite of the laugh. She gasped as he aroused her and made the moisture pour from her, his fingers bringing pleasure and pushing her toward satisfaction.

Her knees buckled, but he caught her, backing her up until she felt the bed behind her. He released her and Isabel fell backwards, the wide expanse of the bed catching her. When she thought he would step between her legs and enter her, instead he knelt between them and lifted them over his shoulders, opening that heated place to his scrutiny and his touch. She leaned up on her elbows to watch him.

His head dipped and she waited for the feel of his tongue there. Instead, only his heated breath touched her skin. Another second passed and still he did nothing, but her body did not care—her heart raced and her breath caught. She was ready to beg him when his tongue flicked deeply between the folds. With nothing more than that first touch, she screamed out as pleasure overwhelmed her and she found the satisfaction he'd denied her earlier. As she gasped out his name, he licked her again.

Her hips arched, trying to keep him there and she could see only the top of his head. He laughed, the sound vibrating through her. His only response was to find that swollen bud and tease it to life again. Isabel fell back, trying to stop him and urging him to continue at the same time. It was too much, too much. The center of her spun tighter and tighter until she believed she would shatter if he continued.

She did shatter, her body tightening and shaking as wave after wave of pleasure and bliss washed over her. But Duncan did not relent until she became a mindless, melting woman unable to form the words to make him stop. Only when her body gave out and a final keening scream filled the chamber, did he lift his head from her.

Instead of plunging his hardness deep into her and seeking his own pleasure, he urged her back to life, kissing his way along her legs, over her stomach to her breasts. Isabel thought herself emptied but his kisses and caresses refilled her hollowness and her sated body began to answer him again. The hours melded together as their bodies did, blurring in a tumultuous night of temptation and satisfaction when every pleasure of the flesh was offered and accepted. So dawn found them tangled in complete exhaustion and fulfillment.

Duncan fell asleep before she did, for no matter his urging to do otherwise, Sigurd's warnings lay imbedded too deeply to ignore. Though her body dragged her toward it, she could manage only to drift in and out of sleep, never quite letting go while Duncan was there. Only when his arm encircled her body and he dragged her close with a whispered order to take her rest did she finally give in and follow him into sleep.

When she next opened her eyes, the sounds of men working in the nearby fields made her realize the lateness of the hour. However, her body would not follow her mind's commands to rise and dress and seek Duncan out. Her muscles ached from their intense joinings throughout the night. He had warned her of what he wanted and he had done it, for in their passionate bouts he had taken her every way a man could take a woman and she had lost track of how many times and where his body ended and hers began.

Isabel knew the true danger in that situation—she would never survive with her defenses intact if he continued to make her feel that way. If her pleasure mattered to him, she understood what would happen—she would lose her ability to remain separate and to consider him only a task. Truthfully, it had already begun. As she began to fall asleep again, she offered up prayers that she could be strong in her resolve.

Now that mutual pleasure seemed his intent, Isabel knew she must begin her work on Sigurd's plan and discover some weakness to use against Duncan. As much as she might regret it, that was the only way to satisfy Sigurd.

And Sigurd must be pleased or too many would suffer.

Isabel slept for several more hours, clutching tightly to the memories of being held close to Duncan's body, until she knew she must rise and be about Sigurd's business. Dressing in the clothing Duncan had given her, she left the bed-chamber and found Ornolf and Gunna outside waiting for her.

Duntulm Village

Sigurd strode around the main chamber of his house not even trying to hide his anger. Duncan had taken Isabel away so swiftly, Sigurd had not been able to make arrangements to follow her. Lord Davin, the fool!, would only say that Duncan's lands were near Uig and that gave Sigurd little to go on. He sent out two men by boat to Uig to track her if she showed her face in the village. If they did not find her there, they would begin searching the nearby farms for any sign of her and continue until they located her. She would know what to do then.

Once he discovered the man's secret and the nature of his importance to Davin, Sigurd would be able to control him. One more added to the growing numbers who would support him when he overthrew Davin and took command of his lands and power. All in time for the Norse king's return to the island from his voyage south. The king recognized and rewarded strength, and with Sigurd's display of it, he knew he would be granted the whole of the isle in the king's name.

He chortled, completely satisfied his plan could not and would not fail. The slut knew how to follow his commands and soon the knowledge he needed would be in his hands. She did it because she thought it the only way to protect his daughter and he would let her think that for as long as it worked. He knew she thought she would stop whoring for him once Thora was settled in marriage, but he had no inten-tion of ending an arrangement that was so lucrative and bene-ficial . . . for him.

He called out for a cup of wine and one of his servants crept over and handed one to him. Sigurd backhanded the stupid wench for being so slow, then drank it down. His empty cup was filled quickly, proving that dumb, ignorant creatures only learned through pain. Some, like Isabel, learned only after extensive rounds of punishment. As with all of them, he'd determined just the right mix of pain and threats to Thora to keep Isabel useful.

Once granted the king's favor, he would arrange a favorable marriage for his daughter, send her off to live elsewhere, and continue to bend Isabel to his will. If punishment and pain were the only effective tools once Thora was married, so be it.

Sigurd peered out the window, looking up at Duntulm Keep, knowing it would soon be his. His plan, put in place years ago, would come to pass. Though moving slowly went against everything in him, he knew it was the best way. Just as he had bided his time to get Isabel's mother to wed him after she first refused him, he would be patient. All things would come to him.

If he had to kill a few people or use Ariana's daughter to whore her way to the information he needed, so be it. Ariana's attempts to avoid marrying him had simply caused a delay in his plans. Ariana was rotting in the ground with her first husband and her only daughter was using her flesh to obtain secrets for him. It seemed fitting somehow.

He swallowed down the last mouthful of wine and wiped his sleeve across his mouth to remove any excess.

Within weeks, a month at the longest, his plans to take control of Skye would be done. He would rule it for the Norse king. Sigurd would rise in esteem and power, and those who opposed him along the way would be dead.

Chapter Twelve

The next days passed by at a dizzying pace and Duncan was never gone from Isabel's side for very long. Though careful to be discreet when near his people, he missed no opportunity to swive her. He sought pleasure at any time in most any place where he knew no one would see them.

She laughed, remembering a few exceptions to that thought. Yesterday, she'd stood at the fence watching the horses within the yard being trained when he'd walked up behind her. With a quick glance to ensure no one was paying them any heed, he helped her climb onto the first rail of the fence, bunched her skirts up out of his way and pulled her onto his hard cock. After the shock of such a thing passed, she found his arms surrounding her, under her skirts, and his hands playing between her legs. It took little time to heat her blood and less time to find his way deep within her flesh. The difficult thing had been not screaming out in pleasure when he drove her relentlessly to satisfaction.

Duncan seemed to like to have her before him when they tupped. He used his hands to tease and torment her to release after release before spilling his seed. Like a stallion to her mare, he would bite her neck as he plunged as far and as hard as he could into her heated, readied flesh.

Once, he'd entered her in that other place, pushing his way in slowly, his hands teasing moisture from her cleft that he used to ease the tightness as he moved farther and deeper within her. It brought about a maddening level of pleasure, one that left her unable to move or to focus her thoughts while he pleasured her.

As she waited for Gunna on the outskirts of the village, thinking on the ferocity of such joinings made it hard to breathe and harder yet to ignore the way her body ached for more. If he should appear, she feared she might throw him to the ground and demand he satisfy the growing need she had for him. Waving her hand to cool her heated cheeks, she wanted to laugh at the turn of events and attitudes. She'd sworn not to be swayed by his passion and now was completely a prisoner of it. What kind of whore was she to forget that passion and pleasure were commodities to be bought and sold and not savored?

Well, the weeks would at least provide pleasant memories to enjoy when she needed them. She stood, expecting Gunna when she heard someone approach on the path back from Uig. One look at the flush in her face, and the woman would know what she'd been thinking. All those living on Duncan's lands and in his house turned a blind eye to their actions, but they all understood what was between them.

Isabel turned to greet Gunna and found instead one of Sigurd's men. Surprised, though she should not be, she greeted him, trying to erase her disdain and gather her control.

"Godrod." She nodded to him as he walked closer. His eyes flickered back and forth like a rodent looking for its next meal. When they came to rest on her, examining her flesh like it was meat, she fought not to shiver or show the fear that raced through her veins.

"Isabel," he greeted her but continued to search the area around them. "It was difficult to find ye." He tilted his head and pushed his matted hair from his gaunt face. Where Sigurd had bulk behind his strength, Godrod had height and a wiry, muscular frame.

"He has kept me close to him," she said. "He only allows me this far and not into the village." A lie, but a necessary one to cover the fact she'd made no attempt to contact Sigurd. She glanced back over her shoulder as though worried he would arrive.

"Getting the full worth of his coin, eh?" Godrod said with a leer. "Keeping ye on yer back and well-plowed, I would think, after what he's paid for ye."

She longed to slap him, but he spoke the truth—a whore was worth nothing unless she was on her back with her legs spread. Still, his words stung. Isabel nodded in reply.

"Sigurd grows impatient for news." He rubbed his hands together. He liked to use his fists on her when she was slow in answering Sigurd's questions or doing his bidding. Godrod knew how to cause pain with his blows and yet leave few marks—a useful skill when bruises would raise questions. Her ribs ached just then, reminding her of his abilities and his duties for Sigurd—he was an enforcer.

"I have learned little," she revealed. "The only thing I have heard is that he is a healer of some sort." She took a step away, trying to move out of his range, but he followed her.

"That does not sound like much to pass on to Sigurd, whore. When he is unhappy, we all suffer." He entwined, then stretched his fingers; the crackling sounds startled her. "Are ye certain there is no more?"

He took a menacing step closer and Isabel watched his

hands. Not as fast as Sigurd, Godrod was more deadly. She'd been forced to watch him kill a man with those hands, so she knew the danger that was always ready to strike out.

"Something is going to happen next week, when the moon reaches fullness," she confessed hurriedly. Her stomach threatened to rebel, but she forced out what she knew. "He can heal people during the full moon. He will have some kind of power. I will know more after that."

He surrounded her before she could even think, his immovable arms encircling her chest, forcing the air out and not allowing another breath in. He clutched her throat in one hand while he wrapped the other in the length of her hair and yanked her head back against his chest, his fetid breath making her want to retch.

"I think yer lying to me, whore. Sigurd said ye might not cooperate and gave me permission to get information out of ye however I please," he threatened. Godrod arched his groin against her back, letting her feel the erect cock that would be his weapon.

He began to drag her toward a small wooded area just off the path and Isabel knew she must stop him. Sigurd had made certain she knew all about Godrod's ways of coercing women, and men, into revealing hidden truths. He'd used that knowledge as a threat against her when she did not follow his orders. Godrod would force and tear his way into her, using and degrading her. Then he would repeat it until she either relented or died.

Isabel stumbled over a rock and managed to loosen his grasp enough to draw in a breath. "Cease this!" she whispered in a hoarse voice. "Duncan has me watched and he will know what you have done."

In answer to her prayers, the sound of someone approaching on the path made him let her go. "Do not think to disobey

Sigurd in this, whore." He stepped back into the shadows of the trees but whispered another warning. "I will be back after the full moon. Do not disappoint me or ye will suffer for it."

"Are you speaking to someone, Isabel?" Gunna asked as she came around the last curve in the path between them. "I thought I heard a man's voice."

Isabel shifted her gown and let her braid fall around her shoulders, obscuring what must be a hand-print on her neck from Godrod's grasp. Positioning herself to block the road behind her, she gave Godrod a chance to hide himself from view.

"Nay, Gunna." Isabel took one of the baskets from her. "I was but singing a tune I have been trying to remember."

"Tell me the words," Gunna said. "I may know the song."

Isabel stumbled over some words, trying to concoct a lie to satisfy the woman, but she could not. She let out a breath. "There was a man," she admitted.

"From the village? Duncan will not be pleased if someone has accosted you, Isabel."

It amazed Isabel how that timid young woman could turn into a lion in her defense. But she did not want Gunna caught in the middle.

"I did not ask him, but he left as soon as you approached, so there was no harm done." Holding the basket out before her, she pretended to look through the items Gunna had bought in Uig. "Did you find the candles you needed?"

Gunna did not answer her, so Isabel was forced to meet her gaze . . . her very knowing gaze. "I pray you, let it go," Isabel begged quietly.

"Duncan said we should be back before noon, so we should hurry." Gunna's mouth curved into the smile that said she understood. As they walked she chatted about village gossip, naming this man or that woman and sharing the news about them as though Isabel knew them—or cared.

Isabel pretended attention, all the while watching for signs that Godrod was nearby. She knew his assignment—find her, follow her, watch her for compliance, send messages back to Sigurd, and give her orders. They'd done it before.

She hated it. Sharing the information she'd given him felt like betrayal of the worst kind. Of Duncan.

But it was only the first of many to come, she knew.

Sigurd would ask and she would provide the answers to save herself and to save Thora. Strange, she did not fear death itself, she only feared what would happen in those minutes or hours before dying. Spent with a man like Godrod, it would be like centuries of pain and torment before death released her. So, she would tell him whatever she could discover because she feared that kind of death more than anything else.

They reached the farm and Duncan stood waiting near the path. His horse stood next to him, a sack tied to the saddle. Isabel stopped without warning Gunna, who ran into the back of her and they tumbled to the ground. Duncan laughed as he helped them to their feet, but Isabel never took her eyes off the horse.

"You should give some warning when you plan to stop like that, Isabel," he teased.

"Your pardon, Gunna." Isabel picked up some of the things that spilled from Gunna's basket when it hit the ground. "I did not expect"—she pointed to the horse—"that."

Duncan helped Gunna inside, asking Isabel to wait on the path for him. She took several steps away from the monstrous beast and awaited Duncan's return, praying he did not mean for her to ride it somewhere.

"The day is still fair and I'd promised you a visit to the glen." Gathering the reins in his hand, Duncan mounted the horse.

"We need not," Isabel said, as close to a refusal as she dared.

"The prize will be worth the ride there, Isabel." When she did not rush to offer her hand to him to help her mount, he guided the horse to her and leaned down. "Trust me, sweetling," he said with a mischievous smile.

Her fear of such animals kept her from joining him in that bit of merriment. Watching the glint in his eyes and the inviting way he held out his hand to her, she knew exactly how the devil tempted good souls into wicked behavior. Duncan had not been cruel to her and he was kind to Gunna, so Isabel accepted his hand and closed her eyes as he pulled her up to sit before him.

She did not open her eyes for some time, fearing the view from high up off the ground. At his prodding, she finally did and was gifted with a panorama of the expanding valley before them. He talked as they rode, explaining the changes of the seasons, the borders of his property, anything and everything to ease her fear.

"Mayhap I should teach you to ride by yourself?" he asked as they reached a split in the path and he guided the horse to the south. She clutched his arm.

"I have no need of such skill, Duncan. When I return . . ." Duncan's eyes darkened and his jaws clenched together.

Isabel did not mean to anger him. He'd been nothing but kind to her, seeing to her every comfort and need while she stayed with him. Though she must reveal his secrets to Sigurd, she did not want to see Duncan hurt. She'd plainly ruined whatever pleasant time the excursion had been meant to be.

She turned slightly and said over her shoulder, "I have never stayed with a . . . with anyone like this, so it all feels like a dream." She tried to explain her own confused feelings. "This will end, Duncan, as it must and I will return to Duntulm. But I did not mean to ruin your plans by reminding you of such things." She carefully leaned into him. "How can I make this up to you?"

Instead of easing the tension between them, Isabel felt a momentary stiffness in him before he relaxed in the saddle again. Did he have other plans? Or did he think to negotiate with Sigurd for additional time with her? Something was wrong, for he urged the horse faster so she would hold on.

They rode along in an uncomfortable silence until they reached the place where the path dipped down as the stream quickened and tumbled over a ledge. The waterfall created by the rushing water collected in a small pool where the ground leveled out once more. He stopped near it and climbed from the horse's back, helping her dismount.

Whenever she was near water, Isabel's spirit calmed. She walked to the edge of the pool and crouched down to feel the water. It was cold, but not as frigid as the sea. She cupped her hands and dipped them in, lifting water to her face. Isabel drank, then did it again, quenching her thirst before turning to see where Duncan was.

He stood off a few yards watching her. She filled her hands and offered water to him. 'Twas his turn to hesitate but he soon accepted her gesture. He knelt next to her and let her bring the water to his mouth. Though some spilled down the front of his shirt and tunic, he drank most of it. She repeated it until he waved her off, though still no words were exchanged.

Watching the splashing water, she wanted to enter the pool, but he forestalled her.

"Come," he said abruptly as he mounted the horse again. "This is not the place I wanted you to see the most. It lies another hour or so from here."

She did not argue, but climbed back up, trying not to let her fear of the horse show. There was anger in his eyes, and she knew she'd caused it somehow. How could she make it better between them? Isabel decided to watch for an opportunity and be ready to appease him.

What she did not want to admit to herself was she cared that he was upset. The realization struck her in the silent moments as the horse plodded on toward the surprise. Just as he did not have to take his whore on an outing to please her, she should not care why or what he did or did not do, so long as the coin was paid.

But she did.

Could she allow him to know it?

Before she could come up with dozens of reasons not to, she leaned into him, grasped his hands, and said quietly over her shoulder, "I thank you for taking time for this excursion when you have other matters to see to, Duncan. I have angered you in some way and beg pardon for whatever thoughtless thing I said or did."

He hugged her to him, the heat of his body warming hers. "I cannot tell if that apology is coming from the whore or the woman."

Ignoring the warnings sounding in her mind and mayhap answering the guilt she felt over reporting to Godrod, she revealed a bit of herself to him. "The woman," she whispered, admitting the truth. She did care, damn her weak heart, that she'd hurt him when he was being considerate. Regardless of their arrangements, she did care.

"You did nothing, Isabel," he said softly, his words tickling the skin of her cheek. "Difficult times are coming and my bad humor is about that, not about you."

"Is there something I can do?" she asked. "To ease these difficult times."

He'd bought her for sex, but he wanted more than just that from her. He wanted explanations and reasons she might not even know she had inside her. He wanted to know why she was different. Why she whored and spied for Sigurd when he would have shared his secret with her if she'd only asked?

He'd known for days she was being watched. Strangers in the small village were noticed quickly and their questions about him had alerted him to their search for her. He did not want to believe she was a spy, but he felt it was the truth. Sigurd had agreed to let her go for a month because he would gain more than the gold paid in return for her.

"Just your presence eases me," he said, in spite of his suspicions.

'Twas the truth. Having her near seemed to temper the effects of the coming full moon and its ritual. Since months before, the weeks prior to the full moon were filled with unsatisfied physical needs and fear of the approaching power. This month, she gave him release and relief from the burgeoning sexual needs the rising power caused within him. Somehow, she made it possible for him to gain control over the impending storm. He did not understand why it was she who had the ability when dozens and dozens of others had not, but simply holding her eased his mind and body, and allowed him to feel the normal desires of a man for a woman.

He lifted her hand and kissed the palm of it. "We approach the glen I spoke of, but the path becomes steep. Hold on," he advised her. When she leaned against him, grasping his hands again, he laughed.

"How can you be so fearless about swimming in the sea and so frightened of horses?" he asked. Duncan did not expect an answer, so her words surprised him.

"I fell from one once and was nearly trampled. I cannot rid myself of that fear."

Another admission from the woman. What had happened between them that she felt at ease admitting such things to him? He gathered her closer so she did not shift as the horse descended the final part of the path leading into the glen, hoping his gesture comforted her. He knew the moment she took in all around her for she gasped at the sight in front of them.

He'd found the place by accident months ago, but had not returned because of the disturbance he felt there. He felt it again as they entered the hidden valley, but the excitement pouring from Isabel tempered it for him. Without explanation, her presence made a difference. The path led along the stream, which emptied into a small lake. As though untouched by weather or storms, the hills of the glen remained green and blooming. But those hills were unlike any others he'd seen in his travels around Skye, the other islands or even the Scottish mainland, for they looked sculpted, as though flat layers of earth had been cut and stacked in ever-narrowing piles until they formed cones.

They rode along the path until they reached the lake. From there the ruins of an ancient stone tower were visible to them. Like a guard tower, it sat high above on a ridge overlooking the glen, though no one had ever claimed possession of it. If he approached from the road that led to Uig some miles away, the tower seemed to warn travelers of the strange place. He reined in the horse and climbed off its back, then helped Isabel down.

Without hesitation, she walked away from him, heading for the edge of the lake. Wonderment filled her expression as she gazed this way and then that, taking in every aspect of the glen. Though the same forboding he'd experienced before began again, her sense of excitement and interest pushed it away and Duncan followed her.

"How did you find it?" She turned around and around, making him dizzy.

He grabbed her and stopped her, but the expression in her eyes, the way they seemed to glow, caused the healing power to rise within him.

It tickled his skin from inside, pushing and testing its way, seeking a release. Duncan shook his head, surprised at the feel of it, how it tempted and teased him to call the power forth and not wait until the full moon only days away. More frightening was that he wanted to bring it to the surface, to share its power with her, in that place.

"I walked for days when I received these lands, to learn the extent of them, and stumbled into this place." He looked back along the path to confirm something before speaking. "It is like a hidden world. Very few have found their way here without me to guide them."

Isabel walked toward one end of the lake without looking back at him. Her expression when she turned spoke of something important. "This is it!" she cried out, glancing from the lake to him and back again. "This is it!"

He thought she was confused until she ran to his side and grabbed his hand. "This is the lake where I fell in!"

Duncan found it difficult to believe, considering she was a wee bairn when the accident had occurred and could not possibly remember its location. But when he glanced at the lake and noticed the flickering lights that seemed to approach where she stood by its edge, he began to think otherwise.

"Do you remember where you lived?" he asked.

She did not notice the lights under the surface, but crouched at the lake's edge and dipped her hand into the water. "'Tis warm! Come and feel it, Duncan!" she urged, laughing.

Her face took on a shimmering glow and he wondered over the origins of the place. As she moved her hand through the water, the lights gathered, much like fireflies in the air. Still, she did not see them.

How could he? He shuddered from the power of something preventing him from moving to the water's edge. He could not ignore it . . . or pass through it. Strange though, for he swam in the sea and in other lakes, never feeling anything like that barrier before.

"Do you see the lights there, Isabel?" he asked.

She shielded her eyes from the sun's light above and searched the surface of the water. "Nay. I see nothing but beautiful, clear water."

She laughed again in childlike delight and he could not resist smiling. She was a carefree, younger, vibrant Isabel. One who must have existed before she began selling herself for secrets. One before the world, and Sigurd, changed her. One he'd liked to have known.

"May I swim?" she asked, her gaze serious.

"If you can stand the cold. You do not need my permission, Isabel. 'Tis the reason I thought you might like to come here."

She began peeling off her clothing, each layer flying through the air to land haphazardly around her on the ground. He would have helped except she moved too quickly for him. So Duncan stood aside and watched as her naked body was revealed to him. He knew every inch of her flesh, having kissed or tasted or touched it all during their time together, but seeing her exuberance aroused him as never before.

Isabel barely paused by the edge, dipping in her foot, then diving in. The lights spread out, as though shifting aside, for her to enter, then swarmed around her body as she moved through the water. She swam deep and he watched as she melted into the water. Even the bright sunlight that chased away the clouds did not make her visible below the surface and Duncan took a pace toward the edge.

Just as had happened when he'd watched her from the battlements above when she swam in the sea, he began counting out the seconds she remained too deep to see. He tried to get closer, but that barrier held him away. Finally, she broke through the surface, laughing in delight. Pushing her hair from her face, she looked around until she saw him and swam with sure strokes toward where he stood.

"Join me, Duncan," she called to him, holding out a hand. " 'Tis warm."

For a moment she looked like a mermaid of legend, or one of the sirens in those ancient Greek stories, luring men into the sea and to their deaths. For longer than a moment, he wanted to take her hand and follow wherever she led. How could he explain to her what he felt? 'Twas like the barrier he'd felt deep within her when he'd tried to heal her. Frustrated that he could not find or understand the connection that existed, he waved her off.

"Enjoy the water," he called, crouching down to watch her from his spot on the shore.

The wench pushed herself onto her knees, exposing every part of herself to him and flung herself backwards into the water, flipping her feet up and leading with her head. He wanted her, his cock hardened and ready, and every squeal of enjoyment she made caused his body to ache and burn to have her.

Duncan bided his time, knowing she would see to him when she finished. Would the healing effect of the water be as noticeable in her as the last times? Would it erase the mark of a man's hand on her throat and his scent from her hair? He had not missed those or the disturbance she felt because of them. If he asked her about it, she would lie or say nothing, so he did not bother. Instead, he waited and, aye, he hoped the water restored her.

He stood and walked around the end of the lake, wondering if it truly was the same one she'd spoken of to him. Though most would question it, her tale of a magical woman rang true to him. The glen carried something in it that was older than time and a power stronger than any he'd felt before. Had he failed to notice it on prior visits because his own power was not as strong? Did he notice it now because his power was cresting or because she was with him?

Regardless, he would never get the answers from Isabel. She seemed unaffected or unnoticing of the mystical presence in the waters though he could see them clearly. See them, but not approach too closely.

She called his name and he turned to face her.

Chapter Thirteen

Isabel climbed from the water, refreshed and feeling more alive than she had in a long time. The cooler air chilled her body, raising gooseflesh as Duncan walked toward her. The heat in his gaze warmed her even as his actions in taking her there warmed a heart she'd thought long-dead. She gathered her hair together and twisted the water from it so she would not get him too wet.

He did not move, yet she could tell he wanted to come closer. The longing in his eyes and the way they glowed and sparkled called to something in her blood and she began to walk toward him. Isabel needed him. She needed him to wrap his arms around her and hold her as her past and her future threatened to collide in that place where she should have died and had not.

She stood a pace away from him and let the desire she'd always controlled and hidden rise in her blood. Her body ached for him. Reaching across the distance she undressed him. He said not a word as she stripped his garments from him. Shaking from the cold air and the frank need pulsing through her, she fumbled with the ties to his trousers. He brushed her hands away and finished removing his clothing, then he stood facing her, as naked and exposed as she.

When she reached out to touch his erect cock, he pulled her into his arms, just as she'd hoped he would. He possessed her mouth.

She took over and kissed him the way she wanted . . . to within an inch of his life. He fell to his knees and she followed his body down, wrapping her arms around his shoulders and her legs around his waist. He managed to sit without disturbing her and guided her onto his shaft, inhaling sharply as she slid inch by searing inch until he filled her with all of him.

The crisp hair on his chest tickled her breasts as she rubbed against him. Running her hands through his hair, she held his face to hers, never taking her tongue from his mouth, tasting, desiring, possessing him. He slid his hands down and lifted her up. She drew her inner walls tight until he moaned. She smiled against his mouth and did it again and again until she drove him as mad with wanting as she was.

She did not relinquish control—over what they did or how quickly or slowly she moved—drawing it out until they were breathless and hot, unable to wait another moment. When his hands became frantic, touching her and making her ache and throb, and when he urged her on with words whispered into her mouth, she relented and began to seek release. She rocked against him, rubbing his cock inside her cleft and against that tight bud of flesh that swelled, waiting for release.

"Let me?" he asked, his voice hoarse with need.

He moved his hand between their bodies, reaching to touch the spot that would trigger the release they sought. She arched then, allowing him to slide his fingers down and down until he paused. Gazing at him as he touched her, she lost herself to the pleasure of it. One stroke, one caress and she shattered into so many pieces she thought never to find them all.

Isabel screamed against his mouth, then threw her head back, letting her pleasure echo throughout the glen. He rubbed and played until she could scream no more, then turned her on her back and sought his own release, thrusting so deeply inside her, she lost track of where she ended and he began. Falling into the welcome oblivion of release, she took and took all that he offered.

Once she came back to herself, she held onto him, burying her face in his neck and inhaling the scent she craved; the one that poured out of him during arousal and joining as surely as he breathed. 'Twas something she'd never noticed with any other man. Aye, there was always the smell of spent lust and spilled seed, but his scent was nothing like that.

"What is that scent?" she asked softly. Lifting her head, she sniffed the skin of his neck and face and found faint traces of it.

"It is part of my power, Isabel. As the full moon approaches, my body needs release more often so the scent spills out, calling women to me."

Part of her longed to warn him off from speaking about his secrets, so she would not face the choice of betraying him, but she needed to understand what drove him to pay the staggering amount for her.

"How many women?" she asked. She tilted her head up to see his face as he answered. One skill she'd developed was knowing if a man spoke the truth or not. A twitch of the eye, a lifting of the corner of the mouth, a glance off to one side all spoke of lies. She watched his expression as he answered.

"The number would rival, I suspect, the number of men you've had in the last year or so, from what I have been told," he admitted.

That number was . . . it was . . . too many to think about, she decided.

"So this is nothing more than flesh meeting flesh to you?"

she asked, throwing a nod to the area around them and their bodies, which remained joined.

"It began as such, Isabel," he replied with an honesty she felt. "But I think it is changing into something different from what it has been before." He withdrew then and her body screamed out at the loss of his flesh in hers. As he rolled off her, he pulled her along, tucking her beneath his arm and holding her close. "I—"

She put her finger to his lips to stop him from revealing anything to her. Isabel knew she would tell Sigurd regardless of how much she might not want to. But, if Duncan did not admit anything . . .

"Hush now," she warned in the only way she could. "This is nothing more than what you paid good coin for. I am very good at what I do, so you may feel there is more, but there is not." Isabel sat up and reached for her shift, trying not to see the shock and hurt in his gaze. "If you'd like me to pretend there is, I can do that as well."

He did not move for a few seconds, then climbed to his feet and gathered his clothing to dress. They did not speak again until he brought over the leather sack that had been tied to the horse's saddle. Food. He'd brought food for them. Another considerate action that made her regret her words. Still, she could not allow him to think she was affected by their time together, regardless of the things he did for her.

Strange, she'd thought her heart was deadened a long time ago, but it ached in her chest, making her regret not telling him how much his actions meant to her. Not telling him that what had just happened between them was extraordinary. Not telling him she'd never initiated sex with a man because of her own needs and desires before the time spent with him.

Telling him any of those things would result in nothing good and so many things bad. She could not risk it. She reacted politely as he took out bread and cheese and some left-over fowl from last evening's meal and shared it with her. Isabel even managed to speak to him about the journey there without breaking down and crying. She was a good whore indeed.

"Tell me of your childhood," he said quietly as she gathered up the remnants of their meal and placed them back in the sack. "If this is the lake you told me about, you must have lived close by." He stood staring at the lake's surface and did not turn to face her.

She walked to him and placed her hand on his arm. He turned.

"Truly, this is the same one I told you of, Duncan. I remember the look of this place, the way the water felt, the smell of the plants and grasses growing here even now."

"Your home then was in which direction from here?" he probed.

"Why do you ask?"

"I am curious, Isabel," he answered. "An unseemly curiosity is at the root of my questions."

He lied to her. She knew it, could see, and hear it. However, if she lied to him, she could hardly hold him to task for lying to her, could she?

"Did you enter as we did from the north? Or from the other end of the glen?"

Isabel looked around her. She walked several paces away from him, examining the path and the lake and how it was positioned. She'd been but a wee girl when she'd wandered into the place—no more than three or four years had she at the time—but it truly did look familiar to her.

"I think there is a small path over there." She pointed it out to him.

Walking in that direction, she passed by a large collection of boulders and made her way to the bushes behind them. There was a path hidden by the overgrown bushes, one that she believed was the one she'd followed into the glen all those years ago.

"It is here," she called out to him. But he was at her side already. Crouching down he looked through the brush. He glanced back at her and nodded. "There is a path. It is difficult to believe this is the same lake you fell into, but it would seem so."

She laughed then, a mix of nervousness and relief. A part of her childhood that had confused and frightened her for years had been solved. The other part, about the woman in the water who'd saved her, would always remain a mystery. Or perhaps that figure had been conjured up by the imagination of a young child who'd faced death and survived it. Or mayhap she'd dreamed it in a time when she'd needed to be rescued?

Isabel looked back at the lake and caught sight of flickering just beneath its surface. With the sun's rays playing over the swirling waters, she could not tell if it was the light being reflected or something else. Surely not . . .

"Did you see it?" he asked, shielding his eyes from the glare of the sun.

She noticed he did not approach the lake's edge. "See what?" Isabel walked close to the edge and studied the water. If something had been there before, 'twas gone. "Nay, nothing."

They stood in silence, farther apart than ever before due to the lies that lay between them. He was interested in her early years and would not admit it. She wanted him with a dangerous desperation she could not accept or admit. They played to a draw that day, in spite of the pleasure given and taken, and in spite of visiting that magical place.

"We should go soon, Isabel. There are not many hours of light left."

She nodded her acceptance, though it meant climbing on his horse again to get back to his farm. The time she'd spent in the water had refreshed her and she felt little of the fear that had controlled her all the way there. Duncan helped her to climb up and then sat behind her. If she dozed off on the ride back, she did not remember. She only knew his strong arms encircled her and for a short time she felt safe from all the dangers that lay before her.

Duncan knew in the marrow of his bones they'd shared more than just a joining of their flesh beside that lake. Isabel wanted him and gave of herself to him. More than just an even exchange, she'd reached out to him for the first time without his beginning their encounter.

In the days and nights they'd spent together, not once had she refused him a full measure of her passion, not even when playing the whore she thought herself to be. No matter when he touched her or how he took her, she responded eagerly. But he'd watched the wanting and longing in her eyes grow and overwhelm her control as she took what she wanted of him. He'd watched as she offered something of herself while they made love. Only when he began to tell her about the coming days did she change and become the whore once more. He caught sight of a man in the shadows off in the distance as they rode back to his farm and realized what she'd done.

She'd stopped him from revealing something she would have to tell Sigurd.

She shifted in his arms, murmuring in her uneasy sleep about the waters in the lake. He guided her back against his chest and let her settle before urging his horse to a faster gait. Though the watcher kept his distance, Duncan did not know what his plans were or whether they were in danger. He would set his own guards in place to keep the stranger at bay until after the ritual. No one would get close enough to frighten her again.

They arrived just before dusk as Gunna was serving the

evening meal. Isabel woke quickly and began to help her, while Duncan saw to his horse and had a few words with Harald about strangers and Isabel's safety. If the man thought it strange Duncan set guards for his whore, he did not voice his opinion. He nodded and Duncan knew Harald would see to it.

Conversation during their meal was sparse for everyone, save Isabel, knew what approached and the dangers of the ritual. All who worked the farm, save Gunna, had seen the ritual and its effects on Duncan and knew he would face it within two days. They finished eating, cleaned up, and left with very little chatter, allowing him time with Isabel. Though usually he would have been mindlessly swiving any woman who arrived at his door by that time in the month, Isabel's presence had appeased his hunger and given him true satisfaction. It must be that which stemmed his need and allowed him rest when he usually paced ceaselessly in the days before the full moon.

Sometime in the dark of that night, Isabel cried out in her sleep and turned to his embrace for comfort. A nightmare captured her and held her, terrifying her and making her sob. He heard words about the lake, the weight of her clothes, sinking into the depths and dying. He urged her to speak of what she remembered, but she only cried out more. The visit to the lake must have stirred up the child's fears and memories.

He wondered if she knew she cried in his arms. Duncan would like her to trust him as much awake as when she slept, but he understood too much stood between them. With no time left to seek out the reasons behind what she did and knowing he would not be there to see to her safety or prevent her return to Sigurd, a pain tightened around his heart. Strange that he'd finally found a woman he thought might accept the differences in him and be strong enough to love him through the coming ordeal, yet he had to pay for her time. A sound echoing on the wind brought him to full alertness.

If he did not know better, it was laughter that floated outside the walls. A man's. No. The laughter raced like the wind past his house, sounding like the tinkling of hundreds of bells, but also like a chorus of voices. Laughing, then fading off as quickly as it came.

Tempted to curse the fates or whatever had condemned him to live and die without knowledge of his origins or the reasons for his powers, Duncan ignored the urge to investigate and slid back down next to Isabel. She moved closer, kissing his chest as she laid her head there. 'Twas an unconscious gesture but it touched him deeply. Clearly she did not have any reservations while asleep. If only . . .

The laughter echoed in the chamber once more and Duncan decided not to draw its ire again. Turning to his side, he held Isabel tightly, wondering how she would react to what was to come and how it would change things between them.

Would the changes she'd already wrought to his accursed body change his fate as well? Or was he as damned as he'd ever been? Two more days and he would know. As he felt the pull of the moon grow stronger, he wondered if the tides ever considered fighting back or if the fight was as futile as he thought it to be?

Chapter Fourteen

Gunna cried twice during the noon meal and did not even put an evening meal on the table. Worse, she would not meet Isabel's gaze at all.

Harald stomped in and out of the house, whispering to Duncan and listening to his orders with a black expression in his eyes.

Ornolf disappeared into the storage barn and did not come to eat with them.

Duncan was the worst, for he carried the look of a man facing the gallows.

And no one would speak to her about what was going to happen.

The next day dawned stormy and dark, the sun not daring to peek through the clouds. All day, people arrived at the farm and Isabel watched as Ornolf greeted them and led them to the barn. Some walked on their own, but others were carried or carted in. A chilling thought struck her as the third group turned up on the path to the farm. They were all either ill, ailing, or injured in some way. They sought out the man called the Healer—Duncan. Icy shivers traced down her spine and she trembled with fear as she faced the coming night, not knowing what to expect.

When she tried to speak to him, Duncan brushed her aside with an unusual indifference. And that worried her most of all. She found an extra cloak in his chamber, wrapped herself in it, and waited by the door to the house, watching the scene unfold through a crack in the shutters. Once she tried to follow Duncan out, but Harald and another man blocked her path, making it clear she was a prisoner, at least for the time being.

As the moon began to gain prominence in the sky Duncan entered the house, motioning for Gunna to leave them in private and she complied silently.

"Duncan—" Isabel began.

He waved her to silence. "There is no time now, Isabel." His voice took on a strange cadence. "I must . . . see to things and you must remain here."

"What will you do, Duncan? Tell me, I beg you."

He took her hands in his and she jumped from the heat in them. Almost too hot to touch, his skin seem to sizzle where it contacted hers. "I cannot speak of it now. You must obey my wishes in this. Stay here with Gunna and do not leave until Ornolf gives you leave to do so."

"But . . ."

He released her without another word, the air around her losing the heat he radiated as he stepped to the door. She shivered and tried to reach for him, saying his name, but he left without another look or word. When she tried to follow, Harald took hold of the door and stopped her, allowing Gunna in but neither of them out.

She tried to lift the latch, but it was held in place by something and would not budge. Isabel slammed her hands down on the table and let out a vile curse, startling Gunna so much she stopped crying.

"Tell me, Gunna. Tell me what is happening," Isabel begged.

"I cannot," Gunna said. "I am sworn to him, Isabel."

"He brought me here because he thinks I can help him in some way." Gunna's eyes showed her shock at the news, so Isabel continued. "I was able to stop some of the effects over these last days," she argued without knowing how accurate her statements were.

"Harald will stop you." Gunna looked at the door, then back at Isabel. She shook her head and motioned for Isabel to follow her into the small storage chamber located opposite the bedchamber. "Come this way instead." She drew back a cloth, revealing a small door.

Isabel reached to lift the latch. Gunna grabbed her hand. "Are you certain you wish to know the whole of it? Mayhap you should remain here as he—"

"Nay, I will not stay here," Isabel argued. Something terrible was heading toward Duncan and she needed to warn him. A horrible churning in her stomach unlike anything she'd ever felt told her so. She must go to him. She must . . . do something.

"Stay in the shadows of the house until you reach the corner, then duck behind the fence. When you reach the barn, go to the back and find the third plank in the wall," Gunna explained, handing her a dark cloak. "It slides apart and you can enter there, but Isabel, you must not reveal yourself or leave until everyone else has."

Isabel nodded, anxious to get to the barn as quickly as possible. Pulling the hood of the cloak down low around her face, she eased the door open and stepped outside. The moon's light shone down, lighting the landscape and throwing shadows across the yard. Using them to hide her presence, she did as Gunna had instructed and made her way to the barn. Finding the back corner, she counted and found the loosened plank. Holding her breath, Isabel tugged it open only wide enough for her to shimmy through, then closed it behind her.

A wall of wooden storage trunks provided cover as she waited for her eyes to adjust to the darkness before moving.

Ornolf's voice broke the silence and she climbed up on one of the trunks to see into the open part of the building. The center part had been cleared of whatever goods or supplies were usually stored there. Those who were ill or injured were gathered in a small group with their families standing in another circle around them.

Duncan stood in the center of them all, his eyes closed and his arms crossed over his chest. But it was his hands that caught her attention.

They glowed like irons in the blacksmith's fire!

Covering her mouth with her hand to keep from gasping aloud, she watched as he began to change into someone, something, else. No one seemed surprised but she could not believe what her eyes saw.

He took in a deep breath and opened his eyes. They glimmered and flickered like flames, brightening and burning until all the color was gone and only white could be seen. His face changed as well, with other features laying over his as though someone had placed a mask over it. The face was younger in some ways and much older in others as it melded with his own, making it appear as though several people lived in the same body.

"The Healer is here," he said, but the voice was not his.

Isabel shook, fearing what she was about to see.

"Take me to them," he ordered. He held out his hands and Ornolf guided him to the nearest invalid, a man of about two score whose arms and legs had been badly burned. Duncan reached out and placed his hands on the man's arms.

She rubbed her eyes, not believing what she witnessed.

Their flesh seemed to melt together, rearranging itself from burned and ravaged to normal skin. All traces of the burns disappeared as Duncan touched the man. Once the damage on his arms had been repaired, Duncan moved his glowing hands onto the man's legs. Impossible though it was, the skin repaired itself under his touch.

Isabel shook her head, denying what she saw each time as Duncan was guided from person to person. Her chest hurt from holding her breath and her eyes burned with tears as she watched him heal each one, drawing their injuries or their illnesses from them and leaving them whole.

He moved in utter silence. Only the sound of his deep inhalation as he began each healing broke the stillness. Ornolf stopped him once, but he looked out with those flaming eyes and set his gaze on a woman who looked whole. Duncan motioned her closer, but she shook her head, denying the need for his power until he said her name and revealed the truth of her condition to everyone present.

"Margaret, 'tis not a bairn that grows in your womb. It will be the cause of your death," he warned quietly.

The woman began to cry and the sound of her desperate sobbing filled the barn.

"Come to me." His words sounded as though he pleaded with her to let him help.

Margaret took one shaking step, then another until he could touch her, laying his hands across her belly and lower. She gasped and crumpled to the ground. Duncan knelt at her side and whispered reassuring words that only the woman could hear.

Ornolf helped him to stand and tried to lead him away, but Duncan stopped once more and looked across the people assembled there. He shook his head, then turned in Isabel's direction. She ducked lower so she could not be seen above the crates, but she could hear him approaching.

"Duncan . . . Healer, you have done enough this night," Ornolf urged. "Come away now."

"There is another here who is so broken her soul calls to me," Duncan said. "I can feel the damage even now."

She held her breath then. He spoke about her, though no one knew she was there. How could he know? How could he feel such things? She fought to remain silent, to keep from answering his call and begging for his gift to be used to patch her soul and body back together. He would do it. He could, as she'd plainly seen. One touch of his hands and all the pain would disappear forever. She could be whole again.

She could . . . never accept such a gift.

Ornolf spoke to Duncan and she heard them move back to the center of the room. Risking a peek she watched as his hands lost the fire and his face became only his. Those who had been healed began to approach him, murmuring their thanks, trying to give him coin and goods in gratitude, but Ornolf guided them away.

Efficiently, he cleared the room and building, then took his leave of Duncan. She heard the door close and the bar drop into place. Isabel waited, not wanting to reveal her presence and remembering Gunna's instructions to remain until everyone else left. Before she climbed down from her perch as quietly as she could, she risked one more look. What she saw stopped her.

Duncan sat slumped forward on the stool. Suddenly his body shook and shuddered until he fell to the floor. The same fire that had filled his hands took over his body and he writhed in agony as it burned him without destroying him. She could see he fought against it, clenching his jaw and moaning as wave upon wave of terrible pain coursed through him. He rolled to his side, curling himself into a ball, but another wave forced him to his back again.

Until his legs were exposed she hadn't realized he wore only a loose robe, not unlike the one he'd given her but in a sturdier fabric. The fire appeared in his legs, setting his skin on fire, making it blister and burn. She hurried to him before she even knew she'd decided to help him.

But how?

Whatever controlled him was inflicting the very injuries and ailments on his body that he had taken from those he'd healed. Shaking her head, she watched as he clutched the parts of his body he'd laid hands on in the ritual. Was the power he hinted at destroying him bit by bit? Her tears poured out as she watched in helplessness, and reached for him.

He opened his eyes and stared at her. "Get out," he begged through clenched teeth. "Now!"

She crouched down, unable and unwilling to leave him. Touching his face, she fell back from the fiery heat. The tips of her fingers reddened as though she'd touched a scalding cooking pot or iron poker in the fire. How could he live through such a thing?

"Duncan," she whispered. "How can I make this stop?"

"You cannot," he forced out. "Nothing can."

The tremors seized him again and he moaned in agony in the silence of the barn. She sobbed, trying to think of something that could help him or ease his pain.

"I beg you, Isabel. Go now." Then he was lost to the fire that burned him but did not destroy him.

She scrambled away, climbing to her feet and stumbling to the place where she'd entered. Without looking back again, she shoved the board aside and climbed out. Isabel could not return to the house sobbing and hysterical as she was, so she crept away toward the stream, her mind confused over what she'd witnessed. Just before she reached it, she was grabbed from behind, dragged into the bushes and thrown to the ground.

"What happened in there?" Godrod asked, his hand wrapped around her throat, slamming her head down. "What is going on, whore?"

Out of control, she cried and babbled what she'd seen—the fire in Duncan's hands and in his eyes, the strange voices and face, and his ability to heal with his touch. She failed to keep any of it in. If Godrod believed what she'd seen or not, he didn't say. He simply kept throttling her and slapping her until she told it all. When she'd finished the tale, he released his grip and tossed her aside.

"If I go back to Sigurd with such a story, he will have me see to you before he kills me. If yer lying to me, bitch, I will make ye pay for it. Ye will beg for death to end what I will do to ye," he threatened.

She crawled away, trying to find a place to hide from him, from everyone, from everything, but he grabbed her ankle and dragged her back. With his foot on her stomach to hold her down, he reached for the ties on his trousers.

"No reason not to use ye while I have ye."

He fumbled with his laces as Isabel watched in horror. Unable to fight back and utterly confused by what she'd seen, she gave up, throwing her arms over her face. He knelt down, spreading her legs and pushing her gown out of his way, chortling.

Isabel held her breath and waited for the pain.

Nothing happened. Opening her eyes, she watched as Godrod fell over to one side, landing on the ground next to her. She scrambled backwards to get away from him, and only then did she realize what had happened. Harald stood there with a long club in his hand. Looking from him to Godrod, she saw the gash in the side of his head from Harald's blow.

"Come now," he said, holding out his hand to her. "Gunna is overwrought with worry about you."

"How?" she got out before she began to shake and tremble.

He wrapped his arm around her shoulders and guided her back along the path to the house.

"Duncan?" she asked as they passed by the barn where . . . it had happened.

"He wanted you protected, Isabel. That is why he ordered you to remain within. He knew someone was following you."

Duncan had known about Godrod? "Is he dead?" she asked, wondering whether dead or alive was the better thing once Sigurd heard of it.

"I did not kill him. The others will move him to the edge of the village where he will awaken with a terrible pain in his head." Harald stopped and gazed down at her. "If he returns, I will kill him."

She shivered, understanding the man would do anything necessary to protect Duncan—anything. She dug in her heels and made him stop.

"I want to see Duncan," she demanded now that her thoughts began to clear. "He needs help."

"There is nothing that can help him this night," Harald said softly, tugging her along. His strength was too much for her and she found herself walking in spite of wanting to stop. "Do you not think I would have done it if there was something to be done?"

She allowed him to take her to the house, knowing the truth of his words. "How does he survive such a thing. He was on fire." Her mind rebelled at what she'd seen happening to Duncan. "And the pain of it. It could drive a man mad."

'Twas Harald who stopped then, turning to face her. "Do not speak of this to Gunna. She has never seen what it costs him."

"Why . . . ?" Her words faded as she realized the tie that bound Gunna and Harald to Duncan. "He healed her?" Harald turned away before answering her, but she did not need to hear it to know it was true. "What happened to her?"

"I will not tell you his secrets or hers, whore." Harald gasped as he spoke the word, then looked away for a moment.

"Isabel," he went on, "Duncan knows you spy for Sigurd and will take anything you learn back to him. You've already told him"—he nodded toward where Godrod lay—"too much. I will not see you put Duncan in more danger."

They arrived at the house to find Gunna waiting within, pacing and wringing her hands.

"Oh thank the Almighty, Harald found you," she cried out as Harald closed the door behind them. "When I heard them talking about an intruder on Duncan's lands, I feared for you, Isabel."

Harald let go of her and turned back to the door to leave. "Stay inside now, Isabel," he warned. "Until Duncan orders otherwise." The expression in his eyes told her that would not happen soon.

How long would it take for him to recover from what had happened to him? If his ability to heal was tied to the full moon, had it happened before . . . and would it again?

"You too, Gunna," he added in case either of them thought to leave.

Isabel said nothing more as Harald exchanged a wordless message with Gunna before leaving. Looking around the room, Isabel realized she'd never lost control of herself as she had in the last hours. Priding herself on being the one to direct things, she began to shake as it all came back to her. Gunna pulled her to sit at the table, then handed her a cup of wine.

"Aye," Gunna whispered to her. "It happens every month or so when the moon grows full." She answered Isabel's questions without even hearing them.

Isabel lost hold of the cup and dropped it. Gunna knew much more than Harald thought and, for some reason, she hid it from her brother. But did she know Isabel's true purpose there, which seemed no secret to Duncan or Harald? She reached out and righted the cup before placing her hand on Gunna's. The woman had been nothing but kind to her and she would not see her repaid by more deception.

"Speak not of it, Gunna," she warned.

"You should know the truth about him." Gunna poured more wine into Isabel's cup, then met her gaze. So much pain lay behind those kind eyes.

Isabel would not add to it. "You should not trust me," she admitted boldly. "I cannot be trusted."

"Duncan would not have brought you here if he did not," Gunna challenged.

Isabel stood then and shook her head. There seemed no other way to make the woman understand other than to speak plainly about it. "Duncan brought me here to ease his need for pleasure during the weeks before the full moon. He needs sex. He needs sex from many women and decided a whore might be able to accommodate him with fewer questions or expectations than other women would. He told me that much."

Every word was true, but the admission did not have the effect she'd hoped for. Gunna pressed her lips together and shook her head, as though refusing to believe would make it all false.

"He also knows, as does Ornolf and Harald, that I am supposed to report back everything I learn about him and the power he has and how it works."

"It uses him up and is killing him, Isabel. That is how it works."

Isabel gasped at the words, motioning to Gunna to say no more, but she continued heedless of the warning.

"He thought it such a gift at first, you know. He was able to save people from death and illness. Each month he could lay his hands on someone and heal them—how could that not be a good thing?" Gunna drank some from her own cup, pausing but not done yet.

"But each year has seen the power grow and its cost grows, too. His needs, as you said, have become excessive and uncontrolled. What you saw after his healings, the burning, is worse each month and the emptiness deepens and lasts longer."

Isabel could not help herself. "Emptiness?"

"Aye. After he heals, he is afflicted with whatever he drew out of the people he's cured. Then the power burns it out of him, leaving him unable to feel for days and days."

That explained the burns appearing on his arms and legs and the other injuries he'd suffered while she watched. Isabel thought back to the first time they'd met, in Lord Davin's hall, and she remembered that he'd seemed shocked when he'd looked at her. He'd asked her to touch him, to caress his skin, and he was surprised in some way. Had that been when his ability to feel had returned?

"More than just being able to feel, his emotions are wiped clean and he becomes like an empty shell."

Too far into the explanation, Isabel had to hear more. "Where did this power come from? Can he not control it?" she asked, damning her soul forever, for she knew Sigurd would be told what she learned. She had no choice.

"No one knows, for he was a foundling and raised by those who discovered him abandoned some miles from Uig." Gunna shivered and drank more wine. "I have sought for knowledge about him or this terrible curse, just as he has, but can find nothing more than a few strange tales. Nothing that can explain it."

A commotion began outside the house and they ran to the door to see what was happening. It opened just as Gunna reached it, revealing a disheveled and exhausted Duncan. Gunna shook her head and cried out his name, just as he sank to his knees. Harald was there in a moment and helped him inside.

"Duncan! How did you get this far so soon?" she asked, revealing to her brother she knew more than she'd ever let on to him. "Harald, bring him. Isabel, turn down the bedcovers. Ornolf, help him!"

They moved wordlessly, carrying out their tasks, and Isabel could see each of the others was shocked by Duncan's presence there so soon after the ritual had been concluded. Within minutes, Duncan lay on his bed and managed to drink some watered wine before fading off to sleep.

When it looked as though she would be ordered elsewhere, Isabel sat in the chair next to his bed and ignored the others. Gunna, bless her, won the argument and they left Isabel at his side with instructions about his care and warnings about disturbing him. They remained in the other chamber for a short while, whispering amongst themselves so she could not discern their exact words, but she did not miss the tone of their conversation.

Harald wanted her gone.

Ornolf remained neutral.

Gunna argued in her favor.

When they all left without dragging her with them, Isabel knew Gunna had gotten her way. She smiled at the young woman's spine of steel. When it came to doing something she thought was the right thing to do, she would even defy her brother.

An hour passed and Isabel dozed, exhausted by all that had happened. Duncan lay without moving or making a sound. As she sat watching him, she finally felt the dirt in her hair and on her skin from Godrod's attack. She poured water from a jug kept near the hearth into a bowl and tried to clean herself. With a brush, she eased the tangled knots from her hair and removed as much of the dirt and leaves as she could. A full bath would have to wait. As she returned to her chair, she found Duncan watching her.

"You wear the mark of a man's hand on your throat once more, Isabel," he said softly.

The tears welled and spilled over, making tracks down her cheeks. She did not want to lie to him any longer, nor did she want to be the instrument of his downfall. Too much was between them to pretend otherwise.

"You disobeyed me," he accused.

Her body shuddered at the words and what usually followed. She could not believe he would seek retribution against her for leaving the house or going to the barn. But mayhap he would?

"Did you find what you sought?"

She slid to her knees and clasped his hand to her chest. "Send me back now, Duncan. I do not wish to play this out any longer. I cannot."

He did not move his hand and she wondered if the numbness had set in. She stroked the skin of his hand and arm and saw no response at all. Knowing more than she had a moment ago and realizing the danger in discovering more, she begged him again. "Send me back. Tell him you are not pleased. I will take the risk of his anger over—"

"Over betraying me to him?" he finished. " 'Tis true, Isabel. I cannot feel your touch on my skin. I will not be able to for some days, though I suspect fewer than last month."

"Why? Why is it different this time?" she asked before she thought about it. Damn her curiosity!

"Because of you."

He stared at her as though seeking the answer to a riddle, a dispassionate gaze that watched her every move, looking for information. No warmth or wanting dwelled there, only emptiness. It seemed a stranger looked back at her. His claim that she was the reason for the change in him felt false.

"Why me?" she asked.

"I brought you here hoping to find out the answer to that simple question."

"And have you discovered it?" Isabel held her breath, waiting, hoping, praying for something that would help her not betray him to Sigurd.

"Not yet, though I am seeing threads of a bigger web each day."

The man lying before her was not the same one who'd shown her kindness and consideration or the one who'd made her melt with overwhelming, breathless desire and pleasure. This man was a stranger and it frightened her.

"Let me go," she pleaded again, touching his hand.

He moved his lifeless gaze to the place where their bodies touched and shrugged. "I'd hoped it would be different, more different, but I fear even you may be too late."

Isabel leaned her head down on the bed and let out everything that was inside her. The guilt, the shame, the loss and grief, the fear, the helplessness, even the hatred. All of it poured out in a torrent not unlike the storm that had followed them from Duntulm. Through it all, he did not speak or reach out to her, but he did not shun her or order her away. Much as the power burning within him had purged him of all emotion and sensation, the tears washed her clean.

She fell asleep where she lay, never knowing he reached out to her in her grief.

He touched but could not feel.

Chapter Fifteen

He wanted it to hurt, but it did not.

Watching her collapse and cry out sobs reaching down to her soul should make him sad or angry. Instead, he watched and felt nothing. She finally fell into a fitful sleep and he reached out to touch her, resting his hand on her hair, then her head.

Nothing. He could feel nothing under his hand.

At least the pain had relented. The burning agony had eased within him only a short time after the ritual finished, unlike the hours and hours he'd suffered the last two months.

Isabel sighed, drawing his attention. She mumbled something in her sleep, not as she did when the nightmares took over, but words of pleading and supplication that would have caused pity in anyone else hearing them.

But not in him that night.

Duncan suspected but did not understand what linked their fates together. Though he was not sure of the reason, he was certain of the connection. Finding that the lake on his lands was the same one she'd fallen into as a child was too significant to be coincidence. Watching whatever inhabited that lake accept her into its depths convinced him she was more than simply a woman, just as he was somehow more than just a man.

Unfortunately, one other thing he knew for certain—he would die with the next ritual.

His heart had slowed and stopped for longer than last time, for he'd counted the seconds and waited for it to beat again before he lost consciousness. Next time, the power would burn him out completely, leaving nothing but his empty body behind when it was done. That knowledge did not bother him. He thought on things he needed to do before it happened.

He must deal with Sigurd and find a way to free Isabel from him. He must learn her reasons for staying with the man and letting him use her as he did. Duncan was missing something critical there, for a woman filled with the vitality and passion for life he'd found in her would not easily fall into being the pawn of one such as Sigurd.

Duncan lay there, with his hand on her head, planning out his last weeks, knowing much of what he could do for her was dependent on her trusting him. Since she did not, for she trusted no one he could think of save Gunna, he could not take her into his confidence and share his plans with her.

Gunna had spoken with him about Isabel several times since she had arrived and he knew Gunna would help however she could. In spite of never having known a day in her life when she was not valued and loved, Gunna understood Isabel's pain better than he did and urged him to see to her future regardless of how things ended between them.

And he would, once he discovered her truths.

Without emotions to shade his view or protect him from the grim realities of his situation, Duncan found it easier to make decisions and plans involving all those who depended on him.

He spent the rest of the night until sleep finally claimed him setting out the tasks he must attend to before the next full moon.

When he woke again, it was night once more, but he had the strength to get out of his bed. Looking around the chamber, he noticed Isabel was not there. Stumbling a bit as he gained his balance, Duncan made his way to the main room and found her there. Wrapped in a blanket and sitting in a large chair by the hearth, she slept. She'd clearly positioned the chair so she could see into the bedchamber, but no doubt the cozy warmth of the fire burning low had made her drowsy.

He crouched down before her and watched her. When no frown marred her brow and no sadness filled her gaze, she was a beautiful woman. Even without the artificial coloring she'd worn those first few times to make her lips look fuller and her eyes darker and wider, her beauty shone through. Noticing, too, the smudges beneath her eyes, he knew she had not slept well.

Sigurd's methods had trained her not to sleep when with a man, so she found it difficult to relax, he knew. She startled easily and slept lightly, when at all, and it had taken many nights before she would seek her rest before he did. Duncan reached out to touch her cheek, but hesitated to wake her. As he looked more closely, he also saw tiny red speckles that were evidence of the violence of her sobbing.

He paused, realizing how much he wanted to feel her skin and be aroused by the sight of her. He wanted to feel pity and sadness that she'd cried so hard. He wanted to be angry at the man who'd left marks on her neck and fear in her gaze.

Something was quite different from before without her. He was emptied, aye, but not as completely burned out as last month. Though he could not yet feel anything, he wanted to and that was more than he'd expected. He stood, trying to decide if he should move her to his bed. She opened her eyes, and he read confusion in her gaze. He stepped back to give her room to stand.

"Why did you not sleep in the bed, Isabel?" he asked.

"I did not wish to disturb your rest." She pushed her hair out of her face, quickly gathering and tying it behind her head. Smoothing her gown and tunic down, she stood and moved away from him. He watched as she put distance between them, stepping to the other side of the table.

"You should know by now that when I am tired, I sleep and nothing keeps me from it."

She took a step away as he walked around the table toward her.

"You are afraid of me." Duncan stopped and moved back, surprised.

"I-I," she stuttered. "So many things have happened, I was not certain . . ." She shook her head and shrugged, still not moving nearer to him.

"You need not fear me." He reached out his hands to her. "I am just a man now, Isabel. My hands are just hands." He held them out closer to her. "Touch them."

Her hands trembled as she did as he bade her to do. Though he saw her touch him, his skin did not feel it at all. "Are they hot?"

"Nay, no longer," she said. "Do they hurt?"

"Nothing hurts. Nothing aches. Nothing feels at all," he said. "But it will."

Isabel watched his every step, every turn, much as she did when she expected some kind of retaliation for a misdeed or error. As she had in the first days with him.

He changed the topic of their discussion. "How late is it? Is Ornolf still about?"

"Forgive me, Duncan. I was supposed to tell you that he would speak to you as soon as you are able. I forgot—"

"Come here, Isabel."

Silence filled the room and he recognized the dread in her eyes at his command. Yet, as always, it was his will and not hers that would prevail between them. She walked around the table and came to him.

"You saw much that disturbed you in the barn. Many things happened and we should discuss them," he explained, all the time noticing the frown lines across her forehead and the way she twisted her hands together.

She opened her mouth to say something, but a knock on the door interrupted her. Ornolf pushed it open and nodded to him. "Ah, so you are awake, Duncan." The older man stepped inside and closed the door, glancing from Duncan to Isabel and back again, realizing he interrupted something. "I will wait for you outside," he said quietly. With a nod to Isabel, he left more quickly than he'd entered.

"What must you tell me?" Duncan saw guilt flash in her eyes and sadness and resignation there, too. She did not step back, but he could see the tension in her stance that spoke of someone prepared to run.

"Harald will tell you," she began, looking away and not meeting his gaze. "When I left the barn, Sigurd's man caught up with me . . ." She trembled and tried to explain, but soon the shaking became too great.

"I did not want you to see the ritual. I told you not to leave here because I could not be with you and I knew someone was following you." He sat down on one of the stools, trying not to intimidate her so much. "So, you told him about what you'd seen?"

She let out her breath and nodded. "I am sorry, Duncan. I was terrified and he hit me and . . ." Tears fell once more from her beautiful green eyes and he opened his arms to her. She ran to him, kneeling in his embrace, and begged for his forgiveness. "I did not want to know your secrets, because I knew I must tell Sigurd. I could not refuse him. I wanted to, but I could not."

"Isabel," he said softly to gain her attention. When she looked up at him, he explained. "I knew why he let you come with me. It was never about the outrageous amount of gold I paid him. I knew he wanted you to spy for him and take back information he could use to gain my cooperation."

Her face lost all its color, becoming a ghastly, ghostly whiter shade of pale. "You knew?"

"I have watched men like Sigurd as they use their way to power and wealth. They target those weaker and climb on top of them as they claw their way to their goals. He is not the first to use a woman nor the last."

"What will you do with me now that you know?" she asked.

She expected the worst from him. It was clear in her voice and in her body. After what she'd endured, her response was no surprise to him.

"I've always known, Isabel, and it hasn't changed anything between us. We will keep to our arrangement for the time being and Sigurd will think all is well." While he set his own plans in place for a completely different result.

He read the suspicion in her gaze as he stood, bringing her to stand at his side. Seeing the mistrust in her eyes would hurt him when he could feel such things again, but he ignored it and led her to the bedchamber. "I will join you after I have spoken to Ornolf."

"You will?" She searched his face for the truth, so he gave it to her.

"I am not yet recovered from the ritual, so, aye, I will seek my rest soon."

It was easy to speak the truth when no emotion clouded his mind. Even easier was to see where his path would lead.

Isabel would be safe.

He would be dead.

Sigurd would pay first.

Once she'd settled under the bedcovers, he left to meet Ornolf and give him the first task to complete. The one upon which all else would depend. Duncan would trust no one but Ornolf to see it done. The man had been his loyal servant, nay friend, since before his powers began to manifest themselves seven years ago and he'd sworn to be at Duncan's side when all was finished.

It would take Ornolf several days to find the information he needed before Duncan could return to Duntulm for the next step. He needed to speak with Harald as well but that could wait until morning. He bid Ornolf a good night and returned to his bedchamber, all the while being drawn there by something he could not explain.

Empty as his soul was, he knew it was not desire or longing that drew him to Isabel that night. His body felt nothing, neither cold nor heat, and he had no appetite for pleasures of the flesh. What could it be that urged him to be with her.

Unable and unwilling to examine his motives more closely, he undressed and climbed into bed with her. She turned immediately to him and he wrapped his arms around her as she lay against him. Soon, only the soft sounds of her even breaths could be heard in the chamber. Just as he began to drift to sleep, the tinkling sound of eerie laughter echoed around him, making him question all he thought he knew about Isabel and her place in his life . . . and his death.

Chapter Sixteen

As she carried out the tasks Gunna asked of her, Isabel kept her eyes open and her ears alert for the sight or sound of anyone nearby. Determined not to be surprised by Godrod again when he returned, and he would return, she was ever watchful when she was more than a few paces from any of the buildings or the main yards of Duncan's farm. Though she enjoyed accompanying Gunna to Uig, she'd stopped walking with her because she feared his reappearance.

Isabel knew she would pay for his injury. One way or another, it would become her fault and her sin to bear. No amount of explaining would lessen the punishment, so she tried to avoid being caught by him. Duncan repeatedly told her she was safe from Godrod, even bringing in six very stout men as additional guards around his lands.

But she understood what he did not—as long as Sigurd had Thora, Isabel would go back to face his anger and accept whatever punishment he doled out. Until Thora was married and away from Skye, Isabel would obey him and be his pawn. It was only a matter of time before Sigurd called her to him.

A week had passed since that terrible night and Duncan still could not feel. At their evening meal the previous night, he'd sliced a deep gash in his hand and never knew it until the others noticed his blood spilling from it. Two days before he'd stepped into the bath she'd arranged before she could add the cold to temper the steaming water . . . and he'd not noticed until she dipped her hand in and burned it.

She hoped and prayed each day and night he would regain his ability to feel not only pain and pleasure, but also the emotions that had been burned from him. Isabel would have sought the comfort of his body, but he did not respond to any of her caresses or kisses. Her own body did not understand the absence of physical relations after weeks of constant and abundant passion and she found herself tossing and turning more than one night, unrelieved and unable to ignore her restlessness.

Ornolf had slipped up and revealed that two weeks passed after the last ritual before Duncan felt anything, but Isabel kept hoping it would not take that long. Though he talked and ate and walked like himself, Duncan was not the man she'd come to care for. The man she was beginning to love.

That thought occurred to her as she was carrying a basket of wash across the yard to hang it to dry in the breezes and she stumbled and almost dropped it. Righting herself, she closed her eyes and tried to banish such foolishness from her heart. Not wanting to dwell on such a thing for too long, she returned to her task and walked to the place where the rope was strung. She put the basket down.

It cannot be. It cannot be. It cannot.

Isabel chanted the words to herself over and over as she wrung out each piece of clothing and linen and threw it over the rope. She tried to find her way to that empty place inside her soul that used to be her refuge when she could not bear what was happening to her, but she could not find it. Her heart spoke the words she feared the most.

I love him.

Isabel knew she should have listened to the warnings long ago when it came to the man. He'd broken through every defense she'd set up to avoid those softer feelings. He crushed them and pushed through barrier after barrier until she could not keep him out. He did not want her love, he only wanted to use her body to ease the weeks when the power within him surged and needed release. He'd told her that over and over and yet her heart had led her down a hopeless path.

Unlike keeping the memories of their passion for colder, bleaker days, this could not end well no matter what. Isabel only hoped she could keep herself from shattering long enough to reach her only goal.

Seeing Thora happily married.

She finished hanging the wash and stepped back, pushing the hair that had come free from her braid out of her face. The winds grabbed her hair and blew it wildly around her as she tried to gather it all. Laughing at the strange sight she must be, she turned and found him there, staring at her with that empty gaze.

Duncan.

It was too soon on the heels of her heart's revelation. She looked away from him and took a deep breath. She had to fight it, for letting him know gave him another weapon against her. She'd believed herself in love with a man before, believed his words about freeing her from Sigurd, and her heart and spirit had been crushed by betrayal. She could ill afford such a distraction and such emotional ties at the moment. Isabel heard the dirt crunching behind her and knew he approached.

"Are you well, Isabel?" he asked in that empty voice. He said the appropriate things but only from rote and knowing what was expected.

She had claimed to be a good whore, one adept at pretending as need be and she drew on that ability. She needed to pretend he did not affect her as he did. She needed to pretend their arrangement was all that connected them and her heart had not just proclaimed . . .

"Isabel?" he asked once more, closer by several paces.

She needed to face him before her emotions got more out of control. Ill-prepared for anything but casual conversation and trying to keep her true feelings out of her eyes, she nodded and smiled and turned to speak to him.

Their gazes met and he stopped as though struck. His eyes flashed and flared the color of hot coals in the hearth, then his body shuddered. She thought he was having a fit or that his power was pushing through, for another face glimmered over his for a scant moment before disappearing. His eyes became his own, staring at her with all the desire and emotion she'd seen before the ritual had burned all response out of him.

He had the same expression he'd worn the first time they'd met in Lord Davin's hall. The night that ended in breathless, exhausting pleasure and began to tether them together in some unholy, inhuman alliance she could not understand.

He crossed the few paces between them and she expected him to take her in the yard, as their mutual sexual needs erupted, overwhelming their sensibilities. He took her by the shoulders and pulled her to him. Her body answered the call of his blood and his heat as it had so many times before. But unlike the other times when the ravenous hunger tore through their control, the kiss he offered was so gentle tears filled her eyes.

Though their bodies trembled as the desire flowed between them, that kiss was the barest touch of their mouths. His lips tasted hers, his mouth hovered close to hers and she could feel his breath in her mouth. Then he tilted his face and took possession of her, beginning once more with her mouth.

Stunned by what he'd seen shining from her eyes, Duncan felt the power surge within him, pushing its way free, pushing its way to her. Someone else flowed through his mind, some-thing otherworldly, something potent, in that second when he recognized the love in her gaze. Never believing he would be loved as other men were, he allowed it in to warm his soul before she tried to hide it from him.

Fear. Overpowering fear flowed from her and he absorbed it, too, tried to pull it from her, until she put up that wall in her soul that kept him from helping her. As he'd walked to her, his heart and soul were released from the void once more. She had no idea she had been the one to release him from the hell of emptiness, but he knew it. The love in her gaze tore him open.

His body hungered for her, for air to move in his lungs, for the feel of his blood pumping through his veins, for all that had been missing the last days.

He wanted to strip off their clothes and lie skin to skin, plundering every inch of her and feeling the exquisite torture as she touched his hungry skin . . . and his soul with her love.

Moments, minutes, hours might have passed as he kissed her over and over, drawing on her strength, accepting the love she offered even if she did not call it that, feeding on her arousal and controlling his. He wanted her, he wanted to be in her, surrounded by her body, part of her.

Duncan lifted his mouth away and watched as she opened her eyes. He'd not been mistaken, love gazed back at him. He bent down and lifted her into his arms, his intentions clear. As he walked toward the house, he realized the yard had emptied of everyone who'd been working there. Good. They saw and understood, and made themselves scarce. He reached the house, kicked the door open, then closed it the same way. The latch dropped and he carried her into his bedchamber, to his bed, and laid her there.

He stepped back and her eyes followed him. He pulled his shirt off and loosened his trousers, letting them fall. Stepping out of them he let his desire flow, feeling heat in every inch of his skin and in the muscle and sinew of his body. It brought him to full arousal.

Isabel licked her lips and stared at his flesh with lust in her gaze. Would he take her now?

No, he shook his head, answering both her and him at the same time. Her response was to draw her knees up, open her legs, and gather her skirts out of the way, inviting him in an openly carnal manner.

He laughed and shook his head again. "Touch me, Isabel. I need to feel your touch," he begged.

She rose up on her knees and pulled her gown and tunic and shift off in one movement, baring herself to him. As she crawled to the edge of the bed, he watched how her body moved and arched, the curves of her hips and arse tempting him with each passing second. Her breasts, full and rose-tipped, made his hands ache, but he controlled himself, knowing her touch would be the answer to his prayers.

Isabel slid off the bed and came to stand before him, reaching out to touch his erect flesh first. Her hand encircled it and he let out the moan of pleasure he'd held in from the first moment he'd kissed her. She never let go as she slid around him, her skin kissing his, warming his, arousing his. Each moment, each touch seemed to awaken a new feeling. Every inch of him craved her touch.

She stood behind him and released his cock, caressing every part of him with her hands and her body. She rubbed herself across his back and his arse, moving as though dancing around him, arching and sliding over him, this way and that, until she stood before him once more. His skin warmed as though the numbness had never been. The blood flowed into it, heating and nourishing it, making him want her so much it nearly overrode his control.

Nearly.

She took his hardened flesh in her hands again, and he finally lost control. With a growl, he lifted her onto the bed and filled her with himself. Her hands never stopped caressing him even as he thrust into her softness over and over. Her body opened to him, much as he suspected her heart had, welcoming him into her depths, allowing him his way and taking the pleasure he offered. Duncan felt her tightening around him and took her hands in his, entwining their fingers and stretching her arms out above her head. She arched against him, drawing him in deeper, until he could go no further. Her taut nipples teased his chest, her hips canted and her legs wrapped around his, holding him inside and tight as she reached for the promised satisfaction.

"Isabel," he growled as his seed threatened to spill. "Isabel," he whispered into her mouth as he kissed her, opening to her and tasting her as his cock filled her.

She tasted his mouth, then suckled on his tongue as he thrust it into her much as he did his cock. Aroused and ready, he waited for her to abandon control, to find a full measure of gratification in their joining. When she began to scream against his mouth, he moved harder and faster into her until his seed spilled and he moaned in unison with her release.

Neither one moved for some time. Panting and sweating, Duncan tried to move from on top her so she could breathe easier, but she held him with her legs. He smiled for the first time in many days, and kissed her gently, touching her mouth and lips, then her cheeks and neck. The muscles of her inner walls rippled around his flesh and she gasped as another release took her. Arching against him she gasped again and again until her body collapsed beneath his.

As they lay there still joined in the quiet aftermath of passion, he realized a number of differences between that time and the others.

He wanted her more than he'd ever wanted her, more even

than in those days before the ritual. He'd felt nothing like that before, not with any other woman and not with Isabel until now.

Her love gave him control of the power that seethed just below his skin. It was not gone as it had been in previous months after the ritual finished; it remained, banked yet ready to flare to life . . . how and when he knew not.

The last thing he realized as they recovered together was that, in the end, her love changed nothing, for he felt death approaching swiftly.

He had three weeks left and so much to do before he died.

Chapter Seventeen

"If it could be so"—Duncan began to ask, watching her face as she heard the rest of it—"would you stay with me?"

Her eyes widened and he watched as hope flared, then faded in only an instant. Had he not been observing her, he would have missed it. She laughed and leaned up on her elbow to look at him.

They had not left his bed yet that morn, and he did not intend to until Ornolf returned with the information Duncan needed about her. Sent days ago through the glen and down the path she'd pointed out, Ornolf had sought out her childhood home and village and anyone who would remember how Sigurd came to be married to her mother. Duncan had suspicions but needed them confirmed or denied before he approached Sigurd.

"Was that aye or nay?" he asked. Reaching out he tangled his hand in her hair as he liked to do, drawing her head closer so he could kiss her mouth once more.

"Duncan, can we not simply enjoy the time we have together and not think of the rest of it?" She returned to that irritating habit of deflecting questions she did not want to answer. He took her face in his hands and gazed into her eyes.

"Was that aye or nay, Isabel? 'Tis a simple question needing only a simple answer from you."

She sat up and slid away, hanging her legs over the side of the bed, reaching for her shift before saying anything. Without turning back to face him, she gave only a curt nod in response.

"But why would you want a whore living here with you?" She shook her head. "Nay, please do not pursue this, Duncan. I must return to Sigurd and you must go on with your life."

"I could buy you from him," he blurted out.

"He will beggar you, demanding more and more until you have nothing. And for what? Pleasure? Me?" She laughed, a caustic sound. "I am not worth what he will ask for."

"Why do you not let me decide that?" he prodded.

"So you plan to pay Sigurd's price and take me away from him, away from whoring then?"

"Aye, that is what I would like to do," he suggested.

"I beg you not to jest about something . . . so . . ."

"Promising? Hopeful?"

"Foolhardy? Impossible?"

"Why? I have coin to meet his demands," he said. "We could—" Her distraught expression stopped him. He reached out to her, but she moved away.

In a flash, he knew she'd been asked the same before.

"Did someone try to take you from Sigurd? Someone before . . . this?"

She covered her face with her hands and cried, in aching, empty sobs shocking him with their suddenness and their sounds. Isabel quieted as quickly as she'd begun, wiping the tears from her eyes and cheeks and pretending he'd not just witnessed her deep sorrow.

"Your pardon, Duncan. I do not know why that happened." She walked over to the small table and poured a rather large cup of wine, drinking it down in a few mouthfuls and staring off into the corner of the chamber for several minutes before returning to him.

He wanted to know more. He wanted to ease her pain. He wanted to keep her, but he knew the futility of promising her a future with him.

"I should not pry," he offered. "I am just curious about your arrangement with Sigurd."

"Curiosity can be a dangerous thing. Let it be, I beg you."

The more he learned about her—how she thought and her true nature—the more he knew to his marrow that she did not willingly whore and spy for Sigurd. There was something so important to her, she continued playing the whore for him.

"Tell me, Isabel." Plain words.

She sighed, but did not speak. Walking toward him, she stopped and picked up the shift she'd dropped.

"Do you call Lord Davin your true friend?" she asked as she pulled her shift over her head and stood next to the bed.

He nodded.

"The cost of having me will be no less than Davin's life and that of his family." She walked away, picking up blankets and covers tossed aside during their bedplay and laying them neatly on the bed. "I could not live with the thought that I caused another death."

Duncan heard truth within her words and decided he would pursue that admission later. He climbed out of the bed, heedless of his nakedness, and followed her. "Mayhap there is another way. Mayhap Sigurd needs something else from me?"

She stopped moving around the chamber and faced him. Bleakness was all he could see in her eyes. "Aye, because of me and my words to Godrod, he will know the power you have within you and he will seek to use it to his best interests. Mistake not my warning, Duncan. His target is Lord Davin and Sigurd will use me to gain control of your power for his own aims." She glanced away. "And I am not worth that man's life."

He stared at her, for she'd given him more information in that short exchange than she realized. Sigurd would kill her if he knew she'd revealed his ultimate goal to Duncan, though it did not take much in the way of conjecture to know Sigurd aimed high and few were higher in the king's regard than Davin. No lord on Skye was richer, in land and wealth and connections, than he.

She took in a deep breath and looked as though she had more to say on the subject, but she stopped herself. Duncan would have asked her another question, but he was interrupted by a loud knocking at the door of the house. Ornolf called out, identifying himself.

Duncan watched as she dressed quickly, pulling on her stockings and shoes, twisting and tying her unruly black locks in a thick braid and leaving the chamber to open the door. She was gone before he could follow and by the time he'd pulled on trousers and a shirt to greet Ornolf, she was halfway across the yard, never slowing or looking back at him.

Duncan had deeply disturbed her and gotten her to share some of Sigurd's secrets. She'd confirmed his and Davin's suspicions and warned him enough to be able to prepare Davin for what Sigurd had planned.

Ornolf waited for him in the other room. "I would not have disturbed you if not for a good reason, Duncan." He walked over and sat at the table. "Isabel looked upset when she left."

Duncan glanced out the door and watched her. She strode across the yard and leaned against the fence. *Haunted* was a better description of the way she'd looked when she left. He did not want to leave her alone, but he hoped Ornolf's words would give him a better idea of how to help her.

They discussed for hours what Ornolf had found, stopping only when Gunna arrived to make their meal. Isabel remained outside, not venturing back to the house nor too far from where she perched outside. Duncan continued to observe her all the while hearing Ornolf's explanations and suggestions. Though everyone walking through the yard called out a greeting to her, she barely acknowledged them.

Sigurd was proving more dangerous than Duncan had ever imagined, more ruthless and more conniving, too. His stomach turned as he listened to the tale of Isabel's mother and discovered Isabel did indeed have a sister. One who lived like a princess with their father while Isabel was kept in a meager cottage and forced to earn her living on her back. Black fury filled him and he wanted to hit something or someone as he learned far more than he'd bargained for. At the end of all the talking, Duncan remained convinced he could win Isabel's freedom and protect Davin and his family. But could it be done in time?

Ornolf was given his instructions and would leave at first light for Duntulm with Duncan following the next day after all the arrangements had been made.

Isabel did not answer the call to their meal, remaining where she'd been since Ornolf's arrival, waving off any attempt on Gunna's part to attract her attention. After suffering from Gunna's pointed looks and gestures and with a bowl of the still-warm stew in his hand as a peace offering, Duncan headed outside to talk to her.

In many ways, it felt as though she was drowning all over again. Isabel stood where she'd been for the last couple of hours, unwilling and unable to return to him for fear he would ask those questions and make her want to think happiness was possible. For her. For him. Shaking her head and kicking the dirt at her feet, she could see no way out of the mess.

Though he might claim to have already known she was sent by Sigurd to spy on him, Isabel had said too much about Sig-

urd to Duncan. If he used that information in dealing with
Sigurd, her stepfather would know whence it came and she
would pay with her life. And that meant Thora would be at his
mercy. Isabel shivered even thinking about that possibility.

Her legs were stiff from standing, but she did not want to go
inside. Ornolf's arrival did not bode well for her; she could
read it in his eyes as he entered the house.

Drowning. She was drowning.

She'd thought much about it, and the visit to the lake, since
Duncan had questioned her about it. Remembering that day
brought back only memories of how it felt to sink below the
water and tumble down, down, down into the black depths.
Her chest hurt from trying not to breathe. It hurt even thinking
about it. Then all the pain disappeared when the old woman
appeared in front of her and spoke to her with calm words.
The water turned from icy chill to warm and comforting, and
sparkling lights illuminated the depths around her.

That day, someone had saved her. Today, no one would.

No one could now.

Danger pressed on her from all sides and she doubted she
would escape with her life. No phantom woman would appear
and lead her to safety.

So lost in her thoughts was she that until Duncan spoke her
name, she did not know he stood beside her. Isabel gathered
her strength and turned to him, a soft smile lying to him as she
did.

A bowl of Gunna's stew gave off its appealing aroma and her
stomach growled at the smell. They'd spent all night and most
of the day in bed and had not even broken their fast before
she ran out to escape him. He held the bowl out to her in one
hand with a spoon in the other and a contrite expression on his
face.

"Gunna said you must eat this," he lied.

She loved him for the way he allowed her her pride in the small matter of accepting the food from him. She took it and spooned the first bite into her mouth to avoid crying.

"Her food is the best I have ever tasted," she praised. "With the simplest of ingredients, she creates a wonderful meal."

"I tried to get Davin to hire her as his cook, but he refused."

Another lie, but a sweet one—offered to ease her discomfort. They stood in silence as she ate every bit of the stew. Finally, she could hide from him no more.

"Is your business with Ornolf completed?" she asked, keeping her gaze on the horses within the enclosure.

"Aye."

"I should help Gunna clean up the meal. I was not much help with the laundry yesterday." Isabel smiled, remembering she'd left half the wash in the basket. And left the basket in the yard, too. Since there was no sign of either, she assumed Gunna and one of the men must have finished the task when she and Duncan were otherwise occupied.

She turned to go back to the house, but her legs cramped and she stumbled. He reached out to her and she took his hand, allowing him to help her through those first few wobbly steps. Even when her legs moved smoothly, she held on to him, savoring a gesture so simple and yet so priceless.

Another bowl of stew, a huge chunk of bread, and a cup of ale sat waiting on the table for her and Isabel could not refuse. Gunna smiled as she ate the food, but Isabel did not miss several scowls aimed in Duncan's direction. Soon, the dishes were done and everyone left Duncan and Isabel alone.

During the week when he had not needed her, Isabel had begun sewing and repairing garments to keep herself busy. Wondering if she should even try she looked at Duncan. The intensity of his gaze warned her of his intentions, but not soon enough for her to escape him.

"I would speak to you, Isabel," he said softly, as though the volume of his voice could belie the seriousness of the topic he wished to discuss.

They'd stepped into a quagmire earlier and she feared he would drag them back into it.

Chapter Eighteen

Sigurd was an evil bastard.

Ornolf had discovered Sigurd was playing both ends against the middle, misleading Isabel and her half sister in order to keep them both in his control. The younger one had been groomed to be sold to the highest bidder for her virginity while the older one whored and spied to ease his way over his enemies.

A neat arrangement kept in place by fear and love.

The younger one had been convinced Isabel had rebelled against him and taken to whoring as a way to shame and humiliate him for imagined wrongs. To Isabel he threatened to use Thora in the same way unless she did his bidding . . . and whoring. A promised good marriage for her sister was the prize held out to keep Isabel in line.

And it had worked, letting the love they had for each other, and Isabel's guilt over not being able to care for Thora herself after their mother's death, apply just the right amount of pressure to keep both sisters obedient. Integral to his success, Sigurd managed to hold them apart enough so neither learned the whole truth of his plan to ruthlessly use them for his own ends.

Duncan tried to explain it all to Isabel without destroying her, but still expose how she'd been used by the man who'd sworn to her dying mother to protect her.

"I do not wish to speak of Sigurd, Duncan. You do not understand," Isabel said, trying to stop him before he started.

"Then make me understand why you do what you do for him," he countered.

"I beg you not to pursue this." She twisted her hands and shook her head. "I am a whore, there is nothing else to it than that."

He reached out to lift her face so she would meet his gaze, but she startled as though expecting a blow. Still, she did not trust him. She held steady the second time as he guided her face up with a finger beneath her chin.

"You are so much more than that, Isabel. You do not have to do this any longer, if you'd just let me help you."

She slapped away his hand and glared at him—unthinkable actions just weeks ago, he realized. She *was* coming to trust him; she just did not do so willingly or fully.

"Why does it matter to you? Have you not received a full measure of service during my time here? Have you not fucked me in every way a man can fuck a woman? Have I not obeyed your every command and fulfilled your every need?"

"It matters," he said, remembering his threat, or promise rather, of the things he planned to do with her. And he had, they had. "You matter."

"Have I not done what you really brought me to do? I let you use my body to find relief from the terrible need that your power forces on you. I have done your bidding and now I want to return to Sigurd." Her voice rose and he heard a brittleness in it that said she was near to breaking.

"You want to return to the man who uses you to rid himself of his enemies? To the man who will kill my friend to raise himself in the king's regard?" he asked, going to the door of his bedchamber and leaning against the wall to watch her. She had not moved from her seat at the table and he noticed her fingers clutched the edge of the table, her knuckles white with effort.

"Mayhap I was mistaken about that." Her eyes darted to him and away as he watched her try to come up with some explanation for her lapse. "I am only a woman. He does not share his business with me."

Her denial did not work. Though Sigurd would not have shared such important details with her, Duncan had no doubt Isabel—strong, reliant, intelligent Isabel—listened well and put the pieces together.

Whether it was the Healer pushing forward or him simply understanding her better, he felt her terror and the pain within her. In that moment, he remembered part of the ritual when the power flowed through him. Isabel watched from her hiding place but the Healer knew she was there and called to her. She'd held the damage so deep within her soul that to release it would be the end of her. Walling it up had protected her and allowed her to survive the horror of her life.

He must stop probing. He must allow her her defenses. If his plans to neutralize Sigurd did not work, she would have to face the man . . . alone. If he showed her the truth, too much truth at one time, it would leave her worse than he'd found her.

Duncan stood away from the door and nodded. "You are right, Isabel. You are his pawn, one of his many pawns, and he would not confide his plans to you."

Though she wanted to believe his acceptance of her denial, a flicker of doubt darkened the green of her eyes. Her fear pushed the questions from her thoughts and she nodded back.

"You must be tired from standing out there so long. I am ready for bed. Join me?" He held his hand out to her.

She gave him a smile, the placating one she used too often,

and shook her head. "I am too restless to sleep. I have some sewing to do, unless you have need of me?" The whore was back.

"Sew then, sleep when you are ready."

Though he expected his own racing thoughts to keep him awake, Duncan fell asleep quickly. Sometime later he woke to the pleasurable feel of her mouth on his cock, urging it to life. He stretched his body, pushing further into her mouth as his flesh responded to her practiced touch. However, once he was fully awake, he recognized her frantic movements and knew it was not about pleasure—it was about assuaging the terrible fear that grew inside her.

She massaged the sac under his erect flesh and suckled the length of his cock, her expert mouth and tongue dragging him toward release. He tried to touch her but she shifted on her knees, moving just out of his reach. The whore had joined him in his bed, not the woman. And she would not stop. So Duncan offered her the only thing he could to help her.

Oblivion.

He closed his eyes and let the scent pour over her, hoping to give her a short time of mindless bliss instead of the pain the questions had caused, sending her into the frenzy of seeking sex to mask it.

She lifted her mouth from his flesh and met his gaze, understanding what he was doing. Closing her eyes, Isabel inhaled deeply of the scent, allowing it to take control of her. Her eyes, when she opened them, were vague, with no color present. She inhaled again and smiled at him. Without a word, she returned to his cock, allowing him to touch her.

And he did, making certain to give her release before he allowed his seed to spill.

Duncan lay awake for hours after, searching through his mind for solutions to the many problems facing him. Her words, spoken in hushed tones, surprised him. He had thought her sound asleep in his arms.

"His name was Olaf," she whispered into the darkness.

Duncan gathered her closer, letting his touch reassure her that he could hear her truth.

"Olaf's father was a powerful chieftain from the outer isles and he sent him to Sigurd as part of their agreement. I was given to him for the time he stayed on Skye."

Before Sigurd moved his sights on Duntulm, Davin's seat, Duncan knew.

"I foolishly fancied myself in love with him and he assured me he felt the same way. When his father summoned him back, he asked me to go with him. I loved him—how could I refuse?"

Duncan let her speak without interrupting her, sensing she needed to prick the boil festering inside her soul. He felt her warm tears pooling on his chest as she continued.

"Sigurd discovered our plan and sent him home. Then he taught me the folly of trying to be something other than I am."

Damn him, but Duncan had to know. "What did he do?"

"He had my leg broken to prove his point about love not being part of the game. He said a whore did not need to walk and swore to break the other if I tried it again. He brought men to my cottage to use me there just to prove his point. A broken and splinted leg did not seem to matter to them as they took their pleasure on me."

Silence covered them as Duncan tried to calm his rage after hearing her words. His heart pounded in his chest, so she must know how it affected him. Her hand caressed him, as though seeking to offer him comfort. But the worst was yet to come, as he found out when she spoke once more.

"Olaf never reached his father. The story was put out that his boat sank during a storm in the Minch, but I know the truth of it. Sigurd described his death to me in great detail while Godrod saw to my leg."

Broke her leg.

Duncan fought to remain still and hold her as she told him the truth he'd demanded and now wished he had not. How could she endure such things and be willing to return to that life? The real truth lay unsaid between them. Her real reason for staying in Sigurd's grasp remained an unspoken thing.

She would never reveal it to him. Never ask for his help, because she'd seen Sigurd's power over and over again, leaving her with no way out and no one to turn to without risking their death also.

A funny thing happens when you know your own death is impending, and there is no way to prevent it—it makes you want to do foolish things. The Healer within urged him to follow a certain path and Duncan understood it. His death would not be the meaningless end he'd thought, for he could find a way to make things right. For all Isabel had given him, he needed to do it. But would she cooperate with him and trust him to see it through?

"You stay to protect Thora."

Isabel stiffened in his embrace, drawing in a shuddering breath and not speaking for some time. Would she deny the truth now that he had named it? Or could she trust him? His answer came in the bleak words she whispered.

"I would do anything to protect her. Anything."

As he would do anything to protect the ones he loved.

Gunna. Harald. Ornolf. All the family he never had. He would do anything to keep them safe. Isabel was also part of that list and he would see her safe . . . and healed before he gave up his life to the power within him.

He gathered her closer and listened as her breathing evened and grew deeper until she finally slept. It came to him in the dark of the night and he rose carefully so as not to wake her, seeking out Ornolf to discuss the new plan of his.

To save Isabel he must save her sister first.

To save Thora, he must break Isabel's heart.

To heal her broken heart and soul, he would give his life.

Love caused a man to do foolish things and he understood he was a man in love. Since he'd never expected to find it, Duncan savored the moment he realized he loved her. But he would not declare it to her for it would only add to her burdens. She bore too many already to bear another.

But he loved Isabel with every fiber of his being.

Seeing Ornolf off at dawn with his new instructions and knowing what must be accomplished in a short time, Duncan returned to his bed and to Isabel. He spent the day and the next night with her, never referring to anything she'd said and not asking any questions. He knew everything between them would soon change and understood she might well hate him.

He pretended he was a normal man with a woman he loved and who loved him—that all was well in his world. She might think she was the only one who could pretend, but he was a quick learner.

Isabel woke when he slipped back under the covers, his body warming hers as he pulled her close, wrapping his arms around her. She savored how safe she felt in his embrace. His soft snoring told her when he fell asleep, but she could not.

Too much had been revealed. So many rules had been broken over those last few weeks; rules that had taken so long and so much punishment to learn. He thought himself immune to Sigurd's power, probably because of the Healer within him, but Duncan could die just as easily as Olaf had.

She slipped from the bed when she heard Gunna in the other room and went to help prepare their food. If anything had changed, she could not tell from the way the young woman greeted her and accepted her help. Keeping her voice down so she did not disturb Duncan, Isabel lost herself in the daily chores and did not think on anything more than that. Her gaze went to him when the door opened, wondering how things would be between them that morn.

She lost her breath at the intensity of his gaze.

His eyes burned but not with the fires of lust or desire. Something else shone there, something that warmed her, body and soul. Something she could not have. Turning away, she blinked back the tears and went to fill his bowl and cup. She placed them before him as he sat down without a word. She did not allow herself to look into his eyes again.

He did not let her walk away. He took her hand and brought it to his lips, kissing it and touching it to his cheek in a gesture so meaningful her tears threatened once more. The conversation around them faded away and in that moment she could almost believe they were living a life she'd never allowed herself to dream. She shook the thought away and returned to serving the others as they arrived to break their fast.

The meal was enjoyable. Talk about the day's duties and the ongoing harvest of the fields surrounded them, but Isabel was aware of only Duncan. He touched her constantly—his hand on hers as they sat next to each other, his leg against hers when he shifted to allow Harald to sit on the other side of him, his arm around her waist and a soft kiss on her forehead when someone mentioned the laundry basket left in the yard. All of it felt perfect, as though such tenderness was a commonplace thing between a man and a whore.

But she'd awakened with a resolve to let the days flow as they would and to take whatever enjoyment she could from them, from him, for their time together would be over soon and she would need to take another man to her bed and into her body.

Duncan stood when the meal was done and told her he would wait outside for her to finish. Harald followed him out. Isabel helped with the dishes, then grabbed her cloak and sought him. Not knowing what to expect, she found him in a playful mood. He asked her to accompany him while he saw to things needing his attention and she went along.

He continued to hold her hand or keep her close all through the day. He held her in his arms when the sun hid behind clouds and the air cooled, and he stopped in the shadows to kiss the very breath from her. Though she felt the hardened bulge against her when he took her mouth, Duncan never sought more than a kiss from her. As they walked out to one of the farther fields, she was certain he would find a secluded place and seek pleasure, but he did not. Only after their evening meal was concluded and everyone sought their rest did he hold out his hand to her in an invitation to join with him.

Duncan turned to her several times during the night, each joining different from the others, each one emptying her and refilling her at the same time. Only when she could not move, exhausted by the depth of their pleasure, did he stop, seeming content to hold her then. Just as the first light of dawn rose in the sky, he spoke.

"If I can come to some agreement with Sigurd, will you stay with me through the next ritual? You have helped me much during this last one."

She was surprised. She'd thought he would bring up other things.

He seemed to finally accept her true role and asked her to see to his pleasure as the moon grew to fullness. Could she remain with him for two more weeks?

"If Sigurd agrees," she said with a nod, "I will stay and see to your needs. Aye."

He rose from the bed then, gathering some clothes and

dressing. She watched as he moved around the chamber, searching through his trunk for something. Leaning up on her elbows, she saw that he was packing.

"Are you leaving?" she asked, sliding from the warmth of the bed. "Should I pack my things?" She would have little use for the garments she'd worn there, for they would not suit Sigurd's purposes. Looking around the chamber, she comprehended how little of her would be left behind when she returned to Duntulm.

"Lord Davin sent a message that he needs me in Duntulm. While I am there, I will bargain with Sigurd for a few more weeks," he explained, never looking at her as he folded a shirt and stuffed it in the leather satchel. She wanted to ask him so many things, but did not want to disturb the truce they'd reached the last day or so.

"Very well," she said. "When will you return?"

"Two days, three at most," he answered. "You should rest, for when I return, it will be time."

Time for his relentless need of her body. Time to be the vessel that eased the terrible growing power within him. Time to play the whore. If she told the truth, the insatiable hunger she would face was easier to deal with than his kindness and caring.

"As you wish."

"I love to hear those words from your mouth. Remember them when I return," he growled, stalking over to her, kissing her fiercely, then walking out.

Chapter Nineteen

Duntulm Keep

Sigurd climbed the stairs, angry at being summoned like a common servant, yet mollified that he was being received in Duncan's private chambers. He reached the top floor of the tower and followed the man's servant to the door. Godrod waited below, included in the summons, but left waiting until called above.

The servant paused and motioned for him to wait, knocking softly on the door and entering it quietly. A moment or two passed and the door swung open, allowing Sigurd entrance. After closing the door, the servant poured wine into a costly gold goblet and handed it to him. Only when he stepped away did Sigurd get a good look at the rest of the chamber.

'Twas fit for a king!

Luxurious fabrics and tapestries curtained the walls and covered the large bed in one corner. Carved furniture of a wood he'd never seen before filled the room. A huge table that could seat eight or ten on one side of the chamber, three cushioned chairs in addition to the stools around the table, even the headboard of the bed, were all made of the same material and embossed with gold. A large gold pitcher held the wine he'd been served, the quality of it surpassing any he'd tasted at Davin's table.

But Sigurd was enough of a merchant and trader to recognize the ploy—the man was displaying his obvious wealth to set the stage for negotiating. Still, it was difficult not to be impressed with such a show.

" 'Tis a wood found in the far east, brought back and given to me as a gift." The words were spoken from behind him. Sigurd turned to face his host. "It is supposed to last for generations of use."

Sigurd watched as the servant poured Duncan a cup of the same wine and served it to him. After refilling Sigurd's cup, the servant bowed away and stood by the door. Though Sigurd still smarted from having to conduct the prior negotiations for the slut with the servant, clearly the new matter surpassed that in importance.

"My thanks for coming to meet with me, Sigurd," Duncan said. "I hope I have not inconvenienced you?"

"Nay, not at all," he answered. "I am ever interested in hearing a business proposition that could benefit both of us." That was what the summons had mentioned—a proposition that would be to their mutual benefit. He feared for a moment Isabel had failed him and disappointed this man. "Did she see to your needs?"

Duncan looked confused for a moment as though he could not remember her, then nodded. Taking a mouthful of the wine, he swallowed it and smiled. "She is quite talented."

"And this new proposition?"

Duncan walked closer and slapped Sigurd on the shoulder, laughing. "So eager then? The promise of profit is appealing to you?"

Sigurd drank more of the wine and nodded.

"Very well," Duncan said, "take a seat and be comfortable. Ornolf, food for our guest!"

Sigurd shook his head and waved off the servant as he sat in the proffered seat. "I thank you for your hospitality but I have eaten." He did not want to waste time eating. He turned to his host. "About this business . . ."

"Ornolf, wait outside," Duncan ordered.

He looked at Sigurd. "I will make this simple—you have a daughter I wish to marry."

Sigurd choked at the declaration. "You wish to marry Isabel?"

Duncan laughed and shook his head. "The whore? I am no fool, Sigurd. I can pay for the whore when I need her. I want your real daughter to wife. Thora is her name?"

Of all the matters Sigurd had thought the man would discuss, marriage to Thora was not one of them. Why would he want her?

"I am presently in discussions with several for her hand in marriage," Sigurd said, testing to learn Duncan's true intent. "I could not accept any offer until—"

"I will double whatever they have offered." Duncan scoffed at the notion of other suitors. "More than that, I offer you my friendship."

A trick of the light, surely, Sigurd thought as the man's eyes seemed to glow. "Your friendship?"

"The king seeks to back strong men, those strong enough to rule over his far-flung lands," Duncan explained with a sigh. "Davin seems to be falling out of favor and I would offer my friendship and resources to someone high in the king's regard."

Sigurd took and released a breath, forcing himself to remain calm and evaluate the words. Before he could reply, Duncan continued.

"I have been asking about you, seeking information about how you have risen to such a high position. Everyone speaks highly of you and your abilities . . . and your ambitions. I would like to ally myself with such a man as you."

Compliments aside, Sigurd was pleased his machinations and money worked, guaranteeing that what he paid those he controlled to say, they said. And believably, for Duncan had accepted their word.

"And I gain what from this alliance you offer?" Sigurd waited to see what would be offered and whether the true bargaining chip would be put in play at all or left aside for later.

"I know you have sought to learn about my abilities and I think you know what I offer for your use. Ask your man God-rod what he found."

"He has spoken of things that seem unbelievable." Did Duncan know the slut spied for him, too? Sigurd wondered.

"Believe them." Once more Duncan's eyes seemed to be on fire but his voice sounded as though more than one spoke. Sigurd shivered as he faced him and felt some power he did not understand . . . or control. He swallowed several times, his mouth going dry at the sound.

"Better still, call Godrod here and let me show you so you can judge for yourself."

"I do not understand," Sigurd admitted.

"My man said he bashed Godrod with a branch when he found him assaulting the whore who, I remind you, I'd paid good coin to have exclusive use of. There was a bleeding wound." Duncan walked to the door and put his hand on the latch. "Summon him and let me demonstrate what an alliance with me could gain you."

Sigurd nodded. He pulled the door open and tipped his head at his servant to approach from below. Godrod stopped at the door until Sigurd gave permission for him to enter. Duncan waved at his own servant and Ornolf pulled the door closed.

Sigurd had not taken close notice of the wound, but from the look and smell of it, it was infected badly. Pus and blood oozed from the haphazardly-sewn gash. It served the man right for disobeying his orders and trying to sample the girl's flesh before her task was done.

"What do you need him to do?" Sigurd asked, waiting to see if the slut had babbled the outlandish tale or simply lied outright.

"Kneel here." Duncan pointed to a spot in front of him.

Godrod delayed, not knowing why he was there and most likely expecting retribution for overstepping. That would come in good time when he least expected it, but Sigurd commanded him to drop to his knees.

Sigurd stood a few paces away, his arms crossed over his chest, waiting for whatever the demonstration would be. Duncan closed his eyes and leaned his head back, standing in complete silence for several minutes. When he straightened his head up and opened his eyes, Sigurd knew he was no longer looking at something human.

Flames filled the man's gaze and his face glowed, pulsing with heat and power. His hands grew bright. Holding them out, he placed them on Godrod's head. Sigurd expected him to scream in pain, but only their breathing could be heard in the silence. As he watched in total fascination, Duncan's hands seemed to melt into Godrod's skin and reform it, from bloody wound to healed, intact skin.

No wonder the stupid bitch had babbled after watching something like that! And she'd been right—Duncan harnessed a terrible power and used it to heal. His hands held the power of life and death in them! As soon as the healing was over, the flames flickered out and Duncan became a man once more.

Godrod stumbled to his feet, touching his head, searching for the wound that had been there just moments ago. Sigurd knew he must gain control over Duncan and use his powers. Never one to dawdle when an opportunity presented itself, Sigurd grabbed Godrod and tossed him into the hall. Matters needed to be concluded rapidly, for he could already see many possibilities. But he was not stupid.

"Why have you offered to aid me?"

"You are a man who knows how to manage people and can help me profit from whatever this power is. It is reaching its peak and I want enough gold and property to keep me comfortable, and protected for the rest of my life. You will see to exploiting my power wisely and arrange things."

"Why Thora?"

"A wealthy man needs heirs, so I need a wife."

The man was coldly calculating, just as Sigurd would be in a similar situation. He smiled. "And you would pay for her?"

Duncan stumbled a bit, the effects of exercising such extraordinary power. "Name your price."

Sigurd quickly calculated an obscene amount of gold and silver and told him.

"Done. Now, I must rest. Ornolf will bring the contracts to you and we will sign them before witnesses on the morrow. I would see this done within two days."

"Two days? Surely not. Thora is not even here in Duntulm." What was Duncan's hurry?

"Bring her to Uig, to my home. Once the betrothal papers are signed, Ornolf will arrange for payment of her bride-price. I am building a new house there and she should have a say in it since it will be hers to control as my wife."

Sigurd did not speak, not agreeing to the plan or naysaying it.

"If you do not want this alliance, simply say so. I but offered it to you first. There are others . . ."

Of a certain there would be others willing to pay for the chance to use his power. Others Sigurd could name immediately. Hesitation would be costly, so he nodded, accepting the arrangement. It would be difficult to accomplish so quickly, but for so much gold, he would make it happen.

"Ornolf," Duncan called out. His servant entered at his call. "It is arranged—see to it." Ornolf glanced at Sigurd and he nodded his acceptance.

He would have to send his fastest men to his keep in the south and get the girl there quickly. By sea, he thought, as he turned and walked to the door held open by the servant. So many arrangements to be made in so little time. Just as he reached the door, Duncan called out to him.

"Sigurd, one more matter."

Lost in his calculations and estimations and with plans already spinning in his thoughts, Sigurd faced him, wondering what else there was to discuss.

"You have not mentioned Thora's dowry."

He had already determined what he would offer as her dowry when considering negotiations with other rich lords, so he offered the same. Duncan shook his head. "You can keep her inheritance, I want only the whore."

"Isabel? As Thora's dowry? That is not possible!" Sigurd claimed. Who ever heard of such a thing?

"Either she is given to me or I will seek an ally elsewhere."

Sigurd had a sinking feeling in his gut that he had been played. No woman, especially not one used as Isabel had been, was worth the amount of gold, silver, animals, and cloth Duncan was passing up. No matter that she had earned Sigurd much. To him, Isabel was not worth it. Duncan could buy a dozen bed slaves a month for several years with what he was giving up in that dowry.

"Why do you want her?"

"She pleases me."

Sigurd thought of the other complication. "Thora will not be happy to have her sister as your bed-slave or concubine." The girl was so naïve and innocent, she did not even know what the marriage bed entailed. But she loved Isabel and Sigurd knew the arrangement would not work. No woman would want to share her husband with her sister, though it mattered little to Sigurd if Duncan slept with them both, separately or at the same time or gave them to his men and servants for their pleasure. He cared not what the man did in his own household.

"And that matters between men of business? You control the whore so well, surely you can make your well-raised and obedient daughter see the good in this arrangement?"

Standing, half in the chamber and half in the hall, Sigurd could feel their deal slipping away. Not willing to lose such wealth and power over a young girl's sensibilities, he nodded. "I will see to it. The whore is yours."

He hurried from the chamber motioning to Godrod to follow him. Out of the keep Sigurd shielded his eyes against the light, peering up to estimate the position of the sun in the sky. The day had about six more hours of light and he needed to get Thora to Uig. By nightfall, the contracts had been delivered and his men were well on their way to take the girl to Uig to be handed over to her betrothed husband.

Once the contracts were signed and the bride delivered, he would begin to control something other men only dreamed of. If he laughed aloud later that day, who could blame him?

Ornolf had barely closed the door behind Sigurd when Duncan collapsed to the floor, his head burning and throbbing with unbearable pain. Ornolf helped him to the bed and gave him a draught against the pain.

"It went well," he said after swallowing down the putrid concoction.

"How did you do it, Duncan? You have never been able to control it before," Ornolf asked as he helped him to lie down.

"I know only that Isabel is the difference."

"You are depending on her for much. Should you place so much importance on a wh—?" Ornolf stopped before uttering the word.

"She is the key, my friend. Doubt it not." Duncan began to slur his words; the brew was already taking effect. "Since she appeared, I have learned how to let only a sliver of the power through. And she's tempered the aftermath. She is . . ."

As he fell asleep, he hoped the numbness would follow the pain for seeing her face when she found out he was marrying her sister would only be manageable without his emotions to tear him apart.

He signed the betrothal contracts in the morning before Davin and five other men. He did not dare tell Davin too much, so the look of betrayal on his friend's face was terrible to behold. Davin trusted him though and did as he'd asked him in serving as a witness. He would send Ornolf to explain everything later. In the meantime, he'd told Davin to send his wife to her relatives on Lewis and to be on guard.

Four days had passed since he'd left his farm and as he sailed back to Uig with Sigurd and the others who would witness the exchange of vows, all he could think about was Isabel.

There would not be time enough to explain things to her, so she would hear of his betrothal when they arrived. He did not want to die knowing she hated him, but Duncan thought that might happen. He dared not explain anything until Sigurd and the others were gone, but by then it might be too late. A marriage feast, even the small one he planned, would last for days and they would be under scrutiny at every moment. Now that she was his, he could take her to his bed without anyone looking twice at them, but he doubted she would sleep with her sister's husband.

And he needed her more than ever before.

His body was readying itself for the ritual, two weeks away, even though he had called forth the tinest bit of power to heal Godrod. What did she have within her that enabled him to control the healing? As he'd told Ornolf, he knew she was responsible for the change in him—allowing him to pull the power in as though gathering the reins of a runaway horse and bringing it under control. Even as it bucked and tried to throw him off, he held it, feeling it flexing and stretching under his hold.

If only he had found her sooner . . .

If only he understood how he received the power or why . . .

If only their love could save them from the disasters that waited for them in the coming days . . .

The boat turned south, following the coast and he saw the bay tucked in ahead. Sigurd looked far too pleased with himself and Duncan hoped he was not making a terrible mistake. His new will was signed and left with Davin who would see it executed. Under usual circumstances, if he did not consummate the vows, the marriage would be invalid and Thora would have her dowry returned to her. Her bride-price would return to him, leaving her to an angry Sigurd's control. Consummated, their marriage and his death would leave her a widow, protected by his name and with enough wealth to live without Sigurd's interference.

Plans spun in his head, each one with its weaknesses and strengths, each one ended to the advantage of someone, but never to Isabel. The boat's crew prepared to dock and Duncan took a deep breath, readying himself to hold all the threads together while he tried to weave an end that would leave Isabel whole and happy again.

As they climbed on the dock and found Sigurd's daughter waiting there, he also heard that eerie laughter echoing around them. No one else seemed to hear it, but he finally knew what it was—the laughter of the fates as he tried to outsmart them and control his own ending.

Chapter Twenty

Duncan's farm, near Uig

Isabel had tried to keep busy as she waited for Duncan's return and word as to whether Sigurd had agreed to his request or not. If Godrod had passed on her words to Sigurd, he would want to know more about the power Duncan possessed so he could plan how to control the man who possessed it. If allowing Duncan to use her for a few more weeks was the price, Sigurd would acquiesce to the request, knowing a larger prize awaited him.

Two days had passed, then a third and Duncan still did not arrive. With only two weeks left until the next full moon, she grew restless knowing how he must need her. On the fourth morning after his departure, she decided that walking to Uig with Gunna and Harald would ease her. So, they set off in mid-morning for the village.

When they reached it, Gunna and Harald walked on without her. Gunna tried to convince her to accompany them, but Isabel was content to go only that far. The day was a pleasant one, though the cooler autumn winds warned of the impending change of seasons. The harvest was complete, and a feast would be held amongst those who worked the farm for Duncan to celebrate the success of the year's crops. As the year rolled on, Isabel had lost track of the time until Gunna mentioned Samhain's approach.

And the anniversary of Duncan's birth.

He'd shared so few personal details and the fact that he was born on the ancient pagan feast day was one he'd forgotten to tell her. Gunna had planned something to mark the day until Harald pointed out it was also the day when the moon would reach its fullness.

And Duncan would suffer the very torments of hell after using his gift to heal any number of people in need.

If he was correct, their physical relations had eased the effects of the torment caused by the flaring of the power in him. He could not explain much more than that, but it gladdened her heart to think she did help him. The pleasure they shared was something she would always treasure.

Her cheeks felt hot as she thought on that last day together. She would like to think he'd looked at her with love but she did not want to fool herself in that way. He cared. He was considerate in his own way. That was enough and would always be.

Someone approached on the path and Isabel stepped into the shadows, fearing a repeat of Godrod's attack. He had not been seen or heard from since that day, but she knew his methods and ignoring an insult was not his way. He would retaliate at some point. Just as she pushed back into the bushes, Gunna came running up the path.

"Isabel, Duncan has returned. He is on a boat that just docked. Come, let's greet him!" she called out to her, waving her forward. "Harald waits for us ahead."

Isabel considered refusing, but changed her mind. Duncan had been gone for two days more than he'd said and the bed had been empty and cold without him. She followed along, keeping her gaze on the ground ahead of her, not looking at the people they passed. Soon, the noise of the port made her glance up at the comings and goings all around her. She'd never dared to venture that far into Uig. It was an interesting place, even though it was a small village.

"There he is!" Gunna pointed to a large boat being tied up to the dock. A number of men climbed from it and made their way up the wooden path to the main street. Duncan walked next to Ornolf, speaking to him as they moved through the crowd.

And Sigurd followed close behind them.

Her ears buzzed as if a thousand bees were trapped inside them, and she found it difficult to breathe. Sigurd came to Uig? Had Duncan been unable to negotiate as he'd planned? Had Sigurd come to retrieve her? Her hands began shaking and she could not stop them. Then her whole body trembled, stopped only by a voice she'd never expected to hear.

"Isabel? What are you doing here?" Thora asked.

Isabel turned to her sister, shaking her head in disbelief. "Did you come with Sigurd? How did you get here?" she asked in reply.

"Nay, not with him, but to meet him. Father sent word that I was to meet him here." Thora leaned closer and whispered to her. "He has signed betrothal contracts, Isabel! I am to be married!"

Though Thora tried to hug her, Isabel backed away from her. It was too much of a coincidence for Thora to be there just as Sigurd and Duncan arrived from Duntulm together. "I do not understand, Thora. Who are you to marry?"

Before Thora could reveal his name, Sigurd barreled into Isabel, sending her sprawling on the ground. "Whore! I told you not to approach my daughter," he shouted. Placing himself between Isabel and Thora as though even Isabel's glance would contaminate her sister's innocence, Sigurd took Thora by the arm and led her to Duncan.

In shock, and in the midst of the gathering crowd, Isabel climbed to her feet and brushed the dirt from her gown. Gunna was on the other side of the street, unable to get to her. Harald stood on the other side of Duncan. Duncan said nothing to her, his gaze filled with sadness until Sigurd brought Thora to stand before him.

No!

It could not be!

"Duncan, this is Thora, my daughter." Sigurd took Thora's hand and placed it in Duncan's. "Thora, Duncan is your betrothed husband. I wish you much happiness together."

Isabel fell back, rushing away from the scene before her. The last thing she saw was Duncan taking Thora's hand and lifting it to his mouth to kiss it. Pain, black and slashing, struck Isabel then, forcing the breath from her body. The air around her began to sparkle and she knew she was fainting. No one helped her. Many stepped away so they would not touch her as she fell again. The shouting of the crowd, congratulating the betrothed couple, woke her from her stupor only moments later.

The crowd had grown and so she escaped down an alley between houses, making her way out of the village. When she reached the path that would lead her back to the farm, she knew everyone would be going there.

She could not return there and watch Duncan marry her sister.

Confused and desolate, she ran in the other direction, making her way along the narrow walkway to the south of the village where few people were. Small fishing boats lay on the sandy beach waiting for the tides to lift them back into the water. Fishermen worked on their nets, preparing them for the next catch, while the day's catch was cleaned and taken to the village to be sold or fed to their families.

She ran past them all, seeking the edge of the water where she could be alone to make some sense of it all. But standing there as the waves swelled onto the sand did not ease the pain in her heart or the confusion in her soul. Everything blurred around her and she stood in mindless agony. It was worse than anything she could have imagined.

She had no idea how much time passed as she stood there unmoving. She had not the strength to think of what to do. Until someone pulled her back, she had no idea the rising tide washed around her, wetting her feet, her legs and much of her gown. Dragged to higher ground, Isabel recognized Harald, who held her upright as she swayed, ready to fall once more.

"Come, Isabel." He pulled and half carried her along the sand back toward the village street. She did not bother to stop him.

He guided her down several small alleys until he brought her to the door of a small cottage. Harald knocked on it softly and waited for someone to open it. The woman was familiar in a vague way, but Isabel did not ever remember meeting her. 'Twas her name that brought back the memory of how she knew her.

"Margaret, the Healer asks for your help," Harald said.

"Anything, Harald. I would do anything he asks of me."

Isabel glanced up, curious to know who would pledge such blind loyalty to him. It was the woman who'd thought herself increasing at the last ritual. The one Duncan had healed. Margaret moved back and let Harald take Isabel into the first chamber, then farther inside, gently seating her on a chair near the hearth.

"Isabel needs a place to stay for now. Can she bide with you?" he asked.

Isabel could see agreement in the woman's eyes and it made her force words out. "I cannot stay here, Harald. Tell her why."

"Isabel . . ." He looked at her, then at Margaret.

She was ready to tell the woman why she should not take her under her roof and risk her reputation when Margaret took her hand and rubbed it between her own.

"You are chilled to the bone, Isabel. Let me get you into some dry clothes."

With a glance, she dismissed Harald and began to peel off the wet layers of clothing. In silent, efficient movements, Margaret got her undressed and into a clean shift. Wrapping a blanket around her shoulders, Margaret then pressed a mug of steaming cider into her hands and urged her to sip it.

Isabel wanted to refuse, but could not find the strength to do so.

"Do you have need of something, Isabel?" Margaret asked. "Are you ill?"

"I am not ill," Isabel whispered.

It was only that her worst fears had come to pass. Her heart had awakened from its slumber and been stolen by the man she'd feared would be her undoing. Worse, he'd taken her soul and betrayed the love she'd given him. After struggling for the last years to protect herself so she could survive and live, she no longer wanted to.

Duncan had never been so tormented as he was when he saw Isabel in Uig. As he climbed from the boat, Sigurd pointed out his daughter Thora and led them to her, all converging at the same time in the same place.

He read the surprise, then disbelief on Isabel's face even across the distance between them and watched as she reacted to the news Thora must have told her. He'd paused for only a moment to try to find Ornolf or Harald but it was long enough for Sigurd to spy her speaking to Thora. Before he could intervene, Sigurd had tossed Isabel to the ground, then brought Thora to him.

Forced to play the game out, he'd stood and accepted the girl as his betrothed, not allowing himself to seek out Isabel for fear of disavowing his well-laid plans in the face of her heartbreak. As the crowd began cheering the news, many approached to wish him well and it was some time before he could speak to Harald or Ornolf about her. She'd disappeared and he'd sent Harald searching for her, suggesting he look for her in the one place he knew she'd go—near the water.

As they approached his farm, with Sigurd playing the proud father to his demure daughter, all Duncan could do was think about Isabel and worry about her condition . . . and compare her sister to her.

He could find little resemblance between the two women other than their dark hair and light eyes. Separated by about four years, he guessed, neither of them looked at all like Sigurd. Thora smiled and acted interested in everything Duncan said, but he caught warning glances from Sigurd and fear in her eyes more than once on the journey.

She'd been in the hall that night when he'd taken Isabel to his chambers, yet she gave no sign of recognizing him at all when he was introduced to her. That was what a respectable woman would do, of course, and she played her part well, ignoring his baser needs. Ignoring the fact he had taken her sister to his bed.

They crossed through the last line of hills separating his farm from the coast and he watched her reaction as they followed the path down to it. It was nothing like the opulence of his chambers at Duntulm, for he preferred the easy comfort of the smaller chambers and the privacy of separate buildings for those who lived and worked there. The needs that became irresistible each month made it necessary for him to have a place where no one else lived. Those needs grew within him even now, calling to the one woman who could save his body and soul.

Margaret would see her safe until he could speak to her and try to gain her cooperation. Margaret was happy to help, just as anyone living in Uig who had benefitted from his ability to heal would be, if he asked. They kept his ritual secret and told no one who was not invited to it. They'd welcomed him into their midst and given him a place to call home, never treating him as the man without a name or a home that he was. And they would ignore Isabel's past with only a word from him.

They rode into the yard, where his men took the horses from them. Climbing down, he noticed Thora could ride well. Sigurd walked to her side and they spoke quietly as Duncan gave instructions about the sleeping arrangements and the news of his betrothal. Clearly, it did not sit well with those who knew Isabel, but they gave him their begrudging acceptance and went off to carry out the tasks he'd given them. In a short time, he saw Sigurd and Thora settled in Gunna and Harald's cottage while arrangements were made for the rest of Sigurd's men to sleep in the empty barn.

Their vows would not be spoken until the next week, as close to the full moon as he could wait. The wedding would take place before five of the six witnesses who'd overseen the contracts. Davin had not returned to the farm with them, so Duncan would call on Harald who, as a freeman, could witness legal contracts and ceremonies. Gunna would hire a few women from Uig to help with cooking and preparing the wedding feast. Sigurd had asked him to delay so Thora could get accustomed to him before they married. Since Duncan had no intention of actually consummating the marriage, he agreed and made arrangements to take Thora riding in the morning.

They shared a modest evening meal, then everyone settled

for the night. Everyone but Duncan, who paced his house awaiting word from Harald. The knock echoed across the empty chamber. In spite of expecting Harald to be angry, the blow came as a surprise. Shaking his head, Duncan tried to open his jaw to see if his friend had broken it.

"Why, Duncan? Why did you have to treat her like this?" Harald asked.

"Wait until Ornolf arrives, then close the door so we can speak unheard by others who might be about," Duncan advised.

Harald stepped back, but the anger did not fade from his expression. The way he kept flexing his hands and making fists with them, Duncan suspected he might strike again. For someone who had argued against Isabel remaining only weeks ago, Harald had clearly changed sides.

A few minutes passed and Ornolf entered quietly. Motioning for them to sit at the table, Duncan kept his voice down in case Sigurd was skulking about outside. They would have little privacy in the coming days, so he needed Ornoff and Harald to understand their roles.

"You found her?" Duncan asked Harald.

"Aye, she is with Margaret now. Could you not have sent word?" He looked from Ornolf to Duncan.

"Nay. I needed Ornolf with me and trusted no one else to carry such news. The betrothal needs to be public and official or it gains Thora nothing."

"And the bedding? Will that be public as well?" Harald challenged.

Duncan could see no way out of the situation without sharing the whole truth with those two men. "There is no other way to tell you this, so I will speak plainly to you both. I need your word this will go no further. You cannot tell anyone. Not Gunna or Isabel or anyone." When they gave reluctant nods accepting his conditions, he told them, "I will not survive the next ritual."

Neither spoke or looked at him or at each other. The silence was deafening and went on too long.

"Each month I have noticed my heart slows and stops at the end of the healing. As the power to heal ends and I come back to myself, it slows to a halt. Last month I feared it would not begin again. Next time, I know it will not."

"Duncan—" Harald began.

"But Duncan—" Ornolf said.

"The power has reached its apex, burning more and more of me away each month. It is taking my life even as it gives others theirs back."

"You are certain?" Harald asked.

"Absolutely. I have known it was coming for several months now, once I realized the pattern in it. Somehow Isabel was able to stave off the worst of the effects, but not to stop the curse's relentless destruction."

"There must be some way to stop it," Ornolf declared.

"Old friend, you have led the way in seeking out information about the origin of my power. What have you found?"

Silence met his question. He'd known the answer when he'd asked it—nothing. Other than some old folk tales about the sith, no one could explain his ability or how it worked. Messengers sent out brought back no information. Stories of sith curses were plentiful throughout the islands, but there was no way to find out more.

"I wanted to protect Isabel and must protect her sister to do that."

"So you will marry her sister then?" Harald asked. Ornolf already knew the plan so Duncan explained the contracts to Harald.

"I will and I have received Isabel as Thora's dowry, so she belongs to me as soon as the marriage is—"

"Consummated," Harald finished, almost spitting the word out. "So you will sleep with one sister to claim the other?"

Duncan ignored the jibe, telling them instead of how the women would be protected. "As my widow, Thora will be free to marry who she wants, with no interference from Sigurd. She will be a wealthy woman and want for nothing the rest of her life," he explained.

"And Isabel?"

"As my property, my will stipulates her freedom is granted upon my death and I designated that she receive enough gold to see her settled comfortably wherever she wants to live. She will belong to no one save herself ever again." He looked at the only two men he could call friends, other than Davin. "You will all be taken care of when it happens."

"And Sigurd simply prances away with all the gold you paid as Thora's bride-price?" Ornolf asked.

"A small price for the freedom and safety of Isabel and her sister."

The chamber was quiet as they thought on what he'd told them. He waited for any other questions.

"Will you tell her? Of your plan?"

"Nay. If Sigurd finds a reason to challenge the marriage or the agreement, all could be lost. I know she is hurt and does not understand, but she will."

"When you die?" Harald seemed intent on provoking him.

"Aye, when I die."

"With Sigurd and the others here, will you perform the ritual?"

"There will be only one person at the ritual this time. The Healer will call her when it is time."

They realized whom he meant at the same moment, staring wordlessly at him. He'd decided, or understood, who would receive the last healing at the same moment he'd recognized that love lived in his heart for Isabel and that she must be healed to be truly free when he died.

Duncan could think of nothing else they needed to know, so he bade them seek their beds and keep his counsel. They must watch him play his part over the next days and stand by him in death. He laughed when he heard Harald whisper under his breath the easier thing would be to make certain Sigurd had an accident on his way back to Duntulm. Remembering Isabel's story about the young man Olaf and his death, Duncan tucked away that idea to suggest it if his plans did not work as he wanted.

He did not sleep that night and by dawn he was on his way to Uig to bring Isabel back to his farm. She would not be happy but she would obey him. He knew beyond a doubt she understood her place and would follow his orders. She would not forgive him for keeping all from her or for not revealing his true feelings for her, but she would be alive and she would be safe.

Chapter Twenty-one

As soon as the first sliver of sunlight entered the cottage through the small window sitting high in the wall, Isabel shifted on the cot where she lay. She remained unmoving as Margaret rose and began her daily tasks. After a few minutes, Isabel began to peel the covers back.

"You need not rise yet, Isabel. Rest a while. I must go see to the cows."

"Do you live alone here?" Isabel asked. There was no sign of anyone else, but a woman who had believed herself carrying must have a man.

"Aye, now I do," she said quietly in a grief-tinged tone. "Though this was my husband's house before it was mine."

She listened as Margaret moved through the small but cozy house, making her way out to the yard in the back where she kept some cows. Knowing she would never sleep, Isabel pushed back the blankets and stood, wrapping one of them around her shoulders to keep away the chill. The fire had gone out sometime during the night.

She began to fold the bedcovers on the cot and also on Margaret's small bed; it was the least she could do for the woman's kindness to her. The back door opened and closed and Isabel sat on the cot, waiting for Margaret to come into the room. She began to ask her if she needed help milking the cows when she looked up and met Duncan's gaze.

Isabel wanted to be empty—she thought she was—but one look at him was all her stupid weak heart needed to begin pounding against her chest. 'Twas a good thing she sat, for she knew she would have fallen over otherwise.

"Isabel." He greeted, then crouched down next to her. "How do you fare?"

No words would come to mind, then they all did. She was devastated. She was betrayed. She was ruined. She was desolate. But she would say none of them to him. She'd revealed the importance of protecting her sister and look what had happened.

"You must return with me now," he urged softly.

"To your farm? Where Sigurd and my sister are?"

"Aye, though there is nothing to fear from Sigurd now."

She began to laugh at his words, softly then louder, until the sound bubbled out of her uncontrollably. She had forgotten many of Sigurd's lessons, but she would never think herself safe from him until she was dead. Duncan took her by her shoulders, shaking her until she stopped laughing.

"I will keep you safe now, and Thora, too," he promised.

"She will be your wife."

"Aye."

"And I will be what?" she asked, trying to understand what he expected of her in a household where her sister would rule.

"You will be mine," he said. "You are mine now."

"Your whore?" She watched as he searched for words. "I will not fuck my sister's husband." He needed to know that even whores drew some lines and he had crossed hers.

He winced. "Come back and we will sort this out between us." He stood. Taking her hands he pulled her up. "I will not force you to do anything, Isabel."

She smelled it then. The scent poured from him, as it did in the days before the ritual. Since they were in the small village, she would not be surprised if other women began to notice it soon. He held his hand out to her once more, waiting for her to take it. He needed her; his body needed hers. Or any woman's to seek release and to control the coming storm within him.

Isabel could not return before she knew why he believed he owned her and why he thought Sigurd no longer a threat. "Why am I yours now?"

He looked around and found her clothes, handing them to her so she could dress.

"I told you I would bargain for you to stay with me when I left for Duntulm." He held out her gown, now dry, and watched as she dropped the blanket and pulled it over her head. More of the scent surrounded her and her body reacted in spite of her mind's refusal.

"You said you wanted me until the next ritual. Is that the nature of the bargain you struck with him?" She pulled the tunic dress over her head, trying to ignore his physical need for her.

"I offered him that which he could not refuse and he agreed to give Thora to me in marriage."

"And me?" Isabel stared at him, pushing away the intoxicating smell. "How am I part of this?"

"I asked for you as Thora's dowry."

She choked and when he would have tried to help her, she backed away from him. "You bargained for a whore as your wife's dowry? Sigurd would have settled great wealth on you for marrying her."

"You are not a whore," he said through clenched teeth, angrier than she'd ever heard him before.

She knew what she was but did not argue. "I am ready."

If she was Thora's dowry, he would legally own her as soon

as the marriage was consummated. "When do you seal your vows to her?"

"The day before the moon grows full again." Perfectly timed, she thought. It fit her plans, too.

"Where will I stay?" She wanted everything clear between them.

"With me." When she would have refused, he cut her off. "It is the safest place for you—the one place Sigurd will not go."

"And Thora? What has she said on the matter?"

"Sigurd has trained her in wifely duties as well as he trained you to yours," Duncan explained. "She will say nothing, for she has no right to say who I may or may not share my bed with."

With few exceptions, a man could take any woman who would have him, or any that he owned, and his wife had no right to stop him or to refuse his attentions because of it. Concubines and bed slaves were commonplace and only a man's wealth determined how many he could afford and support.

But Isabel had no intention of going along with Duncan's plan. Once he took Thora's maidenhead, Isabel would be gone forever. Her reason for living as a whore would be over, for Thora would be Duncan's legal wife and protected by his name and his honor and his wealth.

And Isabel would be dead by her own hand.

The door opened and closed and Margaret joined them in the main room of her house, ending all further talk. Duncan thanked Margaret for her hospitality and took his leave, holding out his hand, expecting Isabel to take it.

"I will meet you back at the farm," she said.

"I will take you there." He let out a frustrated breath and she took a perverse pleasure in being difficult. "Seek out Harald if I am not there when you arrive then."

He left and she thanked Margaret herself. The woman pressed a small sack in her hand—some bread and cheese to eat on the walk back. Though some were already about their business, the streets were quiet and deserted. Making her way out of the village, Isabel found the path and walked back to Duncan's farm.

She would return to him.

At least he did not have to drag her back screaming or bound. For that Duncan was thankful. But he'd hurt with every word she'd said and every question she'd asked. And when she did not rise to his bait, he wanted to beg for her forgiveness and tell her everything. The ride back across the miles to his farm gave him time to clear his mind and prepare to deal with the coming week.

He had promised Thora they would spend time together in the coming week to prepare her for their joining, so he could not wait for Isabel to arrive. Asking Harald to watch for Isabel, he took Thora for a ride to see his lands. When he looked for Isabel as everyone gathered for the evening meal, he did not see her. Gunna set the food up for the large group in the empty barn and the meal was pleasant enough. No one seemed to hold his arrangements against Thora and they accepted his explanation that she would be in charge of his household very soon. Sigurd sat back, watching everything and everyone with a keen eye. Duncan wondered if he could make it all work out as he'd planned.

Only when he returned to his bedchamber did he find Isabel, asleep in the chair. He tried to ease his arm behind her to carry her to the bed, but she startled at his first touch and clutched the arms of the wooden chair so he could not move her. It would take time he did not have to put her at ease in his bed again.

"Sleep in the bed, Isabel."

"Nay," she said in a husky voice, heavily laden with sleep.

"Isabel, I told you I will not force myself on you."

She seemed to consider his words, but he suspected it was the cramp in her neck that convinced her to move into the bed. She did so without removing her clothing. With guilt lying heavy on his heart, he did not argue.

He stayed on his side of the bed and she on hers, but morning found him wrapped around her body, holding her tightly. She opened her eyes and pushed her way free just as he woke up. They parted, neither seeing the other during the day, nor during the evening meal but only as night fell. She lay in his bed when he arrived.

His body ached for her, his heart bled for her pain, but he would not ask her to join with him. If he did, he was no better than Sigurd, using her against her will. He went to sleep hard and woke up every morning the same way. He lived aroused, craving the comfort only she could offer. But more than the physical pleasure, he wanted her love to see him through the end of things.

The night before he would seal his vows with Thora, he woke in the dark of the night to the sound of her crying into the pillow. He touched her shoulder and she turned without hesitation into his arms, molding herself to him, trapping his erection between their bodies. He kissed her forehead, trying to comfort her but she lifted her face and his mouth touched hers.

That was all it took to ignite the fire that burned between them, in spite of anger and hurt and betrayal. She opened to him, taking off the garments she wore until they lay naked, skin against heated skin. He knelt over her and kissed her, open-mouthed and hungry for the taste and feel of her. Duncan moved his mouth over her neck, licking and tasting every inch of her, moving down and down until he reached the center of her pleasure. He spread her legs, lay between them, then opened the folds of heated flesh so he could drive her mad one last time.

"I am sorry," he whispered against her skin. "I am sorry."

Each time he said the words, he kissed her intimately there, finally finding the hidden bud that lay deeper between the folds and suckling on it. She arched, her body tightening and spasming, until she screamed out her release. He waited for her to calm before beginning anew.

She tried to see to him, but he pressed her back on the bed and continued bringing her release until she could do nothing but moan and sigh. Morning found her sound asleep, lying across his unrequited body. But his heart was lighter for the pleasure he'd given her. He went out to get water to wash with and returned to find her gone.

The tension built within him throughout the day. All those who lived on the farm knew the effects of the moon on him. Those who had come to witness their vows blamed it on a bridegroom's nervousness. If he continued to search for someone in the shadows, no one commented on it at all.

Soon, Duncan and Thora had exchanged vows and rings and the women escorted her to his house. He sat waiting, listening to the bawdy jokes and suggestions from the men until Gunna signaled Thora's readiness for his visit to her.

Chapter Twenty-two

Isabel had one other task to see to before she left. She watched from the shadows of the yard when Gunna took Thora, laughing and running, into Duncan's house. He would take her maidenhead and bind their lives together in a way he could never do with Isabel. Though her heart—and her body—belonged to him Thora was now his wife and would bear his children. If the fates and God were merciful, she would live with him to old age.

All of Isabel's anger and pain did not erase the fact that Duncan had done exactly what she'd hoped—he'd saved Thora from Sigurd's threats—and her sister would never have to face the things she'd had to face over the last few years. Duncan would honor Thora and protect her, taking over the task given Isabel by her mother on her deathbed.

She snuck into the house the way Gunna had shown her to sneak out and waited for Gunna and the others to leave. Catching Gunna's eye, she silently begged for a moment alone with her sister. The young woman who was closer to her than anyone nodded and closed the door quietly. Isabel paused in front of the bedchamber, then knocked softly, saying her sister's name. Thora was not lying on the bed as she'd expected to find her, but stood off to one side of it, staring at the pristine sheets.

"Will it hurt as much as they say?" Thora asked without taking her gaze off the bed.

Isabel did not want to compare her first time with a man to the experience her sister would have in that bed. She offered Thora comfort the only way she could—with the truth.

"He is kind and considerate and giving, Thora. Fear not what is to come between the two of you."

She wanted to hug her sister, but she sensed the fear in Thora, and did not want to worsen it.

"Was he that way with you?"

"Aye," Isabel choked out. "By the morning you will wonder how you were ever worried about what will happen." She walked over to Thora and stood at her side, risking all by touching their hands together.

"I want you to know that he is yours now," Isabel told Thora.

"Father explained how it will be, with me as his wife and you as his bed slave, Isabel. I am not happy with such an arrangement, but it is the way of things with men."

Duncan was right—Sigurd had taught them both to expect the worst of life. Thora was trained to accept nothing but an occasional bedding by her husband and to turn away when he sought other women. Isabel had been trained—the sounds from the gathering grew boisterous and she knew there was little time.

"I will not be here in the morning, Thora. You will not have to share him with me."

"Where will you go? How can you leave him?"

"I cannot play the whore any longer. Worry not though, I am at peace with this."

She turned to leave, but felt Thora's hand grasp hers. Isabel opened her arms and hugged her sister for the last time. She'd spoken the truth about being at peace—she'd never felt more so. Reaching up she smoothed Thora's hair from her face. "Here now, no tears. Be happy, Thora. 'Tis the only thing that makes leaving you bearable."

The sounds of the men approaching grew louder, so with one more quick hug, Isabel left her sister and hid in the corner as the door opened and Duncan was pushed into the house. She waited for him to enter the bedchamber, then left through the side door. No one noticed her, for they were celebrating and the ale flowed freely. She sat against the fence through the night, trying not to imagine what was happening inside that bedchamber, and when the first light of dawn broke through the dark, she was ready to leave.

With the strange calmness of one facing her end, she took his horse from the yard and managed to climb on top of it, guiding it away, down the valley toward the glen and the only place she'd truly known peace.

And where she would find it forever.

Duncan practiced their story once more before he was ready to leave the bedchamber. He pulled the sleeve of his shirt down to cover the new bandage where he'd spilled his blood on the sheets. Thora seemed relieved when he explained he'd wished to give her more time to adjust to their sudden marriage.

They'd shared the bed for a few hours, then just past dawn, he'd risen and prepared the sheets so they could be examined and the marriage declared valid. She was, in the eyes of the law, his legal wife and entitled to inherit his estate at his death.

The moon pulled him and the power began to rise in his blood. His body tightened and ached, tense with the need for

Isabel. There was no time to waste, for he had some final preparations to make. His hand was on the door when Thora spoke.

"Did you do this for her?" she asked.

"For her?" He turned to face Thora.

"For Isabel. I think she loves you."

How strange to be talking of the love of another woman with his wife, he thought. "We should speak of others things, Thora."

"I could see the love in her eyes when she told me she was leaving so I would not have to share you with her."

"What? When did she say that?"

"Last night, just before you arrived. She was trying to ease my fears about what would happen between us. She said she would not be here come today but that she was at peace about leaving."

He did not like the sound of that. If anyone saw her leaving . . . if Sigurd saw her out alone . . . Duncan ran from the house before he thought about it.

Reaching the yard, he realized two of the horses, including his, were gone. Seeking out the men who tended them, he found the black had been missing since just after dawn and Sigurd had ridden out not long after. Worse, Duncan noticed the moon already rising in the sky.

Saddling another horse as quickly as he could, Duncan knew where Isabel would go. If she sought peace, it meant the lake in the glen . . . the fairy glen. Knowing how afraid of riding she was, he hoped to find her before Sigurd did.

She nearly fell off a dozen times, but she kept talking to the animal, begging it to carry her to the glen. Whether it understood her or knew the land well enough it needed no rider to guide it; in a shorter time than she'd thought possible, she saw the glen and the lake within. The sight brought calmness to her soul, and she knew she'd made the right decision.

When she reached the lake, she slid down and landed on wobbly legs next to the horse. Murmuring her thanks, she released the reins and slapped its hindquarters, sending it trotting back into the glen. Alone, she walked to the water's edge and peered down into it.

Currents moved deep within the water and she saw brightness and shadows under the surface. Something twinkled like the stars in the night's sky, and she smiled. It felt familiar to her and she stepped closer. Leaning over, she touched the surface and watched as the sparkling followed her fingers in the water. She laughed at such a thing, feeling the darkness in her soul would soon be gone.

"Will you finish what I started?"

Isabel turned to find Sigurd standing behind her. She could not escape his reach even in trying to meet death on her own terms. But for the first time, she did not feel fear as she looked at him. "What did you start, Sigurd?"

"You were meant to die here that day." His voice, so sure of the claim he made sent chills down her spine.

She frowned at his words. "What do you mean?"

"The bitch needed to learn her lesson. She had refused my suit and married some farmer, so I waited for her to be happy and then killed him." He laughed out an ugly sound. "After your birth, I pressed my suit again and still she refused me."

He was speaking about her mother! "You killed my father?" Now that she'd heard that much, she wanted to know the truth before she died.

Sigurd took a step toward her. "I had plans and that bitch forced me to wait. So, when you were a few years old, I brought you out here and threw you in the lake to drown."

Isabel felt sick to her stomach at his bold proclamation of

his misdeed. She backed away from him, but stayed near the edge of the water.

"I tied a rope around your waist with the other end tied to a boulder. You should have sunk with it, but a few hours later you wandered back to her. Wet and crying and alive."

She remembered the weight dragging her down, but always thought it had been the layers of clothing that pulled her under the surface. He'd wanted her dead and had tried to make it happen. He was a monster.

"Why? Why would you do that?"

"She made me wait. She humiliated me. I paid her back, taking her husband from her, then making sure she knew my plans for you before she died."

Isabel heard sounds behind her and turned to look. The water in the lake churned and swirled. The sparkling lights were gone and something darker, something dangerous, moved in its depths. Yet she did not fear it.

"I took everything she had from her, and she knew it." He laughed again. "Now, it's time to finish this so my daughter never has to think about you again."

"My sister? Thora?" The way he'd said it was strange.

"You do not share blood with her. She is mine alone and I have protected her while stripping you of everything." He stepped closer to Isabel at the edge of the water.

"It is done now, Sigurd."

She turned toward the voice and found Duncan approaching them.

Sigurd laughed again, and pulled a dagger from his boot. "I have killed men bigger and stronger than you, Healer. Go back to Thora and I will let you live for now."

His eyes followed Duncan, who moved closer to Isabel but stayed away from the lake. Suddenly the water exploded behind Sigurd dragging him into its depths.

Shocked beyond words, Isabel watched as he fought against whatever held him under the water until he disappeared beneath the surface. Silence filled the glen and she struggled to understand what had just happened.

Duncan was beside her, pulling her into his arms, holding her as though his life depended on it. The import of what had happened struck her then—Sigurd was dead and no longer a threat to her. For a moment she forgot her purpose there was to die.

"Isabel, I must tell you something." Duncan's voice sounded different. As she looked at him, his eyes began to flash and flare, and his face changed.

"Duncan?" she asked. No, not Duncan but the Healer. Glancing up, she realized the moon was full in the sky above. She touched his cheek and it burned her skin.

"Sigurd's death frees you more than my plan could have, but you carry the damage of what he did to you so deeply, your soul cries out to me. You must be made whole or you will not survive." His voice was many and one. It echoed across the glen and whispered only to her. His face glowed, other faces layering over his skin, and she knew whatever was in the lake was also part of him.

He reached for her, but unlike what she'd witnessed before, he wrapped himself around her and she felt him in her mind, searching her memories until they were joined as one.

Duncan held onto the part that made him human, the part that loved her, as he allowed the Healer to enter. As he held her in his arms, he pushed deep within her mind and found the black place where she kept the pain walled in. He beat against it, tearing it apart bit by bit, piece by piece, then watched as everything she held inside tumbled out.

Pain. Guilt. Shame. The horrors she'd lived through. The rapes. The overwhelming fear. The loss. The helplessness.

The physical damage keeping her from having a bairn. All of it poured out like a lanced boil that could not be contained any longer.

Duncan poured his love into her body and soul, healing her, warming her, opening her so she could live again. "You are whole once more, love." The damage, all of it, was gone.

He smiled. "You can love again," he whispered to her as he began to separate from her. "You can live, Isabel. Live."

He felt his heart slow, and he counted the beats, each one coming more slowly than the last until he heard and felt no more.

Isabel fell with him, as his weight took her down to the ground under him. She managed to roll him to his side and spoke his name. He did not respond, so she shook him. Placing her hand on his chest, she tried to feel his heart beating.

It did not.

She looked around, down the glen, at the lake, and found herself completely alone. He was dead.

Her heart cried out for him, but he did not answer. Every last trace of him was gone from her and with it all the pain she'd learned to bury so she could survive the life Sigurd had forced on her. His lies and his mad quest for vengeance was directed against a woman whose only sin was that she'd loved someone else.

"Duncan!" Isabel screamed. Her cry echoed through the glen, across the hills and along the stream. She grabbed his shirt and shook him, screaming out his name again.

He'd known he was going to die and he'd called his power forth to save her first. She'd felt the love he'd poured into her while they were joined and knew what he was doing but could not stop him. Whole and healed, her heart broke as she realized she'd never told him of her love. She'd seen his plan while he was inside her thoughts and realized his goal was always to free her.

He'd used the last of his human control to heal her.

"Duncan," she whispered. "I do love you." Her tears fell as she leaned her head on his chest and cried for all the possibilities that would never be realized for them.

"You were never meant to die here."

A voice cut through her sorrow and she lifted her head to see a creature of infinite beauty standing near the lake. He wore garments that shone like the sun and the air around him sparkled as though someone had pulled all the stars from the sky and thrown them in around him.

"Who are you?" Isabel rubbed the tears from her eyes.

"No matter what the other one said, you were always protected. We let you learn to survive and we sent you strength through our connection to you."

"I do not understand." She leaned back to look at him. Other voices, sounding like hundreds of bells tinkling, joined his. Turning to look at the lake, she found others watching her, including the face she remembered from all those years ago, the one who had pushed her back to the surface and saved her life. The one whose voice she heard when she swam in the sea.

"He needed you to survive, so we kept you alive until he found you," the one who looked like royalty explained. "Then he could heal you."

"Was his power from you?"

"Aye, he is from us."

Confused and shocked beyond rational thought, Isabel wondered if she was going to wake up from a bad dream and find herself in her bed. "Then why did you let him die? Can you not heal him?"

Without seeming to move, the being hovered above Duncan's body. "We cannot call him back from death, but your love for him did."

The heart beneath her hand began to beat and Duncan

drew in a breath, then another. He opened his eyes and whispered her name. "You do love me, even though you thought
I'd betrayed you." Not a question, a declaration as though he
still saw inside her mind and her heart.

"How can this be?"

Duncan pushed himself up to his feet and helped her to
stand. The one who had spoken to her watched them and
smiled. In that moment she recognized his face as the one
joined with Duncan's in the ritual. He was the source of Duncan's power.

"Who are you?" Duncan repeated Isabel's question.

The glen quieted and the man, or being, nodded as though
ready to answer him. "We are Sith," Nodding to the others
who seemed to appear and disappear at will, he added, "We
are Sith." He floated over to Duncan and laid his hand on
Duncan's chest. "You are Sith."

The being laughed, causing the stars above to flare brightly.
Reaching out his hand, the Sith placed his hand on theirs and
whispered without his mouth moving. "Learn of the origin of
your powers, Healer. Learn how you came to be."

Isabel heard the words and felt them deep within her as
something surged between the sith and them. The words
flowed into her mind, then a vision of them was revealed in
the glen.

"Many years ago as humans count time, I discovered a
woman in the western isles where she spent many a summer's
day. Her beauty drew me and I went to her in the day and the
night, giving her my love."

Duncan heard the sith change the way he spoke, telling the
story as a human would, referring to only himself alone. He
watched with Isabel as a young woman appeared in the glen
near them, beautiful and filled with life. Then the sith in
human form joined her.

"I took her to my lands through an entrance like that

one"—he nodded at a place between two of the strangely formed hills next to the lake—"and we spent many months there together. I gave her everything," the sith said fiercely, "but she was not happy and asked to return to her mortal world and the man she'd been betrothed to before I found her. She refused my love and found her way back here on that Samhain night twenty-and-eight years ago as you count time."

The sith turned from them and nodded at the place before them and Duncan saw it as it had happened. He thought only he saw it until he heard Isabel's gasp and felt her hold tightly onto his hand and watch as he did.

The young woman appeared again, pushing her way out of the fairy hill. She was huge with child and stumbled out of the ground, holding her belly and moaning against the pain of the impending birth. She kept looking behind her to see if anyone followed, then ran toward the path.

But she did not make it, falling to the ground as her pains struck. When she looked over her shoulder before gaining her feet once more, the Sith stood on the fairy hill.

"Do not leave," he said. "I gave you my love."

Duncan thought the creature did not seem capable of such mortal emotions. His love and pain were clear though as the sith spoke.

"Come back with me now." He held out his hand to her but she turned away, trying to run.

"I cannot live with you. I do not love you." She gasped for breath as another pain struck. She howled in pain but still turned away. "Let me go!" she screamed.

The Sith's rage and pain exploded then; flashes of light and waves of heat pierced the night sky as he lashed out at the woman who'd betrayed him.

Isabel trembled and Duncan gathered her close.

"They are mine." The Sith pointed at her huge belly. "They are gifted." Something flashed from his hand to the woman's belly and she

screamed in pain. "But they will be cursed for your betrayal, for when they use their Sith powers, they will suffer. Their powers will grow and their mortal bodies will be tormented. When their powers peak and end, they will wither and die."

"No!" she screamed. "Please! Do not make my bairns carry the punishment for my sins against you," she cried out, pulling herself up onto her knees and reaching out her hand to him. "Spare them, I beg you!"

The Sith approached her and crouched in front of her, placing his hand on her belly for only a moment.

Duncan stared at the scene and watched some indescribable emotion fill the Sith's face as he felt the bairns inside her womb.

"They will be taken from you, for you are not worthy to raise them. They will not know of their power or the source of it and you cannot tell them or the Sith will strike you all down," he commanded.

She began to crawl away as though to escape his sentence, but he shook his head at her and waved his hand. Four others appeared around her, holding her and keeping her from running.

"Unless they find true love, given and spoken by one called enemy or betrayer, their Sith nature will destroy their human one and they will live in our world forever. If they find that true love before their powers end, their mortal nature will control their Sith side."

Duncan stood motionless as the story explaining his life played out before them, like a vision. The scene sped up, as Isabel grasped his hand and they watched the woman give birth to three bairns, all boys. As each was born, one of the other sith took the babe and disappeared. When the birth was finished, the last sith faded away, leaving only the woman and her lover alone.

The Sith shook his head at her. "You will not find what you seek with him. You will suffer this loss and more by refusing what I offered you. Only one of the three can help you find the happiness you seek."

"No," the woman keened out. "No more!"

"I do not curse you, Aigneis," he said softly. "I only see what the failure of your mortal heart will cause."

Duncan found it impossible to speak as he watched the sith walk to the fairy hill. The vision of that long ago Samhain night faded, until it was the present day and the moon shone high in the sky overhead. Finally they understood the power that had controlled Duncan's life and the reasons behind it.

The sith's eyes glowed as he turned to face them once more. "That was your past, born of betrayal. You are half sith, half mortal. Destined only to survive in this mortal world if you could find the one thing I could not."

"And my mother? Does she yet live?" Duncan asked.

The sith, his father, smiled. "She lives."

"And his brothers?" Isabel asked when Duncan did not. "Do they live?"

The sith raised his face to the sky and closed his eyes. He nodded, answering her question and confirming Duncan's brothers had survived, and found love, as he had.

"Connor and Gavin live and have faced the same challenge you have—to find love born in betrayal before the power destroys you."

Duncan took Isabel in his arms and hugged her. "I have brothers!" He laughed, swinging her around in a circle. "We must find them."

"She will help you harness your power to find them."

Isabel looked startled that she would play a part in the story. The sith, his father, confirmed it. "You have found favor with the sith." He touched her belly with his finger. "Your daughter will be favored as well. Gifted as only a female can be."

Duncan watched as Isabel glowed under his father's touch. He did not understand what was meant by those words, but if it meant creating a baby, a girl who would be as beautiful as her mother, he did not need to know.

"Seek out your brothers while your power is high on the day of your birth."

Samhain. He'd been born on Samhain.

The glen grew brighter and brighter as though the sith had brought the sun into the middle of it. Then they were gone and Duncan stood holding Isabel alone among the fairy hills.

"We should go back, Isabel. There is much to be seen to now." He was thinking of the wife he must divorce and the woman he must claim as his and only his—legal matters he would have to attend to while trying to control the power he could feel surging within him, ready to be called forth, at his command.

They ran through the glen, laughing as only those in love can. It took them hours to get back to his farm, all the while trying to understand what they'd learned, but there were still many hours left in Samhain for him to seek out his brothers.

Epilogue

Isle of Skye
Samhain night, 1099 AD

He could not wait any longer. Duncan thrust deep into his wife's body and pushed her to find her release. As the moment was on her, he allowed the power within his veins to flow out, searching once more across the expanse of space and time. Isabel was with him, joined in heart, body, and soul, urging him along until he saw—they saw—his brothers.

Isabel and Duncan seemed suspended in the air high above the coast of the inner islands, over a tower that sat by the sea. A man looked at them and waved to them.

"Connor!" they said in one voice, mystically certain of his identity.

Then they were above the northern islands, flying over Orkney toward the coast of Scotland. A man walked out of a huge cave at the edge of the sea and looked up at them, calling out to them by name.

"Gavin!" Duncan called out and he heard Isabel echo the name in her thoughts.

They came back to themselves as they reached the moment of complete satisfaction and he poured his seed, his love, and his power into her. She took everything he offered and gave him more in return. They collapsed on the bed, unable to speak for some time, never letting go of each other.

As the last spasms rippled deep within her flesh, he felt them caressing him, and the air around them began to sparkle and shine. The laughter touched them, moving over their skin and into their bodies.

"She is favored," the sith said within their thoughts. "This one shall be called Ariana, for her silver eyes."

Duncan pulled Isabel to him, kissing the breath from her and thanking all the powers that were, for letting him find her and letting her save him.

THE END

ॐ

Kilmartin Glen
Midsummer, 1100 AD

Duncan and Isabel had followed the words he'd heard in countless dreams, arriving on the Scottish mainland near the ancient hill fort of Dunadd some days ago. He'd shared Connor and Gavin's words with her, as well as his wonderment at having brothers—and a mother. After buying supplies, a small cart, and horses for the journey, and guided by his brothers' voices, they followed the main road through the glen, past countless standing stones and markers left centuries in the past. They needed to sail across the lake that lay at the northern end to find the others.

Though large with their second child, Isabel never slowed and never lost her excitement as they traveled ever closer to his long-separated family. They were just days away from meeting the brothers—and his mother—he'd never known he had until last year.

Other than the vision his father had revealed to them on Samhain night, he'd never heard his mother's voice. He wondered what she would look like and how she would greet them. Since having their first child, Isabel knew more about a mother's heart and tried to convince him his mother would greet him with the love she had not been able to give him throughout his life.

As they boarded the boat that would take them across the lake on the final part of their journey, Duncan found himself growing ever more nervous about meeting her. Isabel slipped her hand in his and squeezed it, offering him silent reassurance about what was to come. The hours passed slowly. He wanted to scream and order the winds to gather in the sails and move the boat more quickly toward their destination. When the village came into sight, Duncan could hardly breathe from the anticipation.

Once again, his Isabel understood. "She will love you as I do," she said quietly, handing their sleeping bairn to him to carry. "Fear not."

Their belongings were taken to the end of the dock as Duncan looked around the small cluster of cottages. A man, tall and large, with his long black hair pulled back, walked toward them. "Duncan?" the man asked.

"Aye," Duncan answered. "And my wife, Isabel."

The man nodded to Isabel, taking a moment to glance at the bairn and Isabel's obvious pregnancy before turning back to Duncan. "The others wait at my house. 'Tis this way." He picked up two of the sacks and walked ahead. "I am called Breac."

Duncan tempered his excitement, taking Isabel by the hand and walking slowly to accommodate her.

Breac glanced back as they made their way along the path, smiling several times, but not saying anything else. Others from the village called out greetings to him as they walked. He was clearly a man of some importance. Duncan knew not who he was. The path turned and a large house sat before them.

Isabel squeezed his hand once more. "Go on ahead, Duncan," she urged. "Give the bairn to me and go."

He would love his wife until he died and forever after that. She understood what he needed to do and allowed him to go on by himself. He handed their daughter to her and hurried on ahead.

The door opened as he reached the path and two men stepped outside. Both were very like him in appearance, tall, with fair hair and pale eyes, though one had blue eyes and the other green.

His brothers.

Duncan swallowed, trying to ease the tightness in his throat. He was a man who'd never thought to have a wife let alone siblings and a mother, and he had all of those and more—a beloved daughter and another bairn on the way.

From nothing to everything he'd ever desired.

"Connor." He held out his hand to the one who'd appeared most often in his dreams. Connor strode over to him and pulled him into a rough hug. Turning to the other, Duncan said his name, "Gavin," still not believing what was happening.

Their embrace was interrupted by the soft voice of a woman. "Duncan."

He held his breath, unable to stop the tears in his eyes as he faced his mother for the first time in their lives. For a woman of more than two score, she looked incredibly youthful. Her grey eyes shone brightly, from tears and an inner vitality that made her seem much younger than she was.

She opened her arms and he ran to her, not fighting the emotions that filled him. She held him, touching his face and his hair, murmuring his name over and over until she simply cried. They remained that way for several minutes until Breac called out to her.

"Aigneis, this is Duncan's wife." He escorted Isabel to them. "And their bairn," he added with a smile.

'Twas the warmth Breac had for Aigneis that made Duncan realize who the man was—his mother's husband. Duncan released her and brought Isabel and their Aigneis to meet her.

Soon Connor's wife Moira and Gavin's wife Katla joined them, bringing their bairns out to meet their kin, and the gathering grew boisterous and excited. Aigneis held the bairn Aigneis, touching her hand often as the hours passed, as though not quite believing she was real. Duncan's heart eased as he got to know his brothers and their wives.

Connor cleared his throat. Following the direction in which he looked, Duncan and his brothers watched as a small disturbance in the air near them swirled and twinkled like the stars in the night sky. It lengthened and widened until a man stepped through it and stood before them.

Their father, the sith prince, looked at them through ageless eyes, letting his gaze touch each of those gathered there, before landing on their mother. His expression softened for a moment before he began to disappear as quickly as he'd appeared. He stopped when their mother called out a strange word to him.

His sith name.

Though Breac tried to stop her from approaching the sith, Aigneis nodded at him and he released her to let her go to the prince. She had not spoken to the father of her children since the night she'd given birth and caused the terrible curse to be laid on their souls. She knew she needed to speak to him of the past and of their sons' futures.

He was magnificent, as stunning as the first time they'd met on Mull when she was but sixteen. Even in human form, it hurt to look on him for too long, but to see him in his own land in his own form was to see the perfection of the sith. She could only imagine what he must think seeing her so much older.

"I am sorry," she began, offering words to show she accepted her part in what had affected so many lives, but he shook his head.

"Even the sith can err," he said in her thoughts. "Expecting you to remain with me was one mistake." His admission shocked her, but his next words were even more surprising. "My curse was another."

"Did you know what the outcome would be when you set it all in motion?" she asked. The sith could see into the past and the future, so she did not doubt that he had.

"I hoped."

A word foreign to the sith. Another one was—

"In my way, I loved you, Aigneis. Never think otherwise."

He reached out and touched the tears that fell, turning them into sparkling crystals which he caught in his hand. He gave them to her as he began to float away.

She would have said something else, but his form dissipated before she could. She spoke his name again. When nothing glimmered in the air before her, she knew she would never see him again. Aigneis turned to find Breac walking toward her.

"Never think otherwise." The words echoed on the breeze and a warm caress touched her cheek as a final farewell from the father of her sons.

Breac reached her and took her in his strong arms, holding her close to his heart. From despair and hopelessness to a full life with a man who loved her more than she deserved. From losing her flesh and blood to finding them all and retrieving the bits of her heart and soul she'd lost with them. From grief to bliss, Aigneis's life had come full circle. Her family had the rest of their lives to spend together. And to love.

So, Duncan, Gavin and Connor, now called MacShee, discovered the truth the sith knew all along—the only power stronger than their magic was the love in a human heart.

AUTHOR'S NOTE

When I was working on this Storm trilogy, I searched for areas to use as locations for my stories. I needed places that had Viking/Norse influences or history, legends tying them to the sith, or the Fae as they're called in other places, and a time period that worked with both (Vikings and sith).

I was led to the Hebrides and Orkney.

I'd done a lot of research to set up the stories at the beginning but in the autumn of 2009 I had the chance to visit Scotland before writing the novella, the second, and third books. I'm glad I did it then!

Connor's story is set on Mull, Gavin's in Orkney and the north coast of Scotland, and Duncan's is in one of my most favorite places to visit—the Isle of Skye. Although there is a rich history in all those places detailing the influence and control of the Vikings, Skye has a place related to the sith that has centuries of legends to explain it.

The fairy glen in my story is a real place near Uig on Skye. If you follow a small road off the main one leading into the harbor at Uig and go past a couple farms, you will find it. Although the road goes right through it, you have to walk it to feel the specialness of the place and to get the best views.

As Duncan described it in this story, it is unlike any other place in Scotland, formed as though the hills were built up in layers and covered with grass as a decoration. The ruins of a lone tower stand watch over it. The surrounding hills seem to lead to a small lake.

I found this glen when reading a book of Scottish folk and

fairy tales about Skye. It seems that in days of old, a fiddler from the village of Uig was asked to play at a ceilidh in the glen. Paid well, he went and played all night at the boisterous event, returning to his home in the morning—only to discover three months had passed and he'd been playing for the sith in their land, where time passes differently!

Photos of this glen are all over the internet if you'd like to take a look at the place. If you visit Skye, take time to stop there . . . and make sure to listen for the laughter of the sith which is still heard in that glen.

Good girls should NEVER CRY WOLF.
But who wants to be good?
Be sure to pick up Cynthia Eden's latest novel, out now!

Lucas didn't take the woman back to his house on Bryton Road. The place was probably still crawling with cops and reporters, and he didn't feel like dealing with all that crap.

He called his first in command, Piers Stratus, to let him know that he was out of jail and to tell him that there were two unwanted coyotes in town.

The woman—Sarah—didn't speak while he drove. He could feel the waves of tension rolling off her, shaking her body.

She was scared. She'd done a fair job of hiding her fear back at the police station and then at the park, at first anyway. But as the darkness had fallen, he'd seen the fear. Smelled it.

Sarah had known she was being hunted.

He pushed a button on his remote. The wrought-iron gates before him opened and revealed the curving drive that led to his second LA home. In the hills, it gave him a great view of the city below, and that view let know him when company was coming, long before any unexpected guests arrived.

When the gate shut behind him, he saw Sarah sag slightly, settling back into her seat. The scent of her fear finally eased.

Like most of his kind, he usually enjoyed the smell of fear. But he didn't . . . like the scent on her.

He much preferred the softer scent, like vanilla cream, that he could all but taste as it clung to her skin. Perhaps he would get a taste, later.

With a flick of his wrist, he killed the ignition. The house was right in front of them. Two stories. Long, tall windows.

And, hopefully, no more dead bodies waited on the steps here.

He eased out of the car, stretching slowly. Then he walked around and opened the door for Sarah. As any man would, Lucas admired the pale flash of thigh when her skirt crept up. And he wondered just what secrets the lovely lady was keeping from him.

"We're going in to talk." An order. He wanted to know everything, starting with why the dead human had been at *his place*.

She gave a quick nod. "Okay, I—"

A wolf bounded out of the house. A flash of black fur. Golden eyes. Teeth.

Shit. It wasn't safe for the kid. Not until he found out what was going on—

The wolf ran to him. Tossed back his head and howled.

Sarah laughed softly.

Laughed.

His stare shot to her just in time to catch the smile on her lips. His hand lifted, and almost helplessly, he traced that smile with his fingertips.

Her breath caught.

Lucas ignored the tightening in his gut. "Shouldn't you be afraid?" After the coyotes, he'd expected her to flinch away from any other shifters. And Jordan was one big wolf, with claws and teeth that could easily rip a woman like Sarah apart.

She looked back at the wolf who watched them. "He's so young, little more than a kid. One who is glad you're—"

No.

Understanding dawned, fast and brutal in his mind. *I'm more than human.* She'd told him that, he just hadn't understood exactly *what* she was. Until now.

His hands locked around her arms and Lucas pulled her up against him. Nose to nose, close enough so that he could see the dark gold glimmering in the depths of her green eyes. "Jordan, get the hell out of here." He gave the order to his brother without ever looking away from her.

The wolf growled.

"Go!"

The young wolf pushed against his leg—*letting me know he's pissed, 'cause Jordan hates when I boss his ass*—and then the wolf backed away.

"Now for you, sweetheart." His fingers tightened. "Why don't we just go back to that part about you not being human?"

Her lips parted. She had nice lips—sexy and plump. He shouldn't be noticing them, not then, but he couldn't help himself. He noticed everything about her. The gold hoops in her dainty ears. The streaks of gold buried deep in her dark hair. The lotion she'd rubbed on her body—that vanilla scent was driving him wild.

He was turned on, achingly hard, for a woman he barely knew. Not normally a big deal. He had a more than a healthy sex drive. Most shifters did. The animal inside liked to play.

But Sarah . . . he didn't *trust* her, not for a minute, and he didn't usually have sex with women he didn't trust. A man could be vulnerable to attack when he was fucking.

"You know what I am, Lucas," she said and shrugged, the move both careless and fake because he knew that she cared, too much.

"*Tell me.*" Her mouth was so close. He could still taste her. That kiss earlier had just been a tease.

If you liked this book, try Dani Harper's
CHANGELING DREAM,
in stores now . . .

What kind of woman runs after a wolf?

W James was no closer to answering that question than he had been many hours before when he had paused in the clinic loft, two bounds away from the open window, and listened to the human calling after the white wolf. He had been startled to find the woman up and around so close to dawn, but more surprised by her reaction when she spotted him. She should have been terrified, should have been screaming. Instead she had stopped still, remaining quiet until he melted back into the darkness—then had plunged forward in a vain attempt to follow him. She acted as if she knew the wolf, but how could that be? There was something else too; something in her voice had almost compelled him to—what? Answer her? Reveal himself? He didn't know. The woman had gone from room to room then, switching on every light, searching.

He wasn't surprised when she didn't check the loft. After all, it was fifteen feet above the ground floor and accessible only by a vertical ladder. A wolf couldn't climb it, and she had no way of knowing that what she pursued was not a wolf and that the ladder was no impediment to him at all. The stack of bales outside, from which he had initially leapt, was more than thirty feet from the loading door of the loft. Only a very large tiger might cross such a span. Or a Changeling.

James felt a strange disappointment tugging at his senses, almost a regret that the woman had not found him. *Who are you? Why do I know you?* Within his lupine body, James chuffed out a breath in frustration. *And why do I care?* The angle of the fading light told him it was time to hunt, that deer would be on the move. Weary of human thoughts and human concerns, he relaxed into his wolf nature and disappeared beneath it.

"What a tourist I am!" Jillian berated herself for not bringing a cell phone, for not paying more attention to the time, for traveling in the bush alone, for not packing at least a chocolate bar. Two chocolate bars. Maybe three. The energy bars she'd brought tasted like wet cardboard. She made a long mental list of the things she was going to do to be more prepared for the next hike, because as difficult as the trail was, she simply had to go back to that rocky plateau, had to see if the wolves would return. Was it part of their territory or were they just passing through?

The sun was long gone. Stars were pinning a deep indigo sky, and a full moon was floating just above the horizon. It had climbed enough to glimmer through the trees and lay a broad swath of light over the surface of the river when Jillian finally found the marked hiking trail. Compared to the goat path she'd been traveling, the graveled corridor was like a wide paved highway, level and free of overhanging brush and fallen logs. It promised easier, faster travel in spite of the darkness. She was still two and a half, maybe three, miles from the truck she had borrowed from the clinic, but at least now she had a direct route.

The flashback broadsided her without warning.

It might have been the crunch of gravel beneath her feet, the rustle of leaves in the trees, or the scent of the river, but whatever the trigger, she was suddenly on another trail by another river. Phantom images, sounds, even smells burst vividly upon her senses. Jillian stumbled forward and fell to her knees, skinning them both right through her jeans. She rolled and sat, but clasped her hands to her head rather than to her wounds. "Don't close your eyes, don't close your eyes. You're not there, it's not real, it's over. Jesus, it's over, it's over and you're okay. You're okay." She spoke slowly, deliberately, coaching herself until the shaking stopped. "It's a different place and a different time. I'm not back there, I'm here. I'm here and I'm okay." *I'm okay, I'm okay.*

But she wasn't, not yet. She rocked back and forth in the gravel. "My name is Jillian Descharme and I'm a licensed veterinarian and I'm okay. I'm thirty-two years old and I'm in Dunvegan, Alberta, and I'm okay. Nothing is threatening me, nothing is wrong, I'm okay." She drew a long shaky breath and rubbed her runny nose with her sleeve like a child. "I'm okay. Jeez! Jeez goddamn Louise!" She was cold, freezing cold, her clothes soaked with sweat and her skin clammy, but the fear had her by the throat and she couldn't move. She had to think of something fast, something to help her break away from this terror, break out of this inertia or she'd be here all night. And then it came. The image of the white wolf—the memory, the dream, flowed into her, warmed her like brandy. Jillian clung to that mental picture like a life preserver in rough seas, let the wolf's unspoken words fill her mind and calm it. *Not alone. Here with you.*

She rose at last on trembling legs and cursed as her knees made their condition known. The sharp stinging cleared the last of the flashback from her head however, banished the nausea from her stomach. She stood for several moments, hugging herself, rubbing her hands over her upper arms. She sucked in great lungfuls of the cool moist air until she felt steady again, and took a few tentative steps along the dark path—but had to resist the impulse to run. If she ran, she might never stop.

"Think of the white wolf, think of the white wolf." Calm, she had to be calm. Take big breaths. "Walk like a normal person. It's okay to walk fast because I'm busy, got things to do, places to go, people to see, but I don't have to run. I can walk because nothing's wrong, I'm okay." She was in control, she would stay in control. As she walked, however, she couldn't stop her senses from being on hyper-alert. Jillian's eyes flicked rapidly from side to side, searching the darkness, her ears straining to hear any rustle of leaf or snap of twig. She noticed the tiny brown bats that dipped and whirled in the air above her. She noted the calls of night birds, of loons settling and owls hunting. A mouse hurried in front of her, crossing and re-crossing the path. A few moments later, a weasel followed it, in a slinky rolling motion. Jillian was keenly aware of everything—the blood pounding in her ears, the sound of her footsteps in the gravel, the liquid sounds of the nearby river—but not the tree root bulging up through the path.

She yelled in surprise, then in pain as her knees hit the gravel again. She rolled to a sitting position, cursing the sharp stinging and her own clumsiness—hadn't she *just* successfully negotiated a rugged game trail down a steep hillside for heaven's sake? She couldn't see much even with the moon's light, but a quick examination showed both knees were bleeding, her jeans in shreds. She cursed even more as she picked out a few obvious shards of gravel, but cleaning and bandaging were just going to have to wait until she reached the truck. At least it wasn't anything worse. Annoying, damn painful and embarrassing, but not a broken ankle or snakebite. Her eyes strayed to the underbrush in spite of herself—there weren't any poisonous snakes this far north, were there? "Good grief!" Jillian yanked her mind firmly away from *that* train of thought and was pondering whether it was possible to stand without bending her knees when she heard the howl.

She sat bolt upright as if an electric current had suddenly passed through her, every hair on end, every sense alert. The call came again, closer. Deep, primal, long and low. Drawn out and out and out, an ancient song, mournful yet somehow sweet. When it fell silent, Jillian felt as if time itself had stopped. And she found herself straining to hear the song again, fascinated, even as her brain told her to run and instinct told her to freeze.

The moon was higher now. The pale light filtered down through the trees and laid a dappled carpet of silver on the stony path. There was no wind, no breeze. Jillian held her breath, listening, watching, but all was still. Her heart was pounding hard with both excitement and fear. Normally she would have loved to get a glimpse of a wolf in the wild, but the idea was a lot less attractive when she was alone in the dark. There were few recorded incidents of wolves attacking or killing humans, but all the data in the world wasn't very re-assuring when she was sitting there bleeding. Immediately she wished she hadn't thought of that. It was just a little blood, but she struggled to get the image of a wounded fish in a shark tank out of her head.

A movement at the edge of the path beyond seized her at-tention. A pale shape emerged from the shadows, seemed to coalesce in the moonlight and grow larger until it was a vivid white creature of impossible size. Jillian's heart stuck in her throat as the great wolf slowly turned its massive head and stared directly at her.

Oh, Jesus. She had studied wolves more than any other wildlife, but only from books and captive specimens. Wolves don't attack humans, she reminded herself. Wolves don't at-tack humans—but there had been cases in Alaska. She gritted her teeth and sat perfectly still, afraid to breathe as the wolf began to slowly move in her direction. The creature approached within ten feet, then abruptly sat on its haunches and stared at her.

It was enormous. She swallowed hard, realizing if the wolf attacked there would be nothing she could do. Nothing. She wouldn't even manage a scream before it was on her. Not one bit of her martial arts training would help, especially when she was sitting on the ground. Nevertheless she scanned the ground with her peripheral vision for anything she might use as a weapon. Her fingers inched toward a rock, closed around it as the wolf rose, took a slow step toward her, into a pool of moonlight. Instantly its snowy fur gleamed and its eyes were . . . its eyes were . . .

Blue.

Jillian felt as if the air had been knocked from her body. The rock rolled out of her palm. Trembling, shaking, she reached a tentative hand toward the animal. "You. It's you," she choked out. "Oh, my God, it's you, isn't it? You're real."

The wolf closed the gap between them and licked her outstretched fingers. *Omigod, omigod.* She couldn't move at first, both enthralled and terrified—until the animal nudged its head under her hand like a dog asking to be petted. Jillian moved her fingers lightly across the broad skull, scratching hesitantly at first. Then fear fell away, and she worked both hands behind the sensitive ears, into the glossy ruff. The wolf stood panting mildly, the immense jaws slack and the great pink tongue lolling out in apparent pleasure. Jillian had no illusions about the animal's power—it might behave like a big dog but those jaws could easily crack the leg bones of a moose, those teeth could tear out the throat of a bull elk in full flight. And as surely as she knew those facts, she knew the wolf would not hurt her. It wasn't sensible, it wasn't logical, but the certainty was core-deep. Instinct? Intuition? Insanity? She didn't know and didn't care. The wolf held steady as Jillian wrapped her arms around its great neck and buried her face in its thick white fur. "I thought I dreamed you. You came to me. You came when no one would come, but they all told me I dreamed you because no one saw you but me. And I looked and looked for you, but I couldn't find you."

Here now. Found you.

The voice in her mind was real. The fur beneath her hands and face was real. The heat radiating from the wolf's body was real. Her voice hitched as joy overwhelmed her. "You're in my dreams all the time. I'm so glad that you're here, that you exist." *And that I am not crazy.* Although her rational brain told her there was certainly something crazy about being in the forest at night, hugging a giant wolf. But she couldn't think about that right now; she had this moment in time and she had things to say. "I owe you a lot; you don't know how much you've done. You saved my life all those years ago, but you saved my sanity too. When things were hard and horrible, and I didn't want to face them, I thought of you and it helped me get through. I got through the hospital and the counseling and the therapy and came out on the other side, because of you." She wiped her cheek on the soft fur, but couldn't stop the tears. "I thought I was done then, I really did. But after a while I felt like it wasn't enough to be alive, that I hadn't really survived until I started living my life again. And you helped me do that too. I thought about what to do with my life and it was so plain to me—I wanted to work with animals, work with wolves. Because of you, I found that dream inside me. You did that for me, and I can't tell you how thankful I am, how grateful I am that you were there for me. Even now, just handling ordinary life, I feel like I'm never really alone."

Not alone. Here with you. The wolf nuzzled and licked at her hair, then lay down beside her. Gradually the tears subsided, and Jillian tumbled into an exhausted sleep with her arms still around the wolf's neck.

Don't miss DEAD ALERT by Bianca D'Arc,
Coming next month . . .

Fort Bragg, North Carolina

"I've got a special project for you, Sam." The commander, a former Navy SEAL named Matt Sykes, began talking before Sam was through the door to Matt's private office. "Sit down and shut the door."

Sam sat in a wooden chair across the cluttered desk from his commanding officer. Lt. Sam Archer, US Army Green Beret, was currently assigned to a top secret, mixed team of Special Forces soldiers and elite scientists. There were also a few others from different organizations, including one former cop and a CIA black ops guy. It was an extremely specialized group, recruited to work on a classified project of the highest order.

"I understand you're a pilot." Matt flipped through a file as he spoke.

"Yes, sir." Sam could have said more but he didn't doubt Matt had access to every last bit of Sam's file, even the top secret parts. He had probably known before even sending for him that Sam could fly anything with wings. Another member of his old unit was a blade pilot who flew all kinds of choppers, but fixed wing aircraft were Sam's specialty.

"How do you like the idea of going undercover as a charter pilot?"

"Sir?" Sam sat forward in the chair, intrigued.

"The name of a certain charter airline keeps popping up." Matt put down the file and faced Sam as his gaze hardened. "Too often for my comfort. Ever heard of a company called Praxis Air?"

"Can't say that I have."

"It's a small outfit, based out of Wichita—at least that's where they repair and maintain their aircraft in a company-owned hangar. They have branch offices at most of the major airports and cater mostly to an elite business clientele. They do the odd private cargo flight and who knows what else. They keep their business very hush-hush, *providing the ultimate in privacy for their corporate clients,* or so their brochure advertises." Matt pushed a glossy tri-fold across the desk toward Sam.

"Looks pretty slick."

"That they are," Matt agreed. "So slick that even John Petit, with his multitude of CIA connections, can't get a bead on exactly what they've been up to of late. I've been piecing together bits here and there. Admiral Chester, the traitor, accepted more than a few free flights from them in the past few months, as did Ensign Bartles, who it turns out, was killed in a Praxis Air jet that crashed the night we took down Dr. Rodriguez and his friends. She wasn't listed on the manifest and only the pilot was claimed by the company, but on a hunch I asked a friend on the National Transportation Safety Board to allow us to do some DNA testing. Sure enough, we found remnants of Beverly Bartles' DNA at the crash site, though her body had to have been moved sometime prior to the NTSB getting there. The locals were either paid off or preempted. Either option is troubling, to say the least."

"You think they're mixed up with our undead friends?"

They were still seeking members of the science team that had created the formula that killed and then turned its victims into the walking dead. Nobody had figured out exactly how they were traveling so freely around the country when they were on every watch list possible.

"It's a very real possibility. Which is why I want to send you in undercover. I don't need to remind you, time is of the essence. We have a narrow window to stuff this genie back into its bottle. The longer this goes on, the more likely it is the technology will be sold to the highest bidder and then, God help us."

Sam shivered. The idea of the zombie technology in the hands of a hostile government or psycho terrorists—especially after seeing what he'd seen over these past months—was unthinkable.

"If my going undercover will help end this, I'm your man." He'd do anything to stop the contagion from killing any more people.

Sam opened the flyer and noted the different kinds of jets the company offered. The majority of the planes looked like Lear 35's in different configurations. Some were equipped for cargo. Some had all the bells and whistles any corporate executive could wish for and a few were basically miniature luxury liners set up for spoiled celebrities and their friends.

"I'd hoped you'd say that. I've arranged a little extra training for you at Flight Safety in Houston. They've got Level D flight simulators that have full motion and full visual. They can give you the Type Rating you'll need on your license to work for Praxis Air legitimately."

"I've been to Flight Safety before. It's a good outfit." Sam put the brochure back on Matt's desk.

"We'll give you a suitable job history and cover, which you will commit to memory. You'll also have regular check-ins while in the field, but for the most part you'll be on your own.

I want you to discover who, if any, of their personnel are involved and to what extent." Matt paused briefly before continuing. "Just to be clear, this isn't a regular job I'm asking you to do, Sam. It's not even close to what you signed on for when we were assigned as zombie hunters. I won't order you to do this. It's a total immersion mission. Chances are, there will be no immediate backup if you get into trouble. You'll be completely on your own most of the time."

"Understood, sir. I'm still up for it. I like a challenge."

Matt cracked a smile. "I hear that. And I appreciate the enthusiasm. Here's the preliminary packet to get you started." He handed a bulging envelope across the desk. "We'll get the rest set up while you're in flight training. It'll be ready by the time you are. You leave tomorrow for Houston."

"Yes, sir." Sam stood, hearing the tone of dismissal in the commander's voice.

"You can call this whole thing off up until the end of your flight training. After that, wheels will have been set in motion and can't be easily stopped. If you change your mind, let me know as soon as possible."

"Thank you, sir." Unspoken was the certainty that Sam wouldn't be changing his mind any time soon.